DANCE WITH THE WIND
Book 1 of City of Virtue and Vice

A singer with forbidden magic.

An undercover renegade.

**How can she keep her magic a secret
if it goes wild every time they dance?**

On Ylena's first day inside the Shining City, a mysterious woman tricks her into auditioning for a magical ritual celebrating the Goddess. Every year, the young singers and dancers compete for the honor of performing in the enchanted ceremony, but with the ruthless High Priests in charge, a single wrong note is blasphemy.

If learning her role wasn't hard enough, unexpected emotions make rehearsals even more complicated. There's Wilder, Ylena's flirty costar who knows more about the city's dark secrets than he's willing to tell, and Caed, her dance instructor, a priest who isn't what he seems.

When Ylena manifests magic that makes her a threat, can she escape the spotlight at center stage before the High Priests discover her secret?

I0587781

DANCE WITH THE WIND

CITY OF VIRTUE AND VICE
BOOK 1

SUSANNAH WELCH

DANCE WITH THE WIND

CITY OF VIRTUE AND VICE
BOOK 1

SUSANNAH WELCH

CONTENTS

Cover Concept and Design by Art Muse (Patrisha E. Badalo)
Editing by Red Loop Editing (Victoria Basnuevo)

eBook ISBN: 978-1-7365770-0-4
Paperback ISBN: 978-1-7365770-1-1
Hardback ISBN: 978-1-7365770-6-6

www.susannahwelch.com

ALSO BY SUSANNAH WELCH

City of Virtue and Vice Series

Dance with the Wind

Dance with the Night

Dance with the Dawn

Fight with the Wind

Fight with the Dark

Fight with the Heart

For Kent,
You are the heart of all my Happily Ever Afters

THE SHINING CITY

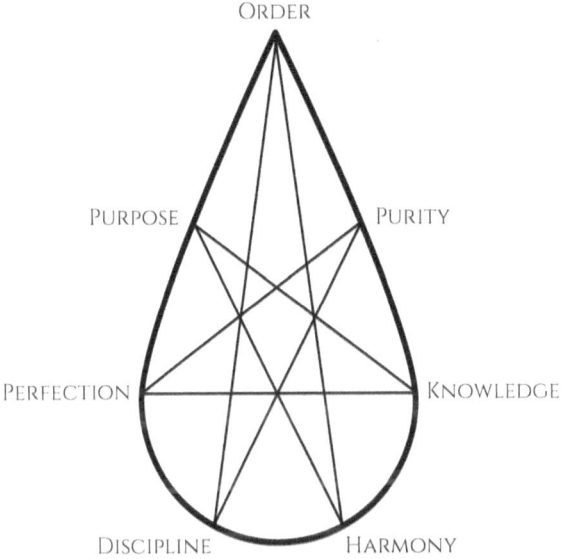

ORDER

PURPOSE   PURITY

PERFECTION   KNOWLEDGE

DISCIPLINE   HARMONY

PRELUDE

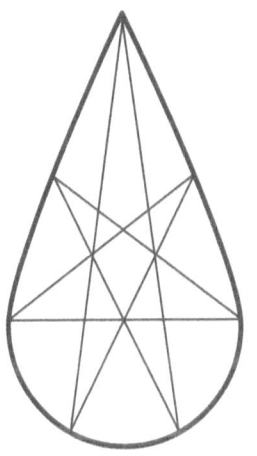

1

Ylena clung to the side of the mountain, gazing down at the Shining City as the sun rose. Her mountain perch gave a clear view of the glowing crystal spires that gave the city its name. She liked to wake early and watch the sun as it crested the mountains and filled the lingering shadows untouched by the crystals' glow.

She wondered if the sunrise looked this beautiful to the people inside the Shining City. The soft morning light touched her face, and she sighed as the sky lit up in red and gold. Icy wind nipped at her cheeks, so she pulled her fur hood close as she began her descent back down the mountain.

When she was young, she asked her grandfather why the two of them lived in a mountain cave instead of inside the glowing city. He'd said, "The Shining City looks beautiful from up here, but inside, it's dead."

Just another cryptic statement he never explained.

She heard the familiar sound of the waterfall long before she could see it. The waterfall wasn't the largest one she had seen on her discovery of the mountain, but it was enough to hide the small cave she and her grandfather called home. She pushed through the dense pine trees and found her grandfather fishing at the calm edge of the water-fall's stream.

He set down his fishing supplies and strained as he stood. "Climb a bit further than usual this morning?"

She followed him behind the waterfall and into the cave, where she took the bucket with two trout from his hands. "How did you guess?"

"You always seem more relaxed the higher you climb."

He lowered himself onto the bench by the fire pit and warmed his hands, then flexed his fingers as if the cold pained him. Grandfather seemed to have an endless well of energy, so she often forgot he was getting older. His light gold complexion matched her own, but deep worry lines wrinkled his forehead. He removed his hat, and she wondered when his dark hair had gotten so gray. She remembered when it had been just as black and sleek as her own.

Ylena sat down next to him. "Looking at the City calms me," she said carefully. "I think life would be easier with more people around."

He grunted. "Trust me. More people just means more problems."

She sighed. "We can't live up here forever, Grandfather. I'd like to have friends ... maybe even fall in love someday ..." She peeked at him under her lashes to judge his expression.

"Ylena, I know you just turned eighteen and feel like an adult, but the Shining City is a dangerous place. The false religion of the Goddess killed your parents, and it would have killed you, too."

She took a deep breath to launch into more questions but was interrupted by a voice outside the cave. "Hello? Brynn? Ylena? Are you in there?"

Ylena gave her grandfather a puzzled look. The few visitors who journeyed to their cave arrived on the same day each month. They weren't due for another week.

Grandfather stood up slowly. "Ched? Is that you?"

Ylena followed her grandfather out of the cave and saw a rugged man wearing leather pants and a thick, fur-lined coat. Ylena had met Ched several times, but he wasn't carrying the large pack he usually brought for trading. In his thirties, Ched was the youngest and most attractive of the visitors that traded with her grandfather. That wasn't saying much, since most of the other visitors were grizzled men and tired women. They all seemed overly sensitive to the cold, so she assumed they must not live in the mountains; however, they seemed a lot rougher than she expected the City's people to look.

"Brynn, I need to speak to you." He looked at Grandfather, and something unspoken passed between them.

"Come inside. Ylena, please go tend the garden."

Ylena opened her mouth to protest, but Grandfather was already leading Ched behind the waterfall. She allowed herself one huff of irritation before she walked to their small garden at the edge of the stream. It wasn't unusual for her to get kicked out of conversations when Grandfather had visitors. That had happened since she was a child. Visitors would bring supplies to trade for the tea and herbs they harvested. She was allowed to listen while they traded, but at some point, she was always assigned a chore that pulled her away from their conversation.

She gathered a couple potatoes and headed back to the cave entrance. The crashing sound of the waterfall made it difficult to eavesdrop, but she did her best.

"... were anxious even before he died." Ched's voice was quiet but persistent. "This will propel them to act. You need to be there if you want to influence their decision."

3

"You're right. I need to go. But Ylena will stay. I don't want her involved ..."Grandfather's voice faded out. She sneaked closer to the entrance, but her grandfather hurried out with his hands full. "Ylena. Good. You're here." He shoved clothes into a small sack, which he then slung over his shoulder. "I'm going to the City ... Maybe for a few weeks. I'll be back as soon as I can."

"Wait, a few weeks? What's wrong?" Ylena followed him as he began walking with Ched into the trees.

"Everything's fine, Ylena. I just need to check on some things. That's all."

"You haven't been feeling well, so I'll go for you! Ched can show me the way, and I'll check on whatever you need, then come right back."

Ched looked her up and down slowly, then raised an eyebrow. Despite the cold air, her cheeks grew warm. Grandfather gave Ched a sharp look, and the man shrugged, then walked a few steps away, where he waited with arms crossed.

Grandfather turned toward Ylena with a kind smile. "I appreciate your desire to help, but I need you to stay here and keep an eye on things. Can you do that for me?"

She grasped his arm. "This is my chance to visit to the Shining City. Please let me come with you."

"No, Ylena." Grandfather's voice was firm. "Now is not the time. Stay here, and don't worry about it." He patted her on the head as if she were a small child.

Ylena watched him catch up to Ched and disappear into the trees. What was so important to cause Grandfather to leave like that? He'd gone into the City only a few times over the years and prepared Ylena for weeks in advance on what to do if someone discovered their cave. She always found that a particularly strange precaution, considering she had never seen anyone other than the few visitors who arrived right on schedule. But this time, there was no warning. He was just gone.

Her anger at the unanswered questions bubbled up, but she pushed her feelings down as she had her entire life. They lived in solitude on the mountain, and nothing would ever change. She should just forget about her dream of a life in the Shining City. She shoved her clenched fists into her pockets and felt the potatoes she had gathered earlier. Her footsteps were heavy as she trudged back inside the cave.

She tossed the potatoes into a bucket of clean water and scrubbed them roughly, welcoming the distraction of preparing a meal. Grandfather had taught her how to cook and fish and hunt, yet when it came to the City and her parents, he continued to hide the truth from her.

Don't think about it. Forget about all the unanswered questions.

She slammed the potatoes on the table and started chopping. Beyond the constant sound of the waterfall, the silence was overwhelming. She sang a lullaby her mother used to sing, which made the emptiness feel a little less lonely. Grandfather said her mother died when Ylena was too young to remember, but she recalled the song clearly.

As she sang, she tried to imagine her life if her parents had survived and she had grown up in the Shining City. Maybe she would have brothers or sisters, or she might have friends her own age. Maybe she would have even fallen in love. If she had someone else in her life, she wouldn't be so alone now that Grandfather was gone.

She finished the song, and her dream faded away, leaving only the sound of her rough chopping. How could he leave so quickly and with no explanation? What could he possibly need to do in the Shining City? He had lived in this small cave for her entire life. Before that, his life was a mystery.

Her knife slipped, nicking her finger. As she sucked on the small cut, the anger she had pushed down bubbled back to the surface. If she stayed hidden on this mountain, she would never find the answers to her questions.

Ylena had waited long enough. She doused the fire, packed up a few of her things, and set off to follow Grandfather into the Shining City.

Ylena assumed that, since she was younger and faster than her grandfather, she would catch up to him, but after several hours of hiking, she realized how foolish that idea was. Grandfather had taught her how to walk through the rough mountainside without leaving a trail, and it was obvious both he and Ched had that skill. She didn't allow the thought to discourage her, though, because she only had to focus on one direction—down.

Even though she had taken many long trips climbing the sheer slopes of the mountain, she had never traveled this far away from home. The thought was both thrilling and disconcerting. She had lived her whole life with the cave under the waterfall as the center of her existence, and now, she felt pulled free. She was exhausted from the hike but had never felt more alive.

She followed a stream as her guide down the mountain, watching as it joined with smaller streams along the way. She was sweating underneath her heavy furs, but her hands and feet were so cold she kept wiggling them to make sure they were still there. She pulled her hood closer to warm her cheeks and pushed on ahead. She didn't realize how close she was until she heard voices.

"Be careful, Jer! That log is slick, so stay alert."

The men didn't notice Ylena standing near the tree line.

Through the branches, she could see the stream she was following poured directly into a grate on the City's smooth, white wall. A large tree was stuck in the grate, interfering with the flow. A bushy-haired young man balanced on the tree as he wrapped a chain around the trunk while an older man connected the chain to the harness of a horse.

Ylena caught her breath. A horse? She had heard about them but had never seen one. She inched closer when she heard a yell.

The young man had slipped and was trapped between the tree and the grate. Rushing water slammed into him, pinning him in place, and he couldn't keep his head out of the water. Ylena dropped her bag and jumped into the stream.

The shock of the cold water stole her breath. The water moved so fast that swimming wasn't an option, and she immediately found herself pressed up against the tree. She relied on her climbing skills to cling to the branches and pull herself out of the water. She gripped the trunk tightly with her legs, grabbed one of Jer's flailing arms, and pulled his head out of the water. His panicked brown eyes finally noticed her, and he reached out with his other hand.

They maneuvered across the fallen log, then stumbled their way to the shore. The older man rushed to their side, chanting fervently, "Blessed Goddess, forgive me. Blessed Goddess, forgive me."

Jer violently coughed up water, and Ylena bent down to steady him. The older man whispered, "It happened so fast. I turned around for a second, and he must've slipped. I told him to be careful! Blessed Goddess, forgive me ..." He continued chanting under his breath.

"I'm okay," Jer said as Ylena helped him stand. He shook his head, and cold water dripped from his thick hair. "I just need to catch my breath."

The older man's attention finally snapped to Jer. He grabbed him by his broad shoulders and looked into his eyes. "You're okay? I'm okay? There was no sin here?"

Jer gave him a steady look. "There was no sin here."

They both turned questioning eyes onto Ylena. She had no idea what they were talking about but sensed they were looking for a response.

"There was no sin here?" She gave them a little smile.

Their shoulders relaxed, and they walked toward the horse to finish their job. Ylena picked up her pack and watched them pull the tree completely out of the water and unhook the chains.

Jer handed the chains to the older man, then turned to Ylena. "You saved my life," he said quietly. "Thank you."

She was shivering with the cold but smiled. "You're welcome. I mean, it's what anyone would have done."

He looked over his shoulder at the older man who tended to the horse while still chanting prayers under his breath. Jer walked Ylena to a wooden door near the grate. "I'm guessing you aren't from inside," he whispered.

She bit her lip, unsure how to respond.

"You saved my life, so I'll say this to hopefully save your life in return. Don't tell anyone you came from outside the walls, follow every rule to the letter, and stay far away from the Priests."

Jer turned away sharply, leaving Ylena staring after him, her breath frozen in her chest at such a cryptic warning. She wanted to ask more questions, but both men were pointedly ignoring her.

Ylena studied the unassuming wooden door just big enough for the horse to fit through. From her height on the mountain, she hadn't seen an entrance to the Shining City, but this wasn't what she imagined. She peeked inside the door into a large storage room filled with tools and chains

8

and extra harnesses. As she stepped across the threshold, the cold wind disappeared. She looked for a roaring fire but didn't see one.

Only one door led out of the storage room, so she walked toward it, trailing wet footprints on the stone floor. She cracked opened the door and stepped out, fully inside the City. The sky was the same blue it had been on the mountain, but the wind blowing across her face was warm and sweet. Tall bushes surrounded her, and she could hear people but couldn't see them. Water flowed from outside through the grate into a round pool with pipes that disappeared underground.

"Oh, child, you are soaked!"

She turned to find a tall woman with chestnut hair piled in thick curls atop her head. The full skirt on her sapphire dress rustled as she hurried to Ylena's side.

"Did you fall in the pool? No, don't confess that to me." She looked around anxiously. "Come with me. You're close to my granddaughter's size. I think I can find dry clothes to fit you."

The woman led her onto a stone path lined with bushes on one side and a wall with doors every few feet. She passed several doors, then opened one and ushered Ylena inside. The late afternoon sun slanted through windows and lit up the room with colors of fabric Ylena didn't know existed.

Ylena's clothing had always been extremely practical: sturdy leather boots and pants, simple linen shirts, warm wool sweaters, and heavy fur coats. Her mind couldn't comprehend the colors and shapes of the clothing hanging neatly around the room. Shirts with ruffles on the collars and sleeves, shoes with tiny heels, and dresses with layers and layers of fabric. How could you move or climb in that?

The woman came around the corner, carrying a white dress that fluttered as she moved. "This isn't new, but it suits you. Plus, it's dry." She ushered Ylena into a small, curtained room, hanging the dress on a hook inside. "Hand me your wet clothes, and I will take care of them for you."

The woman's voice was kind but firm, and Ylena obeyed the instructions without thinking twice. She handed the woman the heavy jacket dripping with freezing water and peeled herself out of every soaked layer.

The woman passed her a towel through the curtain. "Dry your hair before it drips all over the dress."

The towel was softer than anything Ylena had ever felt before. She dried herself off, wrapped the towel around her head, and passed her wet clothes and boots outside the curtain. She pulled on the dress, running her fingers down the smooth fabric.

The woman's voice was muffled as she rummaged around the shop. "It looks like you wear the same size shoes as my granddaughter."

Ylena was trying to figure out how the long pieces of trailing fabric fit together when the woman pulled back the curtain. "That's just lovely! Let me help you." She showed Ylena how to gather the fabric and twist it around her waist and across her shoulder to trail down her back, then handed Ylena a pair of soft slippers.

The woman clapped her hands. "Beautiful! You feel much better right?" The woman lifted the towel off Ylena's head and used it to soak up the last bit of water. "Hmm ... where is that brush?" She began digging through cabinets again.

"Oh, I have a comb," said Ylena as she pulled it out of her bag.

The woman took the comb from her hands. "Let me help."

Ylena found the woman's behavior strange but didn't

stop her. Her grandfather hadn't combed her hair since she was a small child, and she found the brushstrokes soothing.

The woman combed out all the tangles until Ylena's hair fell in a shining, dark sheet down her back. She returned the comb and said, "Let me get you a dry bag for your things." She found a sturdy but soft bag of dark blue leather and held it open as Ylena emptied her few items into it.

The woman gathered Ylena's wet bag, clothes, and boots. "I'll hang these to dry. Why don't you go outside and relax a bit? There is a concert at the park in front of the shop today, and it's a nice place to sit and warm up." She bustled Ylena outside, closing the door behind her.

Ylena found herself standing on a walkway filled with people passing each other in both directions. Seeing so many people all at once fascinated her. She was amazed at how easily they walked around each other and stepped out of each other's way. Some people gave her strange looks as they passed, and it took her a moment to realize she was like a single unmoving rock in the middle of a stream. She stepped out of the crowd, off the stone walkway, and onto the grass.

In the mountains, the ground was covered with rocks. Growing plants required such extreme care that she couldn't imagine a plant being common enough to step on. Her slippers were so soft she could feel the springy grass through the soles, and she looked down at her feet in awe. The sight of her bare ankles surprised her—she had never worn so little clothing and yet been so warm. Even inside their cave, she was always wrapped in multiple layers of clothes.

She took a few deep breaths, and as her mind relaxed, she realized how strange the experience with that woman was. The woman said she had a granddaughter, but her warm brown skin had been smooth and unlined. Ylena had a hard time imagining she might be as old as her grandfather. She never even learned the woman's name.

She turned back to the shop, and a man in a purple suit took her by the arm. "There you are! Follow me."

He brushed back his short, ash-blond hair with a sigh and pulled her along. "I'm so glad I found you. I moved the others forward a slot, and I've been praying I could find you before the end. I absolutely did not want to confess I had lost one of you."

Ylena tried to interrupt to say he had her confused with someone else, but he kept pulling her ahead like a leaf carried down a stream. He headed toward a vine-covered wooden structure in the middle of the grassy lawn.

"I like the dress," he said. "It's a nice touch. Not everyone who comes to sing has quite the amount of drama required."

The man led her up the stairs and onto a raised wooden platform in front of the vine-covered backdrop. He finally let go of her arm and exhaled deeply. "There was no sin here. I got you to center stage right on time." He made a strange hand motion she didn't understand and said, "Goddess's blessing upon you." Then he pushed her forward and walked away.

An auburn-haired woman wrapped in a turquoise shawl sat at a table in front of the stage. Scattered behind her, people lounged on the grass. Ylena had no idea what was going on. Who did that man think she was? No one was expecting her.

She wasn't sure how to get out of the situation without revealing that she wasn't from the City. She wasn't sure why Jer said to keep that information secret, but he'd said it with such fear that she thought she should take his advice until she figured out why.

The woman in the shawl settled back in her chair and looked at Ylena expectantly. "You may begin at any time."

Ylena had no idea what she was supposed to begin. "Um ... I think you may have me confused with someone else ..."

The woman looked down at the papers in front of her. "Your name is Ylena, correct?" Ylena's eyes widened, and she nodded dumbly. "You're the last one auditioning today, so there's no chance of confusion. What song are you going to sing?"

Ylena's mind was racing. How could they possibly know her name? She hadn't given it to anyone in the City. She needed to be alone and think, but there was no way she could run off without creating a scene. She needed to play along with whatever was happening and then escape as soon as possible.

"What song?" she choked out. "Um ... I could sing the song my mother sang to me as a baby ..."

The woman's thin lips twisted into a smirk, and she set down her papers. "Sure, dear. Sing a little lullaby, and then we can carry on with our day."

Ylena looked out at more faces than she had ever seen in her life and tried to swallow down her fear. She closed her eyes and pretended she was back home. The people in the crowd murmured to each other, and their voices blended into a sound like the waterfall. She took a deep breath and began to sing.

> *"Hush now rhythm in my chest*
> *Peaceful sleep is my request*
> *Love's song from on high*
> *Sings soft with a sigh*
> *As your face looks to the sky*
> *My heart gives its own reply*
> *In all you are blessed*

Singing always soothed her, and with her eyes closed, she entered the peaceful place that music carried her. Her voice didn't bounce back to her like it did when she sang in the cave, but it traveled smoothly on the breeze like it did when she sang on her mountain perch. At the end of the song, she was left with the slight melancholy of a finished song but the sweet satisfaction of the last resonant note.

She blinked open her eyes and fully remembered where she was. Now that she had finished singing, she hoped they would dismiss her, but the man and woman were both sitting back in their chair with their mouths hanging open. She stared back at them awkwardly for a few moments when the people on the grass stood up and began clapping wildly.

The woman ran onto the platform and grabbed Ylena's shoulders. "Oh, child! I had no idea we would discover you today! I thought the dress was a little fanciful, and the bit about a lullaby ... Well, you really teased me with that! Aren't you such a clever young thing!" She grabbed Ylena's chin, turning her head from side to side. "Yes, you are exactly what we need for the Pageant this year."

She grasped Ylena's hand and pulled it high in the air as she announced to the crowd, "We have our Goddess!"

A LITURGY

The Goddess gave to us her Virtues
and a Temple to honor each.

SHE is the Queen of Order.
SHE is the Guardian of Purity.
SHE is the Provider of Knowledge.
SHE is the Incarnation of Harmony.
SHE is the Sustainer of Discipline.
SHE is the Essence of Perfection.
SHE is the Giver of Purpose.

HER Gifts are offered to all,
and through them,
life will be found.

ORDER

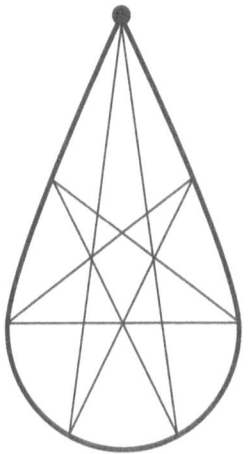

2
_____

The woman kept hold of Ylena's hand and pulled her down the steps of the platform. Ylena felt like she had spent all her time in the City being pulled from one place to the next.

The woman released Ylena's hand to look at her papers. "It says here you are from Perfection Diocese. And you will be *perfect* in the role of the Goddess. This year's Pageant is going to be phenomenal!" She smiled dreamily. "You can call me Madame Director."

Madame Director turned her gaze onto the man who had led Ylena up on stage. "Deven, will you please make sure Ylena gets to Temple Order in time for tonight's meal? I want her to meet the other acolytes as soon as possible. And inform Lira she will be playing the role of one of the Blessed Virtues."

Deven's eyes widened, but his voice was smooth when he replied. "Yes, of course, Madame Director."

The woman adjusted her flowing shawl around herself and strode away.

Deven took Ylena's arm. "Follow me."

She ripped her arm out of his grasp. "Stop pulling me

around!" Her voice was louder than she intended, and a few people gave her strange looks as they walked by. Deven stared at her with his mouth open.

"I'm sorry," she hurriedly said. "I've just been pulled around a lot today. I need to catch my breath."

His expression softened. "Of course. This is a great honor. I'm sure it's all so overwhelming!"

That wasn't exactly what she meant, but it was close enough. "Yes, thank you," she said. "I need to go into that shop and gather my things."

He sighed. "As long as you are quick. It will be time for dinner soon."

Ylena wound her way through the people on the busy walkway and opened the shop door where she had left the odd woman.

A large man in a tailored jacket greeted her as she walked in. "Good evening, miss. How can I help you?"

She looked around, but there was no one else in the shop. "I was in here earlier with a tall woman with dark hair. She let me borrow these clothes from her granddaughter. I wanted to return them and pick up my own clothes."

The man looked down his nose and smiled even larger. "You must have the wrong shop, miss. I'm the only one who works here, and we don't have any dresses in such a … traditional style as the one you're wearing."

She looked around at the beautiful clothes. "No, I'm sure this is the same shop. Have you been here all day? Maybe she was here while you stepped out?"

His smile immediately disappeared, and his voice dropped to an angry whisper. "What are you implying? Are you accusing me of not working today?"

Ylena was startled by his sudden change and took an involuntary step back. "No, I … I don't know. I guess I … This must be the wrong place. I'm sorry."

He continued to stare at her with hard eyes, and she backed out the door. She flinched when Deven hurried to her side.

"Did you find what you were looking for?" he asked.

"Not quite." She peeked through the window at the man still staring at her. "I guess I should come back another time."

"Good. Let's hurry, then." He started to grab her arm but stopped himself. "Um ... will you follow me?" She nodded and followed him through the crowd.

Ylena's eyes weren't big enough to take in everything that surrounded her. The buildings were made from a smooth, white stone unlike anything on the mountain. They walked down streets with little shops that sold flowers and hats and tea and bread and things she couldn't even identify. And each perfect, shiny shop was filled with perfect, beautiful people.

While the buildings all sparkled white, the people lit up the city with color. Their hair and skin were every shade, but they were all similar in their beauty. Each individual outfit was a distinct work of art with bright colors that contrasted with the white storefronts. When Ylena had first put on the white dress, she thought she would stand out in something so glamorous. Her dress was laughable simple compared to some of the others they passed. Walking down the street was like swimming through feathers and ruffles and ribbons.

Deven glanced in her direction. "Are you okay? Why are you looking at everyone like that?"

Her open mouth snapped shut, and she said casually, "Everything looks very normal to me. Yes. Very normal."

He rolled his eyes but didn't say anything.

Ylena continued to drink in all the sights but tried to be a little more reserved. Jer's words kept ringing in her mind: "Don't tell anyone you came from outside the walls, follow every rule to the letter, and stay far away from the Priests."

Why had her grandfather never told her anything like that? He said she would visit the City with him someday. When was he planning on telling her that information? Jer seemed to believe he was saving her life by giving her those warnings. What had she gotten herself into?

She didn't notice Deven had stopped and almost ran into his back.

"We made it in time! Come on, let's find the rest of the performers." He started to walk again, but Ylena didn't follow. Her mouth fell open as she gawked at the imposing building before her.

Temple Order was a circular building that wrapped around one of the giant glowing spires that towered in the bright blue sky. From her perch on the mountain, she could see all seven crystal spires, but she didn't know what purpose they served. Now that the sun was setting, she could see how the crystal spire would light more than just the surrounding area. The entire temple seemed to glow from within.

She followed Deven up the seven steps that circled the building, then walked through an arch at the top of the last step, whispering to herself, "This is normal. This is normal."

The arches led into a wide courtyard where every surface was covered with vines and flowers. Vines were tightly wound into the shapes of a table and chairs, and someone lounged on the low-hanging branches of a flower-covered tree. Ylena tried to keep her eyes focused on Deven's blond head. Everything around her was so strange, and her eyes couldn't take it all in.

Deven led her through another set of arches into the giant, round building. The room had high ceilings and gently curving walls covered with a lattice of shimmering light. It wasn't the amber glow of the crystal, but a white light streaming from a silver liquid that branched out in a web along the stone. She couldn't stop and stare, because Deven rushed ahead to a large table surrounded by a group of young people talking quietly to each other.

Deven clapped his hands twice. "Good evening, everyone. Congratulations on winning your spot in this year's Pageant. I know the auditions were tiring, but that's nothing compared to the hard work and dedication expected of you over the next few months. The creation of this Pageant is a sacred duty, and you all understand the price of failure."

Ylena didn't know what he meant by that, but several people visibly shivered.

"Tomorrow, your training will officially begin here in Temple Order. You will live in this temple and study this Blessed Virtue while you learn your role in the Pageant. You will then move through each of the other temples, learning and rehearsing as you go. Your fellow acolytes will be your family these next few months, so spend some time tonight introducing yourselves over dinner."

Deven looked around at each face. "Where is Lira?"

A blond girl at the end of the table stood up proudly. "Over here!" She had a gleaming white smile.

"Yes. Lira ..." Deven seemed hesitant for the first time all day. "Um ... Madame Director said you will be playing the role of a Blessed Virtue."

Lira blinked her delicate lashes slowly. "Pardon me, Deven, you must be mistaken." She gave him the most respectfully sweet smile.

"No, Lira. I'm not mistaken. You will no longer be playing the role of the Goddess." At this, Lira's face went completely blank. "The part of the Goddess will be played by Ylena. Come on, Ylena. Don't be shy. Say hello."

Ylena froze as all eyes turned her direction, but she managed to choke out the words, "Nice to meet you."

She risked a glance at Lira's face, and the young woman's narrowed eyes made Ylena feel cold for the first time since she entered the City.

3

Despite Ylena's startling introduction, servers carrying platters of food turned the other acolytes' attention away from her for a moment. She took a seat at the far end of the long table, as far as she could get from Lira's furious eyes.

"I don't think you made a friend there." A petite girl with golden blond hair and warm tawny skin pointed at Lira with the celery stick she was eating. "She has the look of someone who can hold a grudge."

Ylena risked a glance down the table at Lira and quickly turned back to her food. "I'm afraid you might be right. I don't know how I got myself into this."

"Well, you must be pretty good to beat Lira out of the role of the Goddess. I'm Pim, by the way. It's good to meet you." Pim gave her a warm smile, and Ylena couldn't help but smile back.

"It's good to meet you, too. This has been such an odd day, but talking to you feels refreshingly normal."

"I can't say that many people call me 'normal,' so I will definitely brag about that to my mom next time I see her." Pim winked.

Ylena laughed. "I'm probably not the best judge of what's normal, so maybe don't start bragging too quickly!"

Pim ran her fingers absently through her short hair and narrowed her brown eyes to examine Ylena. "Are you from Perfection Diocese?"

Ylena choked on her bite of grilled fish. "What makes you say that?"

"I just thought your flair with wearing a traditional style dress to represent the Goddess seemed like something Perfection Diocese would enjoy. Plus, you know how fun it is to try to guess where everyone is from just by looking at them. You've played that game, right?"

"I guess I haven't played it like that before." Ylena would have loved to admit to Pim that she was from outside the City and had absolutely no idea what she was talking about, but Jer's warning was still ringing in her ears.

"Then let me enlighten you!" Pim said joyfully. She leaned in closer for a conspiratorial whisper. "Let's start with Lira. I'm guessing she's from Purpose Diocese. She seems to have an idea of how everyone should fit in their proper place, and that's probably why she's especially upset that you disrupted that." Pim grinned, and Ylena tried to hide her shy smile behind her glass of water.

"Now, let's take Rowan over there." Pim pointed at a young man talking to Lira. "He is not just healthy—he's unreasonably fit. I guarantee he's training with Priests over in Temple Discipline." She nodded her head at a girl a few seats away. "Then there's Wren. You might guess she lives in Harmony Diocese because of her name."

Ylena gave her a blank stare.

Pim hinted, "Wren? As in the bird? Working with animals in Harmony Diocese?"

Ylena nodded her head as she understood, "Ah, yes, of course. Animals in Harmony Diocese."

"But no, I'm from Harmony Diocese, and I think her name is a bit too blatant for us. I think Wren is from Knowledge Diocese. I noticed her bag was stuffed full of books, and I'm guessing she has spent time in the giant library.

"Now, let's look at Wilder over there." Ylena followed the direction of Pim's nod. Seated at the other end of the table was a guy with deep brown skin and thick hair falling to his shoulders in raven black coils. He looked up, caught Ylena's glance, and gave her a slow smile, and her breath caught in her lungs. She hurriedly looked down at her plate.

Pim giggled quietly at the interaction. "Exactly. I guarantee that beautiful creature is from Purity Diocese. Oh, the painful irony." She sighed dramatically.

Ylena wasn't sure what she meant, but her heart fluttered in a strange way.

~

After everyone had finished eating, Deven stood and clapped to get their attention. "Temple attendants will show you to the rooms that will be yours during this month at Temple Order. We will begin rehearsals early tomorrow morning, so get your rest tonight."

The attendants came to take them up the curving staircase to their individual rooms on the next floor. Wilder was one of the first to be shown to his room, and he winked at Ylena as he closed the door. She stood frozen to the spot, but Pim pulled her ahead with a giggle.

Pim and Ylena had doors right across from each other. As the others walked on, Pim asked, "Do you want to come hang out in here and talk for a while?"

"Today has been a bit overwhelming, and I'd like some time to think about it." Ylena started to open her door but turned back around. "But thank you. That's one of the nicest things anyone has ever asked me."

Pim gave her an odd look. "It's not that big of a deal. We will be spending lots of time together. Maybe we'll hang out tomorrow night!" She smiled and opened her door. "Good night, Ylena!"

"Good night, Pim." She opened her door and slipped inside. She leaned back against the door and closed her eyes with a sigh. She had never been around so many people in her entire lifetime. She was grateful to have this first moment of peace since she arrived at the wall of the City.

She opened her eyes and looked around her room. It was smaller than her cave, but it was filled with so many things! A glowing lamp on the wall lit the entire room. She had heard someone say the liquid crystal inside the lamps was called crystalline. The crystalline lamp was up high enough that she couldn't touch the bright substance inside, and she wasn't sure if that would be a good idea anyway. There was a lever underneath the globe, and when she flipped it, a metal contraption dropped onto the globe and blocked out the light. She switched it back and continued to look around.

She usually slept on a pallet on the floor, but this room had its own bed with a fluffy mattress. She sat down on the edge and couldn't believe how soft it was. She stood up and walked over to the small desk. Inside, she found a few sheets of paper and a pen. She opened the doors of the wardrobe to her right and found several matching sets of clothes. She set her bag inside and walked over to the doorway on her left.

Inside, she found a marvel! In the middle of the room was a giant copper tub, and after a bit of awkward fiddling, she realized the attached levers filled it up with water. One of the levers poured in hot water! She was even more shocked when she realized that the other thing in the small room was a chamber pot with levers to clean it as well.

She turned on the water in the tub, and as it was still filling, she got inside. She closed her eyes and imagined that the sound of the water was actually the waterfall outside her cave. She took a deep breath and tried to settle her mind enough to think through a plan.

She had come to the City following Grandfather, and she had no idea how she was going to find him. If what Jer said was true, not only should she not reveal that she came from outside the walls of the City, she shouldn't mention that her grandfather was also from outside. She had walked through the open gate because Jer and the older man purposefully ignored her. That made her wonder exactly where her grandfather came in.

She considered going back to the wall to see if she could sneak back. Maybe if she could find Jer, he would let her go out the same gate and pretend like she had never been inside. She could hike back up the mountain before Grandfather returned, and she might not have to admit to him what she had foolishly done.

But even as she had the thought, a part of her immediately rejected it. Though she had spent most of her day terrified and being pulled from place to place, she had also seen and heard more than she imagined possible. The Shining City was beautiful and completely different from her mountain home, and she desperately wanted to know more.

With the sound of water soothing her mind, Ylena came to a decision. She would stay in the City and see if she could find Grandfather without revealing that she was from outside. Grandfather had said he would probably be gone for a few weeks, so she had plenty of time to look for him. In the meantime, she could finally explore the City like she had always wanted.

She turned off the levers and sank further into the water. Behind her eyes, she saw hints of Wilder's slow smile.

4

Ylena woke after a night full of tossing and turning. Every time she fell asleep, she woke soon after, confused about where she was and feeling as if she was being suffocated. The pillow on her face plus the softness of her mattress made her feel like she was drowning.

She pulled one of the outfits out of her wardrobe. The top crossed around her shoulders and chest, and the ends draped down along one side of the light brown, fitted pants. It was unlike anything she had ever worn before, but she was able to figure out how to put it on herself unlike the complicated drape on the dress the mysterious woman had somehow tricked her into wearing. She didn't know what to think about the woman who gave her the white flowing dress, but it was hanging in the wardrobe next to the other clothes similar to what she was wearing. In the wardrobe, she also found a soft brown pair of leather shoes and a matching belt that was long enough that she assumed it should loop around her twice.

She knocked on Pim's door, but when she didn't answer, Ylena headed down the stairs, back to the room where they had eaten dinner. She was fidgeting with her clothes as she turned the corner into the room and ran straight into Wilder. "I'm so sorry!" She felt her cheeks getting warm.

"Don't worry about it. I shouldn't have been here lurking by the food." He gave her that smile again, and her cheeks grew even warmer. "I'm having a hard time deciding what to eat. Do you know what you want?" He stared at her with eyes as dark as the midnight sky, and Ylena couldn't do anything but blink.

Luckily, Pim chose that moment to rescue her. "There you are, Ylena! I saved you a spot over here!" She pulled Ylena down into a seat in front of a plate of bread, cheese, and fruit.

Ylena dropped her voice. "Thank you, Pim. What is wrong with me? I couldn't say a word."

Pim directed a wry smile over in Wilder's direction. "I guarantee he knows what his smile does to unsuspecting young girls, and he's really a bit of a rascal for springing it on you so early in the morning. Let a girl get a cup of coffee first, for Goddess's sake!" She pointed at the cup of dark, steaming liquid. Ylena took a hesitant sip, and Pim laughed at her reaction. "Not a coffee drinker, I guess?"

"My grandfather makes me tea every morning. This is much stronger, so it just surprised me."

"Well, you better get used to it. I think they are going to work us so hard preparing for the Pageant that you will need all the energy coffee will give you! Use plenty of cream and sugar if you are too delicate for it full strength." Pim laughed and started smearing butter on a piece of bread.

Ylena picked up her bread and took a bite. It was warm and fluffy and delicious. Ylena tried to hide her amazement at the wonderful food, but it seemed that with every bite, her feelings must be written plainly on her face. She and her grandfather had never been starving, but food was a limited resource. In the winter months, when it was impossible for the visitors to get up to the mountain, they ate sparingly so they wouldn't run out before first thaw. But the City seemed to be overflowing with food. Everyone treated food so casually, and Ylena struggled to not seem out of place.

She picked up a strawberry and looked at it. She had only seen small wild strawberries, and they were nothing like this sparkling red fruit. She took a bite and nearly cried at how delicious it was. She closed her eyes and savored the sweet taste. When she realized that closing her eyes like that is exactly what she shouldn't be doing, her eyes snapped open mid-bite. And of course, Wilder was looking right at her with that charming smile. Ylena choked and grabbed her napkin to cover up how red her cheeks were again. Pim patted her on the back and giggled quietly. Thankfully, all attention turned to Madame Director, who had just strode into the room with Deven at her side.

"Good morning, young acolytes!" Her booming voice seemed a little much, considering everyone was seated fairly close together. Ylena thought that Madame Director must really enjoy the echoing sound in the large room. "Today, you begin what will be the single most significant honor of your entire life: playing a role in the Blessed Goddess's Pageant. I require that each year, we create a more beautiful and touching performance than the year before, and this year is no exception. I demand your full enthusiasm, both body and heart, to accomplish this purpose, our most sacred responsibility."

Ylena realized everyone had stopped eating and was watching Madame Director intently. Madame Director stepped closer to the group and spoke in a slightly quieter voice. "I know there is a lot of pressure to succeed, and I intend to give you every learning opportunity to find your full potential. I will not fail you in that. Will you each promise to give your whole heart to this performance as if your life depends on it?" Everyone around her nodded solemnly. Madame Director looked them each in the eye. "I swear the same to you. If we fail in our sacred duty, we all fail together. Please keep that always in mind."

She shook off her serious expression and smiled widely. "Each of you is highly skilled in one or more areas, and you will receive training in the areas you need help. This morning, you will spend some time learning about Order Diocese, and then this afternoon, you will begin the first of your tests to see what areas you will need to be trained in. Finish your meal, and then Deven will take you out on a tour. I will see you back here after lunch."

Deven led the acolytes out of Temple Order and into the surrounding Diocese. They passed some of the little shops she had seen on her way in last night, but they continued to walk deeper into the City. They walked for some time before they passed through all of the neatly organized streets of shops and arrived at neighborhoods with rows of individual cottages. Each cottage had its own yard with an abundance of colorful flowers, surrounded by a white picket fence. In many of the yards, there were people tending to the flowers or repairing individual pieces of a fence. Ylena was once again struck at how beautiful everyone was.

Beyond the rows of cottages, they came to several blocks of large buildings with people bustling in and out. The buildings each had large doors in front and back, where horses and carts were lined up for loading and unloading. Deven gathered up the group of acolytes so they could hear him speak.

"This is the heart of the City. Or, well, perhaps more

accurately, the City's stomach." He grinned. "All of the food produced is brought here to the warehouses for distribution throughout the City. Many of the people of Order Diocese work in these warehouses to make sure that the food is handled appropriately and distributed to each Diocese fairly. This City requires a massive amount of food, and Order Diocese is responsible for this sacred duty. We will now head beyond the warehouses and into the fields. We are blessed because we will get to see the Priests at their holy work."

They passed carefully through the busy streets of people and horses and carts. Once they passed the last row of buildings, they came upon a grove of trees. Ylena could see this was no normal forest. Trees didn't normally grow in perfectly spaced rows and to the exact same height.

She heard Pim's whisper. "It's so beautiful! It's row upon row of everything I love! Apples, pears, avocados, mangos ..."

Ylena was also amazed, but maybe for different reasons. There was food available in the mountains, but it was never as easy to find as this. Each meal was work—hunting, searching, digging, climbing. This was a feast available for anyone to pluck and eat to their fill. It was incomprehensible.

The stone path passed through the straight rows of trees and opened up onto a giant patchwork of fields. There were beans, grapevines, corn, and more vegetables than Ylena could name. She could see people walking through the fields gathering the vegetables, and she stared at the massive baskets of food they gathered. Deven didn't stop, so the acolytes had to keep moving.

He eventually slowed, and Ylena saw him standing before a woman wearing a sleeveless black dress that trailed along the ground. Her waist was pulled in with a complicated pattern of crossing leather straps, and a braided silver circlet rested on top of her long, golden hair. Ylena realized everyone had bowed their heads and was holding their hands cupped outwardly at their bellies. She quickly followed.

"Good morning, young acolytes," came the kind voice. No one around her moved from their position, so Ylena just held her breath. "The Goddess's blessing upon you."

At those words, the group replied as one, "And also upon you." After their response, the group shifted back into their natural positions and moved to get a better view of the Priest. Ylena took a hesitant breath and decided to stay close to the back of the group.

"Welcome to Order Diocese," said the Priest. "I'm honored to show you the holy work the Priests from Temple Order are blessed to perform. May the blessing the Goddess bestowed on me inspire you as you perform your sacred duty in the Pageant."

Ylena peeked around Pim's shoulder and saw the Priest close her eyes. She held her arms out, palms facing down over the empty field in front of the group. Ylena could barely hear the Priest murmuring prayers underneath her breath. When the Priest reached up and touched her eye, the rest of the group echoed the motion, Ylena clumsily following. The Priest then knelt and lowered her hands to the ground, running her hands through the dark soil.

For the space of a heartbeat, nothing happened. Then suddenly ... life.

Small, green vines threaded themselves through the dirt, starting from the Priests hands and moving outward. They wove through the soil and then sprouted leaves. The vines continued to grow larger and outward. Flowers grew, which blossomed into perfect little strawberries.

Ylena was not alone in sighing at the beauty of what the

Priest created. The others bowed their heads again and cupped their hands, and this time, Ylena followed enthusiastically. No wonder the City had such an abundance of food! The Priest's touch had brought forth life.

The Priest stood slowly, and she turned to the bowing group. "The Goddess's blessing upon you."

"And also upon you," came the reply from all.

The Priest brushed the dirt off her hands. "These berries will be allowed to ripen in the sun for the rest of the day. Tomorrow, workers from this Diocese will gather them and bring them to our storehouses. They will then be distributed through the City for all to enjoy."

Deven bowed his head. "Thank you, Priest, for such a beautiful demonstration of the Goddess's Gift of Order. We will leave you to continue your holy work." The Priest bowed her head graciously and moved on to another patch of bare soil.

The group was subdued on their walk back. Ylena felt that they had experienced something holy and profound, and she wasn't sure what to do about it. Her grandfather was adamantly atheistic in their conversations. Ylena would frequently tell him about her sense of awe and wonder as she explored on the mountain, and he would always grumble and tell her to not believe in fairy tales.

She knew the people in the City had some sort of religion, but only because she heard her grandfather speak disparagingly about it. The previous night, as she was getting into bed, she'd noticed a small book on the bedside table and realized it was a book of their scriptures about the Goddess. She had read through a good portion of it before falling asleep and had started to realize just how connected the City was to their beliefs.

Each of the seven temples was inside a Diocese representing one of the Virtues given by the Goddess: Order, Purity, Purpose, Harmony, Discipline, Knowledge, and Perfection. The scriptures mentioned Gifts given to each of the Priests, and after seeing what the Priest from Order had done in that field, she wondered what the other Gifts might be. She had assumed the words describing this power were metaphorical, not the literal miracle she had seen. Had Grandfather seen this? How could he have been so dismissive of her sense of wonder if he had ever seen a miracle like that?

Her thoughts were pulled away from miracles and brought back to thoughts about her grandfather. Where in the City could he be? In her limited experience, she had heard people mentioning the Goddess in every other breath. Where would an outspoken atheist fit in a City like this? If she knew what he had come to the City to do, she might be able to ask someone about it in a subtle way, but as it was, she had no idea about the first place to start.

They made it back to the temple and found a meal waiting for them. Ylena had never eaten so much food over the course of a day in her life. She was still thinking about her grandfather when she sat down at the table without looking up.

"So ... Ylena, is it? That name is ... interesting." She looked up and realized she had accidentally sat down across from Lira. Her pale blond hair was pulled up in a smooth ponytail, and her delicate ivory skin was touched with the softest hint of rose. She was smiling, but the smile didn't reach her eyes.

"I can't believe I've never heard of you," she continued. "I make it my business to find all of the singers of the City who are blessed with a voice from the Goddess, but I haven't ever heard of you. Where have you been hiding yourself?"

Even if Jer had never warned her, Ylena knew in that moment that revealing she was from outside the City would be the absolute worst thing to say. She tried to think of something sufficiently vague. "I don't usually sing in front of anyone other than my grandfather."

"How ... quaint," Lira drawled. "It's just so unusual that one of the last auditions of the day would discover someone I have never heard of and with the skills to play the role of the Goddess."

"I didn't ask for that. I didn't even really know what was happening." Ylena hoped this would remove some of the blame off her in Lira's eyes, but it seemed to have the exact opposite effect.

"No need to be so humble. Humility isn't one of the Virtues." Lira leaned in closer. "You can be honest. You knew exactly what you were doing by wearing that traditional dress and singing the Goddess's Aria." Ylena's eyes widened at that. "Yes, I heard that you said you were going to sing a lullaby from your mother. How clever of you! I wish I had thought to be so sly. Unfortunately, I only demonstrated my talent but without any of your cunning tricks, so ..." She shrugged and leaned back in her seat.

"I ... I don't know what to say."

"Don't worry, sweetie. There are no hard feelings. We are all in this together, right?" As she walked away, Ylena was sure she had never heard a bolder lie in her life.

5

After lunch, Deven had them sit on the seats at one end of the large, open portion of the room. Within moments, Madame Director swished in followed by a man and a woman Ylena hadn't seen before. Madame Director clapped to silence the group even though they were already quiet.

"I hope your tour of Order Diocese this morning was fruitful." She gave herself a small smile at the pun. "This afternoon, we will see what other skills besides singing you have. I'd like to introduce you to your gymnastics instructor, Miya. She has taught the skills needed for the Pageant for many years, and you will learn a lot from her." Miya's hair was cut in a sleek bob near her chin, and her eyes were dark and intense. She was almost a foot shorter than Madame Director, but Ylena could see she was poised on the balls of her toes. She had an energy about her that made Ylena smile.

Madame Director turned to her left. "And this is Priest Caed." She bowed and cupped her hands quickly, which was followed by the rest of the group. "We are especially honored to have a Priest from Temple Discipline as our dancing instructor. This is the first year we have had a Priest as one of the trainers, and I am sure our performance will be doubly blessed as a result. Even though he is as young as the rest of you, I know you will all offer him the respect he deserves." She bowed her head again, but Ylena sneaked a glance at Priest Caed.

His expression was distant, and there was no kindly smile like the Priest who created strawberries with her bare hands. His light brown skin glowed in contrast to his long, fitted, black jacket over tight black pants. He was Ylena's age, but his brooding hazel eyes and priestly attire made him look intimidating. Now that she knew he was a Priest, she could spot the silver circlet on his head. The other Priests had worn theirs on top of their hair, but his was hidden by his tousled, ebony locks. He caught Ylena looking at him, and she quickly looked down at her cupped hands.

"Thank you, Madame Director." His voice was warmer than Ylena expected. "I'm honored to be part of such a momentous performance." Madame Director beamed at his praise.

"What a blessing!" She straightened out her flowing shawl and turned back to the acolytes. "You will be divided into groups to take turns working with Miya and Priest Caed. I expect you each to give your all."

Ylena was glad when she was assigned to a group with Pim, but unfortunately, Madame Director also added Wilder and Lira to her group, causing Ylena to immediately fall into an awkward silence.

Miya led them through the arches into the courtyard to a wall of the temple with vines crawling upward. "I want to start with a test of balance and strength so you will begin with some climbing." Ylena looked up the wall and noticed that even though it was a steep angle, with the vines, it actually seemed fairly straightforward compared to most of the cliff faces she had climbed. "The wall is wide enough for all of you to have plenty of room, so go ahead and show me what you've got."

Pim gave her an excited smile. "I'll meet you at the top!" Ylena smiled back and started to climb.

Climbing was always a peaceful activity for her. She had been climbing since her tiny fingers were strong enough to pull herself up the side of their cave, much to her grandfather's consternation. He soon learned he would need to teach her how to climb safely because there was no keeping her feet on the ground. She had climbed up the sheer sides of the mountain above her cave almost every day. She never felt more alive than when she made it to the top and looked down at what she had accomplished.

As her hands and feet went through the motions of climbing, she thought again about her grandfather. She wondered if she was being irresponsible by staying here and not just going back to her cave behind the waterfall. She felt slightly guilty about being on an adventure when Grandfather might come back early and be worried about what happened to her. She would have left him a note, except that she'd honestly believed she was going to catch up to him at some point on her way down the mountain.

She brought her attention back to the wall in front of her because the vines had started to thin out and she had to focus more between one handhold and the next. The vines were really sturdy, and Ylena was enjoying the pleasure of climbing when she heard a voice from below. "Okay, Ylena. I think you've demonstrated enough of your skills."

Ylena looked down and realized that, despite the fact she wasn't as high as any other place she usually climbed, the rest of her fellow acolytes were less than halfway up the wall from where she was. Even though there was quite a distance between them, Lira's glare was plain to read. Wilder was a little bit farther ahead than the others, and he gave Ylena an appreciative nod. That was the closest she felt to falling during the whole climb. She began her descent and was grateful that the others were far enough away to not be able to see the embarrassment written plainly on her face.

Even though she was so much higher than the others, Ylena made it back down in about the same time as they did. She jumped her last step off the vine and kept her head down to avoid eye contact with anyone else.

"Nice work, Ylena," said Miya. "It's clear you've had lots of practice climbing!" She noticed Lira narrow her eyes at this. "The rest of you were okay, but we will definitely be practicing more as we go."

"I'm not sure which was more awesome," whispered Pim. "How high you were able to climb or the look on Lira's face when Miya praised you."

Ylena couldn't stop the laugh that bubbled out of her mouth. Luckily, no one had heard what Pim had said, but that didn't stop Lira from continuing to glare.

"Nicely done, Ylena." Wilder was right behind her.

Ylena almost jumped out of her skin. How could someone so hulking sneak up so quietly? "Thanks. I wasn't trying to show off. I just got lost in the moment."

"Don't apologize," he said. "You looked good up there." His playful smile caused her stomach to turn over.

Pim laughed as he walked away. "That's just classic. I guarantee he is from Purity."

Miya put them through a few more tests involving flexibility. Miya asked Ylena to demonstrate how she could do the splits. When Wilder raised a single eyebrow, Ylena thought her cheeks would never stop burning. She purposefully didn't make eye contact as he was doing pushups and smiling in her direction. Pim continued to giggle, and Lira continued to glare, but thankfully, Miya was finally finished with them. She sent them inside to switch with the group working with Priest Caed.

If Ylena had hopes that her dancing lesson would be any less awkward, she was sorely mistaken. She wasn't sure what happened with the other group, but Priest Caed seemed even less pleased than he had when he first arrived. The four of them lined up on the open floor in front of Priest Caed. He sighed and began.

"The Pageant is designed to highlight each of the Virtues of the Goddess, and it is your job to express them with dignity and determination. Over the next few months, I will be teaching you each your individual roles, but today, I would like to get an idea for your beginning abilities. We will first begin with a simple warmup."

It turned out that what he meant by "simple" was anything but. He started with some stretches that Ylena appreciated because they seemed to work out some of the tension from her climbing and other tests of flexibility. But he soon transitioned into movements across the floor, and Ylena was completely lost. He moved his feet so quickly in patterns that made absolutely no sense to her.

To her great embarrassment, she was the only one who couldn't seem to pick up the movements. Lira could replicate each combination easily and almost instantaneously. Ylena hoped that if Lira succeeded while Ylena failed, it might make Lira a little less angry. But no matter how many times Ylena froze during a combination, Lira kept smiling with the same amount of apparent glee.

One of the combinations had Ylena and Lira passing close to each other, and when Priest Caed looked away for a second, Lira ran into Ylena and sent them both into a sprawling heap. Ylena sat on the floor stunned. She knew there was no way that Lira had accidentally hit her. She had spent her whole life with only her grandfather, and she had no idea how to react if someone was purposefully mean. She was still shaking off her shock when Lira stood and said, "I forgive you for running into me, Ylena. I know you are new to this, so it's still really hard for you." This caused Ylena's mind to freeze up even more, and she couldn't figure out how to stand up.

Priest Caed stalked over to her and held out his hand. She took it, and he pulled her to her feet. But instead of letting go of her hand, he leaned in closer and said in a harsh whisper, "Ylena, do you realize how serious this is?" He was staring her directly in the eyes, and she wasn't sure how to respond so she just blinked stupidly.

"There is no room for mistakes. You must be perfect. Do you understand me? You must be perfect, or you will die."

Ylena felt caught in his stare and couldn't breathe. She couldn't believe the Priest growing strawberries had lulled her into feeling safe. Priests like Caed were obviously the reason Jer warned her to avoid them.

His grip on her hand tightened. "Tell me you understand," he said slowly. "Tell me you will be perfect."

She whispered, "I understand. I will be perfect."

He let go of her hand and abruptly stepped back. Ylena hurried back to her spot at the back of the class. She noticed Lira's face was a smooth mask of innocence. Pim and Wilder tried to give her encouraging smiles, but she still couldn't seem to catch her breath.

The rest of the class passed with some more awkward moves on her part, but Lira didn't touch her again. Madame Director gathered up both classes, and the acolytes sat on the floor, utterly exhausted.

"Overall, today was a good showing. Obviously, you have each been chosen by the Goddess, so it's just a matter of refining the raw materials she has blessed you with." She looked to Priest Caed for encouragement, but he just stared ahead blankly.

"Some of you need a bit more rehearsal than others, and you will have specific lessons to fit your needs. Wren and Rowan, you will each have daily lessons with Miya to improve your flexibility." Madame Director suddenly focused her attention on Ylena, so she sat up straight. "Ylena, your dancing skills are not as good as I had hoped." At this, she caught a quiet chuckle from Lira that, of course, no one else heard. Madame Director continued, "As a result, you will have daily private lessons with Priest Caed. I expect you to treat these lessons as a matter of life and death. Do you understand me?"

Ylena nodded numbly. "Yes, Madame Director. I understand." She turned to find Priest Caed staring at her. She ducked her head and hugged her legs into her chest.

6

After such a physically and emotionally draining afternoon, there was nothing Ylena wanted more than to crawl into her quiet room and hide, but of course, it was once again time to eat. She sighed and gathered a small plate of fish and green beans and was careful to sit as far from Lira as possible.

Pim was quick to join her with a plate piled high. "Oh, Ylena, I'm sorry that was so rough. I know Lira is the one who tripped you, but after she pulled that innocent face, I knew there was no way the Priest would believe differently."

"Thanks, Pim. I'm glad to know that I'm not the only one who knows what she did. I seriously don't know how I made her so mad." Ylena picked at her food without eating.

"You don't know?" Pim asked incredulously. "She thinks you stole the role of the Goddess from her."

Frustrated tears sprung up in Ylena's eyes. "I don't even know what that means!" Ylena looked at Pim and realized that she might have confessed more than she intended. She tried to surreptitiously wipe her eyes before anyone but Pim noticed.

Pim weighed her words carefully. "I know that not

everyone has been allowed to see the Pageant before. Sometimes, parents don't allow their children to attend until they are about your age, and sometimes ..." She dropped her voice. "Sometimes there are ... other reasons people have never seen the Pageant."

Ylena replied just as carefully. "Umm ... yeah, my grandfather didn't allow me to see the Pageant before."

Pim smiled and continued more easily. "Some parents, or grandparents, can be a bit conservative, and who can blame them? But while that is still a fairly common reason to have never seen a Pageant at your age, I can guarantee Lira would still give you a hard time about it." Pim gave her a wry smile.

Ylena ducked her head and smiled back. "Understood."

"So, those people who have never seen a Pageant, they might not know how serious the whole performance is."

Ylena remembered the look in Priest Caed's eyes when he threatened her. "I definitely understand this is serious."

"Good," Pim replied. "Those people might also not be aware that the role of the Goddess is the most highly sought after role in the entire Pageant. Some girls train their whole life with the hope of winning the role." Pim glanced meaningfully in Lira's direction. "And if that girl finally wins the role of the Goddess, only to have it stolen at the last minute? Well, let's just say that girl might not respond in the best way."

"I see," sighed Ylena. "Thanks for the helpful explanation. And thanks for your ... understanding."

Pim smiled. "I'm glad to help. Now, I'm going to get some more food. Want me to get you something else, too?" Ylena was shocked to look down and realize that, at some point in their conversation, Pim had finished everything on her plate.

"No, thanks," said Ylena. "I think I'm going to head to sleep early."

Pim already had a mouth full of food, but she waved goodbye.

Ylena escaped into the quiet hallway, and the closer she got to her room, the more her breathing slowed. She was almost at her door when she heard Wilder call her name. She turned to see him hurrying down the hallway in her direction. Her breathing immediately sped back up.

"Hey, Ylena." Wilder looked down and seemed shy for the first time. "I just wanted to apologize for the way I was acting today. I know I can come on a little strong, but I only like it if we are both having fun. When I saw how Lira treated you, I realized you might be more in need of a friend than ... uh ... anything else. Can we start over?"

These were more words than she had heard from Wilder at one time, and it took her a moment to understand what he meant. "Um ... yes, a friend would be nice. Thanks." His face lit up in a smile, and her heart skipped another beat despite what he just said.

"I got this for you." He handed her a water glass with a small flower bud inside. "Now that I'm handing this to you, I realize I'm giving you a flower, and maybe that's a confusing message, considering what I just said ..." His embarrassed smile was pretty adorable. "Oh, wow. Yeah, I probably should have brought you something besides a flower for this conversation." He closed his eyes and rubbed his forehead, which caused a little giggle to rise out of Ylena. He glanced up and smiled. "I mean, we are kind of trapped in Temple Order for now, and flowers are definitely in abundance around here, so hopefully, you can forgive me for that, too?"

She laughed. "I think I can forgive you for that, too."

"Oh, good!" He smiled and handed her the flower bud.

As he passed the glass to her, their hands touched, and she felt her heartbeat flicker again.

He pulled away and took a step back. "Well, I guess I will see you in the morning."

She smiled and said, "See you then."

She made it back into her room without embarrassing herself further and leaned against the door with a long, relieved sigh. She set the flower bud in the center of her bedside table and went to take a long and soothing bath. When she finished, she came out to discover the bud had blossomed into a beautiful flower. She smiled and fell asleep.

Ylena had fallen asleep to good dreams, but late at night, she woke up in a cold sweat thinking about what her next rehearsal would be like. Even though she understood why Lira was mad at her, there was nothing she could do to change anything. She went to breakfast feeling defeated before the day had begun. Pim met her again with coffee, but even that wasn't enough to raise her spirits.

Madame Director rounded them up after breakfast and led them into their rehearsal space. She now had a small table to sit at so they could watch the rehearsal, but she directed the acolytes to take seats in a circle on the floor. Pim and Ylena sat down together, and Wilder gave a small wave and took a spot on the other side of Ylena. Lira sat far away from Ylena, but unfortunately, that meant that she could be clearly seen glaring the entire rehearsal.

"Today, we officially begin!" Madame Director began by walking around their circle. "Deven will be handing out books with the Pageant script to each of you. This script is as sacred as the scriptures. I expect you to treat it as such. You will bring this with you every morning to rehearsal until every line has been memorized."

Lira's hand shot into the air. "Madame Director, I already have the lines for every role memorized."

"Thank you, Lira." She gave her a patient smile. "That is definitely a worthy goal for everyone."

"I wanted to let you know, just in case someone has problems fulfilling their role, that I'm more than happy to take over." She smiled sweetly in Ylena's direction.

Madame Director's head whipped sharply to face Lira. "No one will have any issues fulfilling their role." She turned to look at each of them in turn. "I expect every one of you to dedicate your body and soul to this performance. Is that clear?"

They each nodded, including Lira, but when Madame Director turned around, Lira stared angrily at Ylena once again.

"I'm glad that is understood. Let's all turn in your scripts to the first page and begin reading through the lines." She sat down at her table and listened as the acolytes read.

As they began working their way through each scene, Ylena realized how many more lines she had to say than Lira. Every time Lira said one of her lines, she made it obvious that she was reciting from memory and was just following along in her book out of courtesy. Ylena also noticed that they had made their way through several pages and Wilder hadn't said a single line yet. She started to get nervous as she slowly began to realize why.

Wren, the girl with the soft brown hair from Knowledge Diocese, recited her lines in a calm, clear voice:

"The Goddess brought all of creation under her control.
SHE commanded nature, in power and beauty.
But the Goddess was alone.

The Goddess built the Shining City.
SHE filled it with people, diverse and lovely.
But the Goddess was still alone.

The Goddess created her Priests.
SHE gave them her magic, to build and mend.
But the Goddess was still alone."

The room was silent for several moments until Madame Director cleared her throat pointedly in Ylena's direction. Ylena ducked her head and tried to will the blush off her cheeks. "Who in all creation is mighty enough to be my Companion?"

And then, of course, it was Wilder's turn to reply, his words slow and deliberate:

"My Lady,
My heartbeat pulses with the rhythm of a fiery lute,
and I will strum your spirit to life.

My fingers pluck the strings of a delicate harp,
and I am gentle enough to awaken your soul.

My lips curve around tender notes of love,
and I will breathe a new fire into your heart."

He seemed to need the script as little as Lira did, and Ylena felt his attention directed at her even though she kept her eyes buried in her book. She heard a delighted sigh and looked up to see Wren blushing and hiding her own face.

"That's just lovely, Wilder," said Madame Director. "I think we can pause there for a moment and take a brief break before we read any further."

Some of the acolytes stood to go get a drink of water, but

before Ylena could run off, Wilder turned her direction. "You seemed surprised that I was playing the part of the Companion," he said. "I thought you had already figured out that was my role?"

Since Ylena had no idea what this Pageant even was, she most certainly had not figured that out, but she was reluctant to be as honest with him as she had been with Pim. Luckily, Pim was sitting next to her and she jumped in. "Wilder, I think you stunned all of the ladies with your charming performance. And I'm pretty sure you are already aware of that."

He rubbed his chin to hide his grin. "I appreciate the compliment. I think." He laughed and stood up to get some water.

"I should have warned you last night," said Pim. "I thought you knew what part he was playing, or I would have told you then."

"It's not your fault I have no idea what's going on," said Ylena. "But please tell me, does it get more embarrassing than this?"

Pim gave her a really fake smile. "Umm ...I think you should be prepared for that to be a permanent blush, friend."

Ylena groaned and put her face in her hands.

7

The rest of their read-through that morning passed as it had begun—Ylena reading, Lira glaring, Wilder reading, Ylena blushing. When Madame Director finally dismissed them for lunch, Ylena was exhausted even though she had been sitting the whole morning. As she was standing up to leave, Madame Director pulled her aside.

"Today will be your first private lesson with Priest Caed. I don't think I need to repeat myself about how important this is?"

"No, Madame Director. I understand." Ylena stared at her feet.

"Good." She pulled her shawl tighter around herself. "Eat some lunch. You will need your strength."

She had lost her appetite just thinking about her upcoming lesson but forced herself to eat something anyway. Pim was eating while enthusiastically telling a story to the people seated around her, which distracted Ylena for a few moments. Soon, Deven waved to her, and she followed him out of their usual rehearsal space.

"Cheer up, Ylena," he said. "Dance lessons won't be that bad. You might actually start to enjoy it!"

She forced a smile. "Thanks, Deven. I've just never learned the first thing about dancing, and Priest Caed is a bit ... intimidating. I'm worried I'm not good enough."

"Nonsense," said Deven. "You have a good sense of rhythm, and you are strong and flexible. There is no reason you won't succeed at this. You just need to learn the basic footwork so you know where to start." Ylena nodded numbly.

"We don't usually have a Priest as an instructor, you know." Deven led her underneath the arching trellis to the other end of the circular courtyard. "Most years, it is one of the dance instructors from Discipline Diocese who teaches the lessons, but this year, we have an actual Priest willing to teach. We are very blessed."

"Yes. Blessed. Of course."

He put his hand gently on her arm to pull them to a stop. "I've actually seen Priest Caed dance before. Not just as an instructor in a lesson, but dance using his Gift. It was one of the most beautiful things I've ever seen. I know he is, as you say, intimidating, but if you truly want to learn what it means to dance, there is no one better to learn from." He gave her an encouraging smile. "Are you ready?"

"As ready as ever, I guess. Thanks for the support. I will do my best and learn whatever he has to teach me." Deven pulled back a curtain draped over one of the many arches and ushered her inside.

This rehearsal space was much smaller than their other room, but it still had a lot of space to move. The wall directly in front of her was covered with mirrors from floor to ceiling, and the other wall to her back wasn't truly a wall, just a series of arches leading out into the courtyard. The arches were covered with sheer fabric that billowed in the warm breeze and filtered a soft light into the room. The floors were highly polished wood planks and reflected the soft glow from the crystalline lamps along the edges of the room.

Priest Caed hadn't arrived yet, and she was grateful for the time to herself. In her real life back on the mountain, she spent the majority of each day with just her own thoughts. She did talk to Grandfather, but he wasn't exactly as chatty as Pim, and they would go through most days with only a few conversations over meals and before bed. Since she had been here, she felt like her mind was overflowing with words upon words upon words.

She looked at herself in the mirror and wondered again how she had wound up here. She had often sat on her perch on the mountain and wondered what it would be like to visit the Shining City, but nothing here was close to what she had imagined. From her first step down the mountain, she felt she was being pulled along on an invisible string.

That reminded her of one of the steps she had tried to learn yesterday. She raised onto her toes and leaned the top half of her body to one side and then tried to imagine a string pulling her the other way by her hips. She practiced a few times but kept losing her balance and couldn't see what she was doing wrong.

"You are holding your upper body too rigid." Ylena jumped at the sound of Priest Caed behind her. "You need to keep your core strong but let your upper body follow the trajectory of your hips."

Ylena stood blinking, trying to piece his words together. "I don't know what any of that means."

He didn't seem angry, but he walked toward her with a purpose that caused her to immediately tense up. "See what you did right there?" She shook her head no.

"Look in the mirror," he said. She turned to face herself

in the mirror again. He walked behind her, and she saw her shoulders rise. He held his hands just above her shoulders and caught her eyes in the mirror. "May I?" he asked. She nodded.

He lightly placed his hands on her shoulders and used his thumbs to grasp her shoulder blades, move them down away from her ears, and pull them back and toward each other. She saw the immediate difference in her reflection. She seemed to grow taller, and she looked more confident, too. He removed his hands, and she practiced raising her shoulders and then pulling them back and together like he showed her.

"Wow. That's helpful," she said. "Thank you." She caught his reflection again and saw a faint smile. He walked to stand facing her in front of the mirror.

"It's clear to me that, other than yesterday, you have never danced at all, am I correct?" he asked.

She lowered her head. "That's correct."

"Shoulders!" he snapped. She immediately raised her head and dropped her shoulders back into place. "Good. As I was saying, your lack of training is obvious. However, I am dedicated to ensuring this performance is flawless. I promise to teach you everything you need to survive this Pageant. Do you promise me that you will give it your full dedication?"

She was careful to hold her shoulders in place. "Yes," she said. "I promise."

"Good. Then we start with how to stand." At her blank look, he continued. "You've learned where the shoulders go. Now, it's time to learn everything else."

***

Ylena wasn't sure how it happened, but she left her lesson exhausted from learning how to stand correctly.

Besides the shoulders being down, pulled back, and together, there were a thousand other pieces to think about. Back straight, core muscles tight, hips relaxed but not tilted front or back, neck long, hands firm but relaxed, knees pulled up but not locked ... She used her full body every time she climbed the mountain, but she had never concentrated on each separate piece before. She wondered how Caed could walk at all if he was constantly thinking about each individual part of his body like that. She was imagining the way his powerful body looked as he stalked across the dance floor when she realized she had entered the wrong set of arches and ended up in a different room.

"Hello, Ylena! I'm glad you are finally here. We need to have a chat." The woman who had given her the dress was sitting calmly and drinking tea. "Come, sit." She patted the chair next to her.

Ylena walked forward hesitantly and slowly lowered herself into the seat. "Um ... I have a lot of questions, but the first is, who are you?"

"You can call me Lady Erenne." The woman leaned back in her seat and smoothed the bright green silk brocade of her dress. It was the same color green as her eyes and complimented her warm brown skin.

"Where did you go after the audition? And why did you give me that dress in the first place? I think it was at least partially responsible for me getting the role and ending up here. And did you give my name to Madame Director? How did they know to expect me? How did you know to expect me?"

Lady Erenne calmly sipped her tea and waited for Ylena to stop with her string of questions. Then, she set down her cup and folded her hands in her lap. "These are all very good questions, Ylena, but I'm afraid I can't answer them all to your satisfaction. What I can say is that you are in exactly the place you should be to accomplish my goals."

"Your goals? What are you trying to accomplish?"

Lady Erenne chuckled. "Now that question is much too complex, and I definitely don't have time to answer that one."

"But why did you want me in this Pageant?"

"Now that's a very practical question!" Lady Erenne took another sip of tea. "I put some plans into motion to make sure you ended up right where you are now. I'm not going to claim any meddling in you being awarded your current role. You won that by your own talent. But I will say that you would have ended up here as a cook or a seamstress no matter how you performed on that stage. The dress was just my usual flair for the dramatic, and I'm so pleased to see you lived up to it."

She sipped her tea and folded her hands in her lap again. "As for what I want you to do, for now, I just need you to listen and keep your eyes open. There are some troubling events happening in this City. I need you to help me discover who is involved."

Ylena leaned back in her chair. "What am I supposed to do about troubling events? I have no idea what's even going on here."

Lady Erenne gave her a smug smile. "I don't need you to understand what's going on, because I do. But I'm sure you'll pick up some things as we go along."

"But what's so special about this Pageant?"

"The Pageant is a very powerful moment for this City. It wouldn't be the first time someone has tried to tamper with it. But just so you know, it's not just the Pageant I am interested in. I have eyes and ears everywhere. The Pageant just happens to be the place I want you."

Ylena stood to go. "Listen, I appreciate your support getting me into the Pageant, but I can't help you. My grandfather ... I don't ... I might not be able to stay here until the actual Pageant. I wasn't trying to get into any of this, so ..." She turned to leave.

"You know they will all be executed, right?" Lady Erenne took another sip of tea.

Ylena froze as fear straightened her spine. She deliberately turned back around.

"If you leave, all the rest of them will be executed. Madame Director, Deven, Wilder, Pim ... all of them." She stared at Ylena with a shockingly calm expression.

Ylena sat back down slowly. "What do you mean? What does that have to do with me leaving?"

"If you leave, it will be a sign that your group of acolytes was not chosen by the Goddess, and they will kill every person associated with the current group and start the auditions over again." She leaned forward to look Ylena in the eyes. "Has no one told you that this Pageant is a matter of life and death?"

She thought through how many times someone had something similar. "I thought that maybe they were being a little melodramatic?"

Lady Erenne chuckled darkly. "This City is definitely melodramatic, but no one was joking. If you fail to perform for the Pageant, you will die. If you leave, they will all die." She stared at Ylena with hard eyes. "You probably wouldn't have chosen this if you had known, but it is too late now. You are in. So, what are you going to do?"

Ylena felt the walls closing in. She couldn't breathe. The last few days had been mostly enjoyable, but she still had in the back of her mind that she would be leaving once she found Grandfather.

"I know you will stay," said Lady Erenne. "You won't decide to put all of their lives at risk. You'll find a way to stay and do what needs to be done." She leaned back and began drinking her tea again.

Ylena stood, and because there seemed to be nothing more to say, she walked back to rehearsal.

PURITY

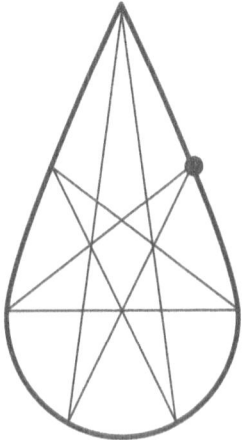

8

After a night replaying Lady Erenne's words, Ylena realized that there was no use worrying about what she would do after she found Grandfather. The best plan for finding him while keeping everyone else safe was to throw herself wholeheartedly into preparing for the Pageant. She was going to devote herself to being perfect. She began memorizing her lines late into the night and taking each rehearsal as serious as possible. This new perspective helped alleviate some of her embarrassment during their read-throughs. When she was completely focused on her lines, she often made it through an entire rehearsal without blushing once.

They spent several days just reading through the lines from their seats on the floor. Madame Director said that she wanted them to take some time to soak in the words before they got distracted with who would stand where. By the time Ylena was settling into a routine, Madame Director had an announcement to make.

"Good morning, acolytes!" she said with her usual clapping. "You have all done a lovely job here in Temple Order. You have been attentive to each word of the script and been able to keep your lines in their proper *order*" she said this with a proud emphasis. "But now it is time to move on. Today, we will be traveling to our next step in your preparation, Temple Purity."

At this, the group cheered. They were all feeling a little restless after so many days indoors rehearsing lines. They went back to their rooms, packed up the few items they had each brought, and began the walk to Temple Purity. From high on the mountain, the crystal spires appeared a lot closer together than they actually were. Ylena studied the next spire and realized they were in for a long morning of walking.

Their group was recognizable as the acolytes for the Pageant, and several people waved or clapped for them as they passed. Ylena realized it was probably the simple clothing they had been given for rehearsals that made them notable. The people they passed all wore so many styles of elaborate clothing that their group in simple clothes stood out.

Even though she had walked down streets with little shops similar to these, she still had to hold herself back from gawking at everything they passed. She still couldn't believe how many shops devoted to food there were. *There is an entire shop devoted to just pastries!* Everywhere she looked in the City, she found food. Even after several days of having regular meals prepared for her, she still couldn't believe how easy it was to find food.

"It's easy to forget how beautiful the City is, isn't it?" She flinched at Wilder's voice. She hadn't noticed him walking at her side.

"What do you mean?" she asked, nervous that she had been caught staring at something that was normal to everyone else.

"Just that after being inside Temple Order for several

days, coming out here into the City makes it all feel new again." He looked at her with a smile. "There is always so much to look at." His dark eyes were locked on her.

She was starting to recognize Wilder's "lines" even when he wasn't reading from a script. "You're right. Just look at that store completely devoted to butter knives. Fascinating." She gave him a wry smile.

He burst out laughing. "Not exactly what I was looking at, but I can see why you find them fascinating."

She liked it when she was able to surprise him. That's when he sometimes dropped his "lines" and talked to her more like a friend. It caused a lot fewer blushes; plus, she enjoyed the conversation.

"I do see what you mean about everything looking new," she conceded. "It is marvelous to think just how much time was spent on each individual cupcake and hat and vase and butter knife." She smiled. "There are so many true artists in the City."

"I agree," he said with an authentic smile.

They spent some time pointing out anything they saw that was either unusually beautiful or silly until Pim ran up to them out of breath.

"Did I miss anything?" she said with a laugh.

"Where have you been?" said Ylena.

"I saw someone I knew!" She skipped along between the two of them. "I was trying to catch up on all the news we've missed while we've been rehearsing nonstop."

"So, what did you hear?" asked Wilder.

She waved them to come close and whispered so quietly Ylena almost didn't hear her. "One of the High Priests is dead."

Wilder's eyes widened in shock, and Pim looked around to make sure no one had overheard them. Ylena obviously knew that it was sad when someone died, but she wasn't sure what Pim meant by a High Priest.

"Do you know which one?" asked Wilder.

"The High Priest of Purpose," she whispered again. "There hasn't been an official announcement, mainly because no one knows what to say."

"What do you mean?" asked Ylena, before she could stop herself.

"Well, what kind of announcement could they make?" whispered Pim. "One of the seven High Priests, who are basically immortal, has died ... for some reason? Makes for a kind of awkward announcement."

"Yeah," said Ylena. "I guess you are right."

Pim shivered. "I don't want to think about that right now. Let's walk and pretend everything is fine, just like we always do!" She put her arms through Ylena and Wilder's and walked between them with a smile that seemed mostly real.

It was easy to tell that they were getting close to Temple Purity based on how close they were to the giant spire at its center. The spires were lit from within with a constant glow both day and night, although the glow looked like a golden shimmer of the sunlight on the crystal during the day. They dwarfed the rest of the City and came close to competing with the height of the mountains that surrounded the City.

As they passed through the last of the shops and a park similar to the one she had auditioned in, they stepped into the open area surrounding Temple Purity. The circular building itself looked similar to Temple Order, but instead of court-yards filled with vines and flowers, this courtyard was filled with a virtual garden of water. As they walked up the steps and under the arches, they stepped onto a clear walkway that lay directly over a slow-moving stream of water. Ylena could see small, colorful fish swimming through the water above a layer of smooth white stones. The feeling of walking on the top of the water was disconcerting, so she couldn't look down as she walked. The rest of the courtyard was filled with fountains with sprays of water forming moving sculptures. She tried to understand how they got the water to flow in such precise patterns. She was soon so transfixed that she didn't see that the rest of the group was moving on without her.

She hurried to catch up and followed them as they walked through an arched door that was hidden behind a waterfall. She smiled and closed her eyes for a moment to savor the sound. She followed them through the archway and found a room strikingly similar to the one they had just left at Temple Order.

"Welcome to our home for the next few weeks," said Madame Director proudly. "Your rooms are up the same stairs as before. Go ahead and settle in, and be back here to begin the next step in your training."

9

After they settled into their rooms, they all met back in the rehearsal space, and Madame Director had Deven lead them through some simple blocking. He had drawn lines on the floor to approximate the size of their stage. As they talked through their lines in the first scene, he showed them where they would stand for each line. He had them practice each line with the movement several times. Ylena thought that the movements felt very stiff and unnatural, but Deven assured them that the more they practiced, the more their movements would begin to feel normal.

They took a break for lunch, and then Madame Director stood for another announcement. "Dearest acolytes, it is now time for you to tour Purity Diocese and learn more about this Virtue of the Goddess. Follow Deven as he leads you on your discovery!"

Despite a good part of their morning spent walking, Ylena was glad to spend the afternoon out in Purity Diocese and not in a classroom with Priest Caed. She had been making progress in her dance classes, but they were a lot more intense than going on a simple walk.

They began their walk through more of the shops that surrounded the temple but soon arrived at a series of large buildings. She recognized a series of pipes leading into each building that looked similar to the pipes she had seen at the pool where she entered the City. They walked along the pathway that ran between the buildings, and on the other side, she found a river flowing through the middle of the City.

Deven got their attention and spoke to the group. "This is the largest waterway that flows from the mountains into the City. This is the main location of the work that the Purity Priests bless us with, although they do work at various other waterways throughout the City. The Priests purify the water that comes from the mountains and give it the life it needs to travel through all of the pipes that connect this City."

He led them to the edge of the water, and Ylena saw a male Priest wearing sharply creased black robes and a silver circlet atop his brown hair step out from the midst of some of the pipes. Her group bowed their heads and cupped their hands.

"Goddess's blessing upon you," said the Priest.

"And also upon you," responded the group as they looked up.

"Welcome to Purity Diocese," said the Priest. He had a no-nonsense way about him, and it seemed like he just wanted to get this over with and get back to work. "I'm honored to show you the holy work the Priests from Temple Purity are blessed to perform each week. May the blessing the Goddess bestowed on me inspire you as you perform your sacred duty in the Pageant." He recited the rote words and then turned back to his work.

The group crowded around the pipes to get a closer look at what the Priest was doing. The Priest closed his eyes and held his arms out, palms facing down over the water, and murmured quiet prayers she couldn't quite hear but sounded similar to what the Priest in Order had said. When he reached up and touched his eye, Ylena was ready and easily mirrored the movement. The Priest knelt and lowered his hands into the water of the stream.

Their entire group held their breath, and then suddenly, there was a great whoosh of sound. The water closest to the Priest seemed to flow straight up and then fall in a gentle rain into the pool connected to all of the pipes. The water swirled in the pool like it was alive until it settled down and was instantly still without a single ripple.

Ylena wanted to burst into applause, but she followed the group into bowing and cupping their hands.

The Priest said, "The water flows into these large pipes and then into the smaller pipes that run in every shop and home. May the Goddess bless you as you prepare for the Pageant."

Deven thanked the Priest for sharing his Gift, then ushered the group to head back to the temple.

Like the time when they saw the Priest's Gift of growing a field of strawberries, the group was subdued on their walk back. Ylena wondered why her grandfather had never told her about what the Priests in the City could do. He'd lived in the City before he moved to the mountain cave with his daughter before Ylena was born. He must have known what they could do. So, why didn't he mention something so magnificent? He was very careful to teach her how to find clean water when they would walk around the mountain. He taught her what kind of illnesses she could get if she drank water that had been contaminated by a sick animal, but he never thought to mention that in the City they had Priests who could simply remove everything that didn't belong from the water?

She was a bit irritated at him for this, but then she had a

thought. If Pim saw someone she knew while she was walking through the City, could the same happen for her?

Instead of focusing on all the shops and amazing creations in the City, this time, she focused on the people in the hopes she would see Grandfather.

After they were more than halfway back to the temple, Ylena noticed something about the people in Purity Diocese that she didn't notice in Order Diocese. The people here were dressed in two very distinct ways. One group was dressed conservatively. The men wore jackets and vests and ties and overcoats, and the women wore so many layers and ruffles that she wasn't sure how any of them weren't suffocating in the heat. The other group was shocking by contrast. While they were still almost all completely covered to a fault, some of their outfits were extremely revealing. One woman was wearing a dress that covered her from neck to ankle and with sleeves to her wrists, but the white fabric was so sheer Ylena could see through it. Her eyes widened so far that she wasn't able to hide her reaction from Pim who laughed at her.

"She's similar to Wilder with all that!" Pim laughed.

Wilder looked at her curiously. "What do you mean?"

"I told Ylena early on that I assumed you were from Purity Diocese. Was I wrong?"

"I'm from Perfection Diocese," he said.

"Well, that's understandable, but in a different way," she said with a smirk. "I just assumed you were from Purity because of the old joke."

Wilder and Ylena both had a confused expression, so she went on with a dramatic sigh. "What? You don't have the same jokes over there? They say there are two kinds of people in Purity Diocese: those who are pure because they don't have a choice." She paused dramatically and looked at

Wilder. "And those who see Purity as a game they intend to win, even if everyone else loses."

Ylena started to laugh, but Wilder stopped walking and spoke in a low voice. "That's a dangerous joke, Pim."

Pim immediately froze in place. She looked terrified, and tears sprang to her eyes.

Wilder's face broke into a smile. "I'm just teasing, Pim. I think your assessment of me is spot on." He gave her a wink.

She laughed, but her smile wasn't as bright as it had been just a minute ago.

10

The next few days fell into a nice rhythm. Ylena's mornings were spent working through their script and blocking, then lunch with Pim and Wilder, then dance lessons with Caed, then back with the group for any projects they needed to finish before dinner. Besides the few times she had to avoid being sabotaged by Lira, her days were pretty good. Things were going so well that she was surprised when she once again stumbled upon Lady Erenne.

"Ylena! How nice to see you!" Lady Erenne announced warmly. "Come sit and have some tea with me."

Ylena sighed and sat down beside Lady Erenne at the small table next to the fountain. "Hello, Lady Erenne. I hope you are well?"

"Aren't you a sweet thing?" she replied. "Yes, I'm quite well, thank you. You've been doing a wonderful job of devoting yourself to the Pageant. I'm quite impressed."

"Thanks. I'm not sure I have much of a choice."

"You always have a choice, dear. Not always the choice you would prefer, but a choice nonetheless." Her hair was unbound today, and she brushed her loose chestnut waves behind her shoulder. "About the other matter we discussed ..." She looked at Ylena expectantly.

"I'm not sure what you want from me," Ylena replied. "I'm working on the Pageant as hard as I can, and that's basically my whole life right now."

"That's good. The Pageant is your number one priority. But are you telling me you haven't heard anything exciting since I saw you last?" Lady Erenne leaned forward like she was awaiting a tasty bite.

Ylena thought through her last days and wondered what she knew that could possibly interest the Lady Erenne. She hesitated long enough that the Lady Erenne spoke again.

"Now, now. Don't hold out on me. I am one of the only people in this City who knows where you are actually from. I think that's valuable enough information that you owe me a little bit of information in return, don't you think?" She smiled sweetly and picked up her tea again. She stared intently at Ylena over the top of the cup.

Ylena immediately felt her chest tighten. She'd almost forgotten that the Lady Erenne had found her soaking wet just inside the gate of the City. Of course she had realized where Ylena came from.

"I heard the High Priest of Purpose died." Ylena said it in a rush and immediately began thinking of a plausible reason she would know this that wouldn't cause her to reveal that Pim had been the one to tell her.

"Ah, yes. Well, it's good to know that information is finally filtering into the City. That seemed to take longer than I would have expected." She tapped her bottom lip thoughtfully. "That is an important piece in the puzzle, so I'm glad you thought to mention it. Did you hear any word on what caused his death?"

Ylena blinked and tried to get her thoughts to catch up. "I don't think I even knew it was a 'he.' I only heard that it was suspicious that he died since the High Priests are basically immortal." Ylena put her head in her hands and sighed. "I don't even know what that means! How am I supposed to tell you anything important when I don't even know what's important and what's common knowledge?"

Lady Erenne smiled widely. "Oh, now that is a smart question! Let me see if I can give you something helpful in exchange for your honesty. There are seven High Priests, one for each of the seven temples that represent each of the Goddess's seven Virtues. I trust you know those from your script?" Ylena nodded. "Good. Each of the High Priests has led their respective temple for more than two hundred years."

Ylena's eyes widened. "Two hundred years?"

Lady Erenne's lips twisted up. "Maybe that seems especially odd to you because you have never seen an old person anywhere in the City?"

"You're right. I haven't. And no children either, but I haven't been able to ask anyone without revealing that I'm not from the City."

"That's very wise of you. The lack of visible children is a different issue for another time. But there are three main reasons you won't notice a truly old person in the City. First, the Priests in Temple Perfection can use their Gift to heal most illnesses and injuries, so people should only die after a long, full life. And second, the Priests have the ability to Perfect people and change their appearance to seem as young as they choose."

Ylena cocked her head in thought, and Lady Erenne chuckled. "Yes, I see you doing the calculations. Maybe some of the people you thought were young are actually old. That's true. But there is a third reason. Aside from the High

Priests, people don't live long because of the leading cause of death in the City: execution."

Ylena was so startled she almost choked. "Excuse me? Execution?"

"I guess you've been sheltered in the temples during your time here and haven't actually viewed one. That is a small blessing, I suppose. You've definitely been threatened with execution enough, though, I daresay?" Ylena thought back on all the ominous statements people had made since she arrived and nodded.

"None of that is simple melodrama, as we discussed before. The High Priests discovered that the best way to keep the control in their hands was to make sure they were the ones with the most power and the longest lives. They have each lived longer than routine healing normally allows, and no one with a shorter lifetime has been able to challenge them. But now, someone has tipped that balance. Interesting, isn't it?" Lady Erenne tapped her lip again and stared off into the distance in thought. She brought herself back with a shake of her head and focused on Ylena again. "So, does that start to make a little more sense?"

Ylena had no answer but to shake her head.

Lady Erenne chuckled again. "No, I guess it doesn't. But don't worry. It doesn't need to make sense to you right now. If I need anything specific from you, I'll send you a letter with instructions. For now, just focus on doing your best in rehearsals, keep your ears open, and let me know if you hear anything else interesting. You'll do just fine, dear." She patted Ylena's hand and then turned back to her tea in a seeming dismissal.

Ylena stood to leave, but as she reached the doorway, Lady Erenne called to her, "Ylena, do you know which Diocese Wilder is from?"

Still numb from their conversation, she answered automatically, "He's from Perfection." Her thoughts finally caught up to her mouth, and she said, "Why do you ask?"

Lady Erenne held her tea close to her mouth. "No reason. Thank you, dear." She took another sip and stared off into the distance.

11

Ylena was still dazed from her conversation with Lady Erenne when she realized she was late for her dance lesson. She had never been late before, but tardiness didn't seem like something that was allowed in the City. She ran through the courtyard of Temple Purity and received quite a few odd looks. She wanted to avoid the judging glares of the people in the courtyard, but her other option was to look down at the clear floor suspended over the water and that was much worse. She skidded to a halt in front of the arches that led into the dance studio. She said a little prayer to the Goddess or whoever was listening that Priest Caed wouldn't be there waiting. She walked in and found Caed standing at the front of the room with his arms crossed. She realized why it might be easy for her grandfather to be an atheist.

"Glad you cared enough to show up," Priest Caed said. She wanted to curl in on herself, but she stood up straight. She had learned that lesson well on her first day.

"Let's not dwell on it." He walked closer to where she stood in the middle of the dance floor. "What were we working on last time?"

"Spotting my turns," she replied. "I was practicing how to do more than one turn in a row without getting dizzy." She was still struggling with her turns. She had felt unsteady and clumsy the entire lesson.

"Yes, we will practice turning more later. You have a lot of turns at the end of the third act, and you need to be able to finish them without falling off the stage."

Ylena's eyes widened in panic, and Caed chuckled. "I'm kidding." She gave a hesitant smile but wasn't convinced.

He continued in his teacher voice. "Today, we are going to learn some partnering. A lot of your scenes involve dancing with the Companion, and I'd rather you start your group dance rehearsals with a little practice under your belt. How does that sound?"

"Yes, thank you," she said with a smile. She was always eager to learn something that would save her from looking like an idiot later on.

He walked to the small record player and cranked the lever a few times until it began to play a waltz. He walked back to her side and brushed his dark hair out of his eyes. He raised his hands to her sides and looked her in the eyes. "May I?" he asked. She nodded. He settled one hand on her waist and signaled with his eyes that she should put her right hand in his.

"One of your dances is a variation of a waltz, and you will begin in this position. In addition to your usual posture, you will lengthen your spine before leaning back and tilting your head to the left. Go ahead and try that."

She arched her spine and tilted her head like he said. She could see their reflection and smiled into the mirror at the lovely shape their bodies created. "Pretty!"

In the mirror, she could see his eyes trail along the curve of her neck. His eyes continued up to the top of her head.

"Good form," he said. "If you tilt your head back too far, it will break the line, but you have it exactly right."

He adjusted his grip on her hand. "Grip lightly, because we will let go for turns, but remember you can come back here to find your center."

He shifted, and she automatically moved to compensate. "Good. The most important thing in partnering is being responsive to your partner's movements. When I move one way …" He stepped his right leg forward, and when his body shifted, she instinctively moved her left leg back. "…you react." He shifted to move both legs together, and when he pulled back, she followed him to center.

"Wow," she breathed. She looked at herself in the mirror again and smiled. "I'm really dancing."

She saw his reflection smile down at her. He let go of her waist and used that hand to gently push her out to the side. She flung her arm out in response and couldn't stop a giggle. He used his left hand to pull her back in and curled her around herself, though she wasn't quite sure how it happened. She ended with her arm and his wrapped around her waist. In the mirror, she saw him looking down at the curve of her neck again, but before she had time to catch her breath, he spun her out to the side, then pulled her back to their starting position.

She mentally worked through the motions of what they had just done. She was exhilarated as she reviewed the math of each move and glanced up at him to ask a list of questions. Every question died on her lips when she looked in his eyes.

Every lesson, week after week, step after step, Caed had taught her with a cold determination. Ylena felt the same determination, so she had seen her skills improve each day. But today, she didn't just feel the satisfaction of doing the right steps; she felt the joy of what it meant to dance. When she looked in his eyes, she saw that same joy, and it surprised her. She thought Caed was someone motivated only by following the rules and doing the right steps, but in his eyes, she saw a fire reflected that she didn't expect.

She realized they had been standing in the same position for several heartbeats, and she suddenly wasn't sure where she should move her body next. Luckily, he seemed to have the same realization, and he smoothly let go of her hand and waist in such a way that the two of them were immediately at a more comfortable distance.

He was able to break the silence before she was. "That was nicely done. I think your first group dance rehearsal will go better than the last one." A hint of a smile curved on his lips.

She instantly was brought back to their first lesson and remembered how she ended up on the floor because of Lira. Her eyes widened as she imagined Lira sabotaging her again.

"Don't worry," he said. "You've learned a lot since then. I'm honestly shocked at how fast you have picked everything up. I'd like to believe that it's because I'm such a brilliant teacher." He gave her a dramatic bow. "But I think it's actually because you have natural talent along with a whole lot of dedication."

She smiled and started to duck her head in embarrassment, but she remembered her posture and stood up straight. "Thank you."

He began to pack up his things as she turned to leave. She stopped before the arches leading to the courtyard. She closed her eyes and savored the exhilaration still flowing through her. She was slightly out of breath, her heart was racing, and her muscles tingled from exertion. Her whole body felt ... alive.

She spun back to face him and said, "Thanks for showing me what it's like to dance."

She could read the same thrill of restless energy in his stance, and his soft smile let her know that he understood what she meant. "You're welcome, Ylena."

≈

After her dance lesson with Caed, Ylena enjoyed a good dinner with Pim and Wilder and then headed back to her room. She caught herself humming again and laughed. Pim had asked why she was in such a good mood, and she said that this was just her usual cheerful self. Maybe Pim was right, though. She did feel a bit lighter than usual.

She did a pirouette into her bathroom and laughed again as she turned on the warm water. Her mind was filtering through every step she had learned over the last few weeks, and she finally understood what it meant to piece the steps together and dance. Everything about her was changing. She had never seen anyone dance before she came to the City, and now, she couldn't imagine going back to a small cave without a dance floor. How would she explain that to Grandfather when she finally saw him? What if he told her to leave the City and never come back? What if she never got to dance like that again?

She tried to push back the tears by lowering herself into the water and closing her eyes. She imagined herself in a flowing dress as she danced across a wide stage. She held out her hand and could almost feel a matching palm meet her own. She smiled as she remembered what it felt like to spin away from Caed and then to have him gently pull her back into his chest. Her hand tingled with the memory of his warm fingers wrapped around hers. She smiled and opened her eyes.

In her clasped hand, she held the water from her bathtub. It was formed in the exact shape of Caed's hand. She gasped and let go. The water crashed out of its shape and splashed across the floor of the bathroom.

12

Ylena was already drinking her second cup of coffee when Pim joined her for breakfast. "You're up early," said Pim. "I'm always eating breakfast long before you show up!"

"I didn't sleep well." Which was an extreme understatement. After cleaning up the water all over the floor, she had tossed and turned all night. "I decided to see if coffee would help."

"Is it working?" Pim grinned behind her cup.

Ylena gave her a wordless glare, and Pim giggled as she stuffed bacon into her mouth.

"Good morning, ladies!" Madame Director flowed up to their end of the table. "I see you are up early. Would you be willing to run an errand for me?"

Pim sat up straight. "Of course! What do you need?"

"I need someone to go pick up a bowl we will need for one of our scenes today. The vendor's name is Tarley, and his pottery stand can be found in the market on the east side of the park. Can the two of you handle that responsibility?"

"Yes, Madame Director," said Pim. "You can count on us!" As Madame Director walked away, Pim shoved another piece of bacon in her mouth and jumped to her feet. "Come on! Let's go! I can't believe she's giving us the chance to leave the temple for a little bit!" Ylena gulped down the last sip of her coffee and followed Pim out of the temple.

Ylena had to admit it was nice to get out of the temple, even if it was just a quick trip over to the park. Their lives revolved around rehearsals and lessons, and the chance to do anything out of that routine was exciting. Pim was so giddy she was basically skipping, and Ylena was trying to get her to focus.

"Let's not get distracted, Pim. I want to do a good job so she might let us escape like this some other time, too." Pim smiled and continued skipping.

Sooner than they had hoped, they found the booth with pottery, and Pim walked up to the man standing in front. He was broad shouldered with strong hands and a quick smile. "Are you Tarley? Madame Director sent us."

His dark eyes twinkled. "Of course she did, young acolytes! Have you been working hard and memorizing all your lines?"

"Yes, sir!" they both replied. His smile was kind and reminded her a bit of Grandfather, even though he appeared much younger.

"Good work!" he said. "I look forward to seeing the Pageant this year! Let me get that bowl. I set it over here."

He turned to find the bowl, and Ylena admired all of the beautiful pottery he had set up. There was a particularly beautiful blue vase that looked like it was made of something that sparkled. She reached out her hand to touch it but didn't notice how it was precariously balanced. She tried to catch it before it fell, but she couldn't. Tarley's strong hand suddenly reached out and gripped the vase before it slid off the table.

She looked up at him with wide eyes and saw him

whisper a prayer to the Goddess. He set the vase in an open space on the table to his right and picked up the bowl he had packed into a padded box. "You better get back to the temple, ladies. It's a bit too dangerous out here for ones as young as you."

Ylena took the box with the bowl carefully in both hands. They both thanked him and started to walk slowly back to the temple. They had just made it a few steps past his booth when they noticed the sounds in the market change. The normal sounds of people talking and laughing just stopped. Ylena looked around, but she couldn't see anything different.

She looked back to Tarley's booth and saw him look up suddenly. He made a quick movement scanning the crowd. He met Ylena's eyes and looked relieved when he located her. He didn't notice that his quick movement tipped over the vase. Ylena saw it roll slowly off the front of the table and crash onto the street.

The street was already quiet, but after the crash, it fell completely silent. Tarley's eyes moved to stare at the vase on the ground, almost like he couldn't understand what had happened. Every person was utterly still until Ylena noticed a ripple of movement. Around her, everyone was suddenly dropping to their knees. Ylena carefully adjusted the box in her hands and knelt.

She lowered her head, but her eyes scanned through the crowd and watched as three figures approached. A majestic woman with dark hair twined through a tall crown walked slowly toward Tarley, who was standing frozen in fear. The woman wore a sleek, black dress with a long, flowing black veil attached to her sparkling crown. At her sides stood two large figures wearing tight fitting, matte black armor. Ylena could only guess they were men by their size, because they were both wearing deep hoods and masks that covered their faces.

The woman looked down at the broken vase. "What a shocking lack of Discipline." Her voice was smooth and carried easily through the silent crowd. "We are so blessed that I was here to discover this disorderliness. The only way we can honor the Goddess is by revering her Virtues. I am her holy emissary."

Her words seemed to be a silent cue, and the two armored men stepped toward Tarley. Their movement snapped him out of his frozen position. He looked quickly between the two of them. One of the men raised his flattened palm in front of his mouth and seemed to breath out. A fine powder flew from his hand into Tarley's face. He coughed and tried to fan it away, but it floated on the air, and he couldn't avoid breathing it in. The effect was instantaneous. His eyes widened, and he stumbled back. He reached for his throat as if he would claw away his skin and be able to breathe. The two armored men grabbed each arm and pulled him away from the table filled with the rest of the pottery. He fell forward onto the ground and thrashed for just a few moments. And then he fell still.

"Goddess's blessing upon you," said the woman, and she walked on through the crowd.

"And also upon you," replied the crowd. Ylena jumped at the reply. It was the first sound anyone had made since the woman appeared.

The crowd began to slowly stand. The two armored men each grabbed one of Tarley's arms, and they carried him through the crowd, following the woman. A young man with a booth near Tarley's had a broom and was sweeping up the vase. Sounds slowly returned, and people began to walk away.

"Come on. Let's get back," said Pim. She pulled Ylena to her feet, being careful with the box.

Ylena was staring at the man sweeping the vase. She couldn't move.

Pim walked to stand in front of her. "Ylena. We have to get back," she said calmly.

Ylena blinked and slowly focused on Pim's face. "What just happened?"

"We need to get back. Rehearsal will start soon." Pim started walking back toward the temple.

Ylena watched her take a few steps, and then she took a few careful quick steps to catch up. "Pim!" she whispered. "What just happened?" She said each word slowly and clearly.

Pim stopped and looked her in the eyes again. She tilted her head and gave a look Ylena couldn't understand. Then, she shook her head and started walking again.

Ylena grasped the box closer to her chest and followed her.

Ylena handed the box with the bowl to Madame Director and took her seat on the floor as Deven talked them through the blocking on their next scene. It had a lot more cues than some scenes, and Ylena was so distracted she had to ask him to repeat himself multiple times. He frowned but walked Ylena through her placement until she had it down. The rest of the group picked up the blocking quick enough to cover for Ylena's difficulties. When they finished, Deven told them he was proud of them and to enjoy their lunch.

The group headed over to their dining area in high spirits after such a good rehearsal. Ylena looked at the rest of her group and had never felt so alone before. She felt like her body was moving while her thoughts were frozen. She numbly sat down in her usual spot and stared at her empty plate.

Pim sat down across from her, turned to Wilder, and said, "Great work in that scene! The look over your shoulder at the end was a nice touch!" She smiled and bit into an apple.

Ylena looked up at Pim like she had never seen her before.

"Thanks, Pim!" he said. "You know I'm always trying to impress, so it's nice someone noticed."

Ylena kept staring at Pim, trying to understand how she was calmly eating an apple and laughing.

"So, Ylena," said Pim, "how have your dance lessons been going? You haven't talked about them lately." She smiled and bit into the apple again.

"How can you just go back to normal like that, Pim? After what we saw—"

Pim reached across the table and grabbed her hand. Hard. She looked directly into Ylena's eyes, her smile never wavering, as she whispered, "Ylena. You need to pull yourself together. Now."

Ylena started to reply, and Pim's smile faltered for a fraction of a second. In that moment, Ylena saw the barely contained fear behind her eyes. She looked down at the tendons straining on Pim's hand as it grasped hers. Ylena took a deep breath and raised the corners of her lips in the approximation of a smile.

"I think my mind is stuck in dramatic acting mode," Ylena said with a little laugh.

Wilder considered the two of them with a questioning look, but he just took another bite and smiled as Pim started telling a story.

13

Ylena finished her lunch and left for her dance lesson with a forced smile. She waved back at Pim and Wilder and stepped out from behind the waterfall into the courtyard. There were a few people seated on the edge of a fountain, so she waved politely and started walking quickly to her lesson. She arrived a few minutes early, so she leaned up against the stone wall and tried to shove down the sob that was threatening to burst from her lips. How did everyone just go back to their life after what happened to Tarley? Everyone acted like what happened was normal.

Her breathing began to slow down as she thought back to her conversation with Lady Erenne. Is this what she was talking about? All the life and death decisions people talked about were real? She thought about the look on Tarley's face when she almost dropped the vase herself. He had been scared for her. He'd probably saved her life at that moment, and she didn't even know enough to thank him. He had told her to get back to rehearsal because it was too dangerous for someone as young as her. She thought that was a silly thing to say at the time, but now she understood. He wanted to protect her.

She felt the tears running down her face, and she hid her face in her hands. Pim had told her to pull herself together. She took that fear and sadness and pushed it away until she had time to deal with it later. She took several deep breaths and wiped her hands dry. She smoothed her hair back and walked into her lesson.

Caed was practicing a complicated combination at the front of the room. His steps were quick, and the wind rustled through his hair and loose clothing. She tried to understand exactly how he went from one step to the next with such precision. His next step turned him toward the back of the room. He saw Ylena and stopped.

"There you are." He smoothed his dark hair away from his eyes. "I was just working on a combination that I think will help you practice precise footwork while keeping your arms where they belong."

She wasn't sure how she would be able to focus on anything, but she didn't want to admit that to him. She forced her voice to sound cheerful. "Sounds good!" She walked out to the dance floor and stood next to him, her eyes watching his feet. When he didn't start moving, she looked up at him.

"Are you okay?" He studied her eyes closely.

"Yes, I'm great." She looked at his feet again to avoid his eyes. "Will you show me the combination?"

He hesitated a moment, but then said, "I will."

He showed her the combination by breaking it down in the usual eight counts at a time. Her brain still felt fuzzy, but she felt like she picked up the steps quicker than usual. Once he had walked her through the full combination, he started the music and stepped back to let her put all the pieces together.

She disconnected from the painful thoughts buzzing through her mind and just ... moved. Her body flowed smoothly from one move to the next. She felt like every step was placed exactly where it belonged, followed by the next step, exactly placed. Her hands flowed through the air slowly like they were met with the barest resistance from a soft breeze. She leaned into the wind and moved her body smoothly to the side, and she could feel every muscle beneath her skin move in tandem to hold her in place, just so. She spun to face the front of the room and felt the wind curl around her as her hair floated down around her face. She took a deep, cleansing breath and looked up into the mirror with a real smile. She flicked her eyes to the left of her reflection to see Caed's reaction. And immediately shrank back in fear at the look on his face.

"What did you do?" He stormed over to her. "How? How did you do that?"

She looked up at him and saw the flicker of the silver circlet he wore hidden underneath his hair. She was immediately back in the market and hiding her eyes from the woman with the sparkling crown. She felt her breath come in short gasps. It reminded her of Tarley's last few breaths. She covered her face with her hands, all thoughts of good posture gone.

She could see Caed's feet as he stopped a few steps away from her. She heard him take a deep breath, and then he spoke in a quiet voice. "May I?"

She looked up at these normal words. He gently took hold of one of her wrists and studied her hand. Then, he stared into her eyes. She felt like he was looking beyond her eyes and into her head. He narrowed his hazel eyes and slowly released her wrist.

"Hmmm ..." He was speaking to himself. "I need to think

about this. Class is dismissed for the day." He grabbed his things and walked out.

She stood alone in the middle of the dance floor without a single clue of what happened.

Ylena didn't feel like seeing anyone after her dance lesson, so she took the back way to her room so she didn't have to walk through the rehearsal space. She hurried into her room and closed the door behind her. She splashed some water on her face to wash off the sweat and the tears, but touching the water reminded her of the strange reaction of the water from the night before, so she dried her face quickly.

She sat on her bed and tried to take a deep breath but couldn't seem to get enough air. She tried to fit the pieces of the day together in her mind, but everything was so jumbled she couldn't make sense of it. Since the first day she stepped into this City, she had felt pulled from one thing to another and had no idea where any of it was leading. She sighed and curled up under the covers and slept.

KNOWLEDGE

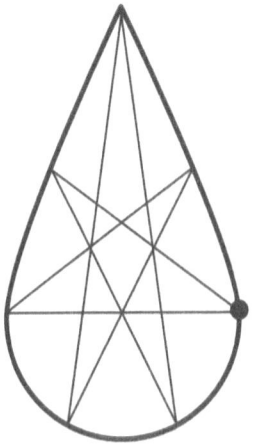

14

Ylena woke the next day and realized she had fallen asleep after her dance lesson and skipped dinner. She couldn't believe she had slept so long. She washed up and headed out to breakfast.

She was getting her coffee when Pim bounced up with a smile. "Good morning! Is the coffee good today?"

Ylena smiled. "It's good every day!" She thought it was strange that Pim wouldn't mention Ylena skipping dinner last night, but then again, maybe that was another thing no one talked about?

She sat down to eat when Madame Director swished into the room. "Good morning, acolytes! Today, we are moving to Temple Knowledge. Eat your breakfast, and then we will be off!"

There was an excited air to the rest of their breakfast, and everyone hurried to get their things. Even though the temples were pretty similar, she was still excited to see what the next one was like. She said a private goodbye to the waterfall in front of the entrance and followed the group outside.

When her foot touched the street, though, her mind

froze. How could they even consider going outside? That's where *she* was! What if they stumbled upon her again? What if someone in their group was the one who made a mistake? Her body was locked in fear, but Pim took her arm and moved her forward.

"It's nice being outside and getting a little sun, don't you think? We always spend so much time inside rehearsing that I forget what it's like to see the sun!" Pim tipped her golden face up to the sky as they walked.

Ylena looked at the smile on Pim's face and couldn't help but smile back. "Thanks, Pim. You always know the right thing to say."

Pim laughed. "I do know I have a *lot* to say. Whether or not it's the right thing, I guess that is debatable."

They continued on, arm in arm, until they arrived at Temple Knowledge.

They walked up the familiar steps, but the courtyard was once again unique. Here, the courtyard was lined with bookshelves and small seating areas where people could be found reading alone. She looked at the bookshelves and wondered how they kept the books from getting wet when it rained.

Then, she stopped in her tracks and realized something. Besides being perfectly warm every day, it had not rained even once since she had arrived. During the summer months in the mountains, it would rain at least once every two or three days. She had been here for weeks, and while she had noticed that some days were cloudier than others, she never saw a drop of rain fall. She wanted to ask someone about it, but if it was true, then bringing it up would automatically reveal she was an outsider. She put it out of her mind for the moment and caught up to the group as they were walking into their rehearsal space.

"Don't get too settled in yet, acolytes," said Madame

Director. "This morning, Deven is taking you straight to the Library."

They dropped off their things in their rooms and headed directly back out. Luckily, the Library was just a short walk from the temple, so there wasn't much time for Ylena's feelings of panic to return.

They passed through the last line of shops surrounding the temple and were standing in front of the tallest building Ylena had seen. The Library was seven stories tall and stretched for an entire block. It wasn't as tall as one of the glowing spires, but Ylena felt dwarfed by it in a similar way.

They walked up the steps and entered into a giant foyer. The center portion of the building was open, and Ylena could see people walking around different shelves of books all the way up on the seventh floor. At her back were rows of windows shining light down onto tables in the center of the room. She could see hallways leading off in every direction, so even the rows of shelves she could see were only a portion of what these rooms held. Her whole group was hushed in awe and respect of the peacefulness of the Library.

A young woman wearing an open, long black jacket over tight black pants came forward and greeted them. They bowed and quietly gave the traditional response. The Priest's braided silver circlet sparkled in her bright copper hair. "Follow me, please."

They followed her through the large open room, past all of the sunlit tables, and into a room off one of the hallways. This room was smaller, but it was still filled from floor to ceiling with books.

"Welcome to the Library," said the Priest. "I know you have seen demonstrations of the Goddess's Gift from some of the other Priests, and if you'd like to have a personal demonstration of Knowledge, I'm happy to assist any volunteers." She gave a crooked smile, and Ylena thought that, of all the Priests she had met, this one seemed the most *normal*.

"But we also thought you might find it interesting to look around the Library and see what you could find. If you are interested in books on a particular topic, I can direct you. Or feel free to wander and see what you discover."

Pim ran up to the Priest and whispered something in her ear. The woman smiled and subtly pointed Pim in the direction of some shelves back in the large room. Pim winked at Ylena and hurried off.

Wilder had already wandered off on his own, so she was left to decide for herself. She had lots of questions about the City, and the Library seemed like the perfect place to research, but how to ask the question to find what she wanted without sounding like an outsider?

She waited while a few others from the group received directions from the Priest until she was the only one remaining. "What are the oldest books about the City you have here?"

The Priest's eyes sparkled. "Such a good question! Our oldest books about the City are over in the West Stacks on the third floor. They were written just a few years after the City was created. You will find so many interesting things there about our history!" Her face was glowing with the excitement of talking about something she loved. "However, those aren't the oldest books in the Library." Ylena cocked her head to the side and tried to understand what this meant.

"The books in the South Annex are from *before* the City was created. Most of those books are in languages we don't even understand, but that hasn't stopped us from being fascinated by them." She gave a dreamy little sigh.

"I've never thought about what happened *before* the City," Ylena said. "Other than what I read in scripture, of course." She had read through the scriptures in her room multiple times, hoping they would help her understand the parts of the City that didn't make sense.

"The scriptures say that, before the Goddess shaped the City, Chaos reigned. And from the few things we have been able to gather from those old books, that much is clearly true. When the Goddess shaped the City, she brought that Chaos under her control with Order and was able to build this marvelous creation." The Priest looked Ylena in the eyes. "I see you are still troubled by this. The Goddess offers the Gift of Knowledge to all. You may ask your question."

Ylena had so many questions, but she asked the one that was currently burning within her. "The City. The way … everything is here. Is this what She wanted? Did She make it this way?"

The Priest sighed and gave her a sad smile. "Ah, child, you are not the first to ask, and you will not be the last. I don't have all the answers, but I can show you what I have learned about the Goddess. Will you allow me to use my Gift of Knowledge?"

The other Gifts Ylena had seen were beautiful, and she really wanted to know the answer. "Yes, please. Show me what you know about the Goddess."

The Priest closed her eyes, and a tear formed on her lashes. She held out her hands and appeared to be waiting. Ylena took hold of her hands.

Ylena blinked up at a clear blue sky. She lay in soft grass, and the smell of violets surrounded her. A warm breeze blew her copper hair to tickle across her cheek.

Her copper hair? Ylena took hold of a copper strand with a hand that was clearly not her own. She was inside the Priest's memory.

She heard a quiet laugh and turned her head to see a green-eyed girl in a simple black top and shorts lying beside her in the grass. On the girl's finger rested a sunshine yellow butterfly. Ylena looked closer and could see the delicate tracery of veins in the wings as they beat a gentle rhythm. The girl slowly raised her hand, and the butterfly took flight. Ylena watched the yellow wings until they were just a dot against the cloudless sky. She sighed with wonder.

Ylena was sitting on a blanket in the sunlit courtyard at Temple Knowledge. She could smell fresh cinnamon rolls and coffee. A toddler in black overalls plopped onto her lap and shoved a cinnamon roll into Ylena's mouth. The icing was warm and sweet, and she laughed in surprise. The little boy clapped his sticky hands together and laughed.

Pink clouds as the sun rose over the mountains ...

Gentle hands braiding her hair ...

The smell of the pages of an old book ...

The soft gray fur on a kitten's belly ...

Chocolate fudge ... A love letter ... New shoes ... Fresh cut grass ... Laughter on the wind ...

Ylena opened her eyes on a gasp. She was standing in the Library with her hands still clasped with the Priest. The Priest opened her eyes slowly and let go of Ylena's hands. Her sad smile was now a contented one. "Those are the hints of the Goddess I've seen. I know it doesn't really answer the question you asked, but it's the best answer I've been able to find so far."

Ylena fought her disorientation at being back in the Library in her own body. Every memory had been a single perfect moment frozen in time. It didn't answer her question, but the Priest's kind face was sincere. "Thank you for the honest answer." Ylena bowed her head and cupped her hands as if receiving a gift.

15

Ylena decided to see what she could find in the oldest books about the City. She didn't think that reading chaotic texts from before the City would help her, but after viewing the Priest's vision, she wasn't sure she would find the answers she sought in a book anyway. She found her way to the West Stacks and took the stairs to the third floor. The books all looked exactly the same, and she wasn't sure what she was hoping to find. She skimmed through some of the titles and pulled out *The City's First Priests*. She walked to the end of the row and ran straight into Caed. She dropped the heavy book, and it narrowly avoided smashing her foot.

"Are you okay?" he asked. His hands were filled with several books, and he looked at her with concern.

"Yeah, I'm fine." She bent down and picked up the book. "Just embarrassed for not watching where I was going."

"You weren't alone in that. I get a bit distracted in here." He hefted his stack of books.

"Look, I want to apologize for ... whatever I did in our lesson yesterday. I had a ... difficult morning and was confused, so whatever I did wrong, I'm sorry."

He stared at her as if he was just seeing her. "You're apologizing. To me."

"Yes. You seemed upset by something I did. I am trying so hard to do a good job, but whatever I did wrong, I'm sorry."

He looked deeper into her eyes. "You are apologizing for doing something wrong. To me. A Priest."

His words finally sank in, and the implications came crashing down in her mind. Even though she had no idea what she had done yesterday, she probably just admitted to doing something much worse than Tarley accidentally dropping a vase. She started to panic but had no idea what to do.

"Breathe," he whispered. He set his stack of books on the end of a shelf and guided her further into the row of books.

"Ylena, look at me."

Her eyes started to refocus, and she turned her attention to his face.

"I didn't mean to terrify you. It's just ... you continue to surprise me. You aren't in any danger from me." He tilted her face up to look into his eyes. "Do you understand? I don't want to hurt you." She nodded. "You aren't in danger from me, but that doesn't mean you aren't in danger. I need you to listen to me closely." He made sure she was focused and dropped his hand from her face. "Not everything in this City is as it seems." She would have laughed at this understatement, but she was still too scared to laugh.

He continued, "There is evil in this City underneath all of the beauty and perfection."

"You sound like Grandfather," she said. "Oh ... I guess I shouldn't admit to a Priest what Grandfather says about the Goddess."

"Oh, I don't believe in the Goddess." He said it in an offhand way that shocked her.

"You don't believe in her?" She shook her head, trying to understand his words. "You're a Priest. How can you not believe your own religion?"

He raised an eyebrow. "You've seen death caused by her High Priests. Do *you* believe?"

She hesitated but admitted, "I don't know."

"That's more sensible than most," he said. "But listen, we don't have much time. There is evil in this City, and I'm trying to fight it. I don't want you to get involved, because it's likely the answers I dig up are going to lead to me being executed." Her eyes went wide. "I know that is how this will eventually end, but I plan on taking out as many as I can before I go. I would spare you from getting involved, but I think you are tied up in this in ways you don't understand. I'm not sure if telling you what I know will put you at more risk or less. I'm worried I won't be able to protect you."

It wasn't until this moment that Ylena realized exactly how close they were standing. Caed was close enough for her to hear his gentle whisper, but that meant he was pressed even closer to her than when they were partner dancing. She suddenly felt too warm and aware of every inch of her body. Just drawing in a breath seemed to move her body closer to his. She saw the same realization cross over his face, and he stepped back quickly. He looked like he might want to say more but shook his head and turned to glance down the aisle.

"You should go," he said. "They will be looking for you."

She nodded and hurried down the stairs without looking back.

16

W hen Ylena made it down the stairs, she found the rest of the group gathering up. The Priest told them that except for some of the very oldest documents, they were able to check out one of the books and take it with them back to the temple. Luckily, the book she had chosen was a reprint of the original text, so she was able to take it with her.

Ylena questioned Pim as a means of distraction from considering why she was still so warm after her conversation with Caed. "So, what book did you check out?"

"It's a book on anatomy." At Ylena's confused expression, Pim opened the book to show her a page she had marked. "It has pictures." Pim giggled.

Ylena was suddenly warm again. "Pim! Are you serious?" She whispered as loudly as she dared.

Pim adopted a fake religious expression. "Ylena, Knowledge is available to all."

Ylena was dumbfounded, but Wilder just chuckled quietly.

"And what did you find?" Pim asked Wilder.

"Love poetry sweet enough to melt a woman's heart." He smiled in Ylena's direction.

"But you didn't bring it with you?" Pim asked.

"I memorized it, of course," he said with a wink.

They made it back from the Library in time for lunch in Temple Knowledge. Ylena ate her food quickly so she could hurry to her dance lessons with Caed. She was tired of not knowing what was going on. If he had information to share with her, she would rather know it, even if it put her at more risk.

She stood up to go when Deven made an announcement. "Today, we will officially begin working on your choreography together as a group. Ylena, from this point forward, you don't have to worry about any more individual lessons. It's time for you all to continue together!"

The group finished their lunch and started moving into the common rehearsal room. Ylena couldn't believe that, after all these weeks of private lessons, they were suddenly finished. She finally felt like she wasn't going to embarrass herself during their group rehearsals, but she was disappointed to give up her private lessons.

"I bet you are glad you don't have to be trapped in a room alone with him anymore," said Pim from Ylena's side.

"Huh? What do you mean?"

Pim dropped her voice. "I mean, he is cute, as far as Priests go, but he always just seems so ..." She looked up and stared right at Caed. "... brooding."

Ylena chuckled. "Yeah, I guess he is that. But it wasn't so bad. I actually learned quite a lot."

Pim turned to her. "Really? Because I don't want to be mean, but ... you were kind of terrible."

Ylena laughed out loud. "Thank you for your honesty, Pim. You are definitely correct."

At her laugh, Caed glanced in her direction. Pim was

right. He was definitely brooding. And her first interaction with him in their group lesson was terrifying. She thought back over what he had said to her that day, and only then did she realize that he hadn't been threatening her. He was warning her. It happened to be a very *dramatic* warning, but she was coming to expect that in the City, especially with people associated with the Pageant.

Madame Director stepped forward. "Good afternoon, acolytes! I hope your time at the Library was enlightening. Today, you will start your group choreography. I will leave you in Priest Caed's very capable hands." Caed looked Ylena's direction, and Ylena blushed. She realized this dance class would be even more challenging than before.

Priest Caed led them through a brief warm up, and Ylena felt some of her tension disappear through the movement. Over the course of their lessons, she had started to feel more comfortable in her own skin, and the simple warm up was enough to remind her body that she was alive.

He started by teaching them the choreography for one of the final scenes in Act One. The dance had a lot of unison movement, so it was a good first piece for them to practice all together. One bit of good news was that Lira was on the opposite side of the stage from Ylena for this portion, so there would hopefully be no "mishaps" today.

After the intentional crash in their first dance class, Lira hadn't tried anything so blatant, but she constantly harassed Ylena any chance she got. Ylena's flower crown had mysteriously disappeared, and she had to make a new one before anyone claimed she lost it. After she noticed a terrible smell in her room, she found a single raw shrimp rotting in the bottom of her wardrobe. Ylena could never prove any wrongdoing on Lira's part. She was too clever to leave any proof, but she always smiled in a way to take credit for every bad thing that happened to Ylena.

"You need more practice so that you all have the exact timing, but that portion is good for now," said Caed. "Let's move on to the next part of that scene with the Goddess and Companion." It wasn't until that moment that Ylena thought through what that meant. And when she did, she knew there was no chance she was getting out of this without a constant blush.

"Ylena, you'll stand here for your song," said Priest Caed. "Then, when you call for the Companion, Wilder will enter from stage left." Wilder swaggered onto the taped stage area, which got him a chuckle from a few of the acolytes and a glare from Caed. "Yes, wonderful," he said drily. "You enter stage left and arrive as Ylena finishes her verse. Then, you turn toward one another and prepare for your waltz."

Ylena raised her arms. Wilder held one hand gently, and she rested the other hand on his shoulder. As he put his other hand on her waist, she realized she had never been this close with Wilder. He smiled down at her and raised an eyebrow. She swore he had read her mind. She stood up straight and then leaned her upper body back and tilted her head to the left, like Caed had told her.

Caed stepped closer. "Yes ... umm ... that's exactly where you start. So, Wilder, you will lead her through the first few steps of a basic waltz. Do you know how to do that?"

Wilder looked down at Ylena and the curve of her neck. "Don't worry. I know what to do from here." Ylena wasn't prepared, but when Wilder stepped forward, her body responded. Her feet moved through the repeated pattern of steps, and she followed him as he led her in a small circle on their stage. He brought them both back to center. He leaned down close and whispered, "Did that feel right?"

Ylena suddenly felt everyone's eyes upon her, and she stood up straight in his arms. She looked to Caed to see if he would rescue her by moving on to the next part, but he was staring at Wilder with cold eyes.

"The steps were accurate, Wilder, but your form leaves much to be desired," said Caed. "I'll be here to make sure you don't embarrass yourself."

Wilder's constant smile seemed to freeze unnaturally. "Don't worry. I promise to practice with Ylena a lot while you are gone."

Priest Caed dismissed their class soon after that, and both he and Wilder seemed to stalk off pretty quickly. Ylena was shaking her head at the whole situation when she saw Pim sitting on the floor, giggling to herself.

"What's so funny?" Ylena asked.

"I did not see that coming!" Pim could barely speak because of her giggling. "You played that so sly I didn't see a thing until Wilder put his hand on your waist. Then, I saw what the brooding Priest was really made of." She fell over dramatically and continued to laugh while she lay on the floor.

"What are you talking about?"

Pim sat up straight and took hold of Ylena's hand. "Honey, I'm from Harmony Diocese, and our Priests are as Gifted with animals as that Priest was Gifted with a field of strawberries. And even with all their Gifts, they would *never* put two bulls in the same pen." She laughed. "This is going to be hilarious."

Ylena wasn't sure she agreed.

17

_____

After dinner, Ylena started to walk to her room, but Pim caught her by the arm. "Want to come hang out in my room for a while? We can read my library book." She waggled her eyebrows.

Ylena gave a scandalized laugh but agreed. "I'll wash up and then head over."

As she entered her room, she noticed a letter on her bedside table.

Ylena,
I have an answer to one of your questions. Meet me in the court-
yard in one hour. Wear comfortable clothes.
_-E_

She reread the letter multiple times and tried to understand what this could be about. She had an endless number of questions, so which one was Lady Erenne going to answer? She wondered if she should just ignore the letter. Ylena had no idea who Lady Erenne was or what her goals were. Maybe she should avoid Lady Erenne's schemes, even though the woman could reveal the fact Ylena came from outside the City. She only considered that thought for a moment before discarding it. Lady Erenne was the only person who knew she was from outside, so she was the only person Ylena could ask for answers.

She walked across the hall and knocked on Pim's door to tell her she was tired after all the walking and dancing today and that she'd come look at the book with her tomorrow. Pim was disappointed but said, "I guess I'll just read it alone tonight." Pim shut the door with a grin.

Ylena went back to her room and read her library book about the City's first Priests, waiting for the time to pass. She couldn't concentrate, but thankfully, the time passed quickly. She put the book away and wondered if she should take anything with her. She laughed about Lady Erenne's line about "wear comfortable clothes." All of Ylena's clothes were provided by the temple, save for the white dress Lady Erenne had given her the first day. They were comfortable enough for her dance lessons each day, so hopefully they would work for whatever Lady Erenne had in mind. She pulled her black hair into a sleek ponytail and went down the back stairway just in case anyone was still in their rehearsal space.

The circular courtyard surrounded the entire temple, but she found Lady Erenne rather quickly, sipping her tea in one of the small reading nooks. The glow from the tall crystal spire gave enough light to see, but since the sun had set, shadows hid the part of the nook where Lady Erenne directed her to sit.

"Good evening, Ylena. Thank you for joining me."

"I wasn't sure I had much of a choice, to be honest."

Lady Erenne chuckled warmly. "I do appreciate your honesty. I had hoped your desire to find some answers would be more intriguing than just simple fear of reprisal."

"I have a lot of questions, but I think there is an even

longer list of questions that I'm not smart enough to know that I should ask."

"I'm afraid you are correct, Ylena. And unfortunately, we don't have time for a long discussion this evening. There is another conversation I want you to hear that I think will benefit the both of us. Have you ever been to the upper floors of the temple?"

Ylena was confused. "No, I've never had a reason to go find out. Plus, I'm not sure if I'm even allowed up there."

"Not being allowed hasn't stopped some of your fellow acolytes from wandering around the temple at night." Lady Erenne gave her a meaningful look as she sipped her tea.

"Which of them is wandering around? And why?"

"I'm sure they have their own reasons, but I wouldn't know. I do know that, tonight, there will be a conversation upstairs that you need to overhear. Do you see the two windows directly over my head?" Ylena looked up and nodded. "That's where the conversation will be happening in less than an hour. You need to get up there, listen to what they say, and then report back to me tomorrow."

"You want me to just walk upstairs and start wandering around in the hopes I can find that room and overhear something? While not getting caught in the process?"

"Walking upstairs won't be necessary. You have better skills than that, Ylena." She gave her a disappointed frown.

Ylena looked back up at the windows, and realization hit. "You want me to climb up there?" She looked at the sheer wall leading straight up to the windows. "This isn't like Temple Order. There aren't any trellises or vines leading up to that window. How do you expect me to get up there?"

"You're skilled at climbing surfaces more difficult than this. I'm sure you will figure it out." She stood. "I will contact you tomorrow to hear your report. Listen carefully to their exact words. And whatever happens, do not be seen. Do you understand?" Ylena nodded. "Good. Well then, have fun!" She smiled and walked out of the courtyard.

Ylena stared after her. "Have fun?" she whispered to herself. "Seriously?" She looked up at the two windows. They appeared to be several floors up but weren't as high as she had climbed up the vines in Temple Order. But how could she get up there?

Everyone had cleared out of the courtyard, but with the glow of the spire, anyone walking by would easily see Ylena climbing up the side of the temple. She walked around the circular courtyard to see if she could find a more hidden way to climb, even if it was further away from the windows.

In the east side of the courtyard, she found a tree whose large trunk was cleverly carved with bookshelves. She could climb trees as well as she could climb a mountain, but with the carved bookshelves, the climbing seemed almost laughably easy.

She maneuvered herself along a sturdy branch toward the temple. The branch swayed with her movements more than she liked, and she hoped this tree was as healthy as all the rest in the City. She didn't know how she would explain any broken bones she got while falling from a cracked tree limb. She got close enough to the temple and hopped onto the ledge, scooted along toward the wall, then began climbing the decorative stonework. She was able to grasp the edge of the roof with two hands and pull herself up. Once she was seated, she took a break to steady herself.

Sitting on the roof, she felt more exposed than at any other time. Up here, she was no longer hidden by the tree or the arches surrounding the temple. She could see out into the City that was lit from the glowing crystal spires.

She had rarely seen the City at night from her mountain,

because her night climbs made Grandfather nervous. She knew the City glowed at night, but she had no idea what it would look like from inside. The buildings cast shadows in some places, but the spires were so massive the majority of the City was bathed in a warm light all night. The streets were quieter than during the day, but Ylena could still see people going from one place to another. She recalled Lady Erenne saying that some of her fellow acolytes wandered around at night, and she wondered what they could possibly be doing.

Her thoughts brought her back to the reason she was on the roof in the first place. She crept over to the portion of the roof above the two windows and lay down on her stomach, close to the edge. Ylena was relieved to see that the windows were open, because opening windows from the outside was not a skill she had learned while climbing mountains.

"... I told you, Jahan. He said he thought he was being followed, but he was never sure who it was." Ylena froze at the sound of the woman's smooth voice. Even though she couldn't see her face, she knew it was the woman with the tall, sparkling crown.

The woman's voice brought back all of Ylena's feelings from the day in the market. She tried to still her breathing and listen closely to their words.

"He was extremely erratic before the end," the woman continued. "I honestly thought he was just paranoid, but now that I've seen the same things, I'm not so sure."

Ylena couldn't see him, but she could hear Jahan answer. "I didn't think it was paranoia. I thought he was playing one of his power games. I thought he was trying to put us on edge so he could jump in and pick up a new market while we were distracted."

"He was shrewd enough to pull off something like that,

but apparently, he wasn't clever enough to keep from getting killed," the woman replied.

"I'd rather not end up in the same situation, so if you have any suggestions, Syrene, I'd love to hear them."

"I trust *you* implicitly, Jahan, but one of the others is not playing by the rules."

"That much is clear. But which of the other High Priests had something to gain by his death? The uncertainty in Temple Purpose is not helpful to any of us."

Ylena could tell Syrene was pacing by the way her voice faded in and out. "Someone must be working with one of the younger Priests in Temple Purpose. They will already have an alliance in place once the new High Priest is raised."

"That's possible. But if so, it is a betrayal to what the seven of us have spent the last two hundred years creating. Whoever did this cannot be trusted with keeping the balance."

Syrene stopped walking. "No. They definitely cannot be trusted. Find out what you can about how the selection for a new High Priest is coming. I will see if I can uncover which one of us has been making trips to visit the younger Priests in Temple Purpose. We have to find out who would betray us like this before they manage to unbalance everything we have created."

After she heard both of them leave the room, Ylena waited several minutes before beginning her climb back down. She made it all the way back to her room in less time than it took her to climb up. As she lay in bed, she realized her body felt as alive as it did after she finished dancing. It felt good to do something active that got her some of the answers she was looking for. She still had so many questions, but she fell asleep smiling as she laughed darkly.

Not even the High Priests had all the answers.

Ylena woke early the next morning and took her coffee and her book from the Library in the courtyard. She didn't know how she would find Lady Erenne to talk to her about what she overheard, so she thought she would make herself easy to find.

In her book, she discovered that there was no record of High Priests in the City's oldest histories. It was unclear from the book when the first High Priests were chosen, but according to the conversation she'd overheard, the current High Priests had been in place for over two centuries. It made more sense why the death of one of them was even more shocking. One of the most powerful people in the City for the last two hundred years was murdered, and no one had a clue who did it.

Ylena was so engrossed in her reading that she didn't notice that one of the women who was restocking books had come up to her nook. The woman held out a thin book to Ylena but didn't say anything. Ylena took the book by reflex but didn't understand. The woman nodded at the book, and when Ylena examined it, she found a small piece of paper inside. The note simply read:

Do they know who did it?
- E

Ylena blinked slowly trying to figure out what she was supposed to do about this. The woman looked at her expectantly. Ylena said, "Uh ... no?"

The woman nodded her head and walked off to continue stocking the shelves.

Ylena only vaguely understood what happened, but she was even more frustrated by the fact that she wouldn't see

Lady Erenne in person and get the chance to ask her more questions. She had so few opportunities to ask, and she felt cheated out of what she saw as the reward for what she had done.

She heard Pim's laugh from the rehearsal room, so she went inside to begin her regular day.

18

Ylena had several days in a row with no word from the Lady Erenne. She had rehearsals finalizing the blocking every morning, and then group dance rehearsal was in the afternoon. She hoped it would get less awkward than the first day, but it only seemed to get worse. She was never able to have a conversation alone with Caed to tell him to lay off his rivalry with Wilder. The more irritated Caed got, the more over the top Wilder became. She couldn't handle how embarrassing it all was. The acolytes would try to hide their giggling, but they clearly found it hilarious. Lira couldn't decide if she was angry that Ylena was getting so much attention or ecstatic that she was constantly being embarrassed.

Ylena was frustrated at her lack of progress when she walked into her room after dinner and found a letter and stack of nicely folded clothes.

Ylena,
Join me in the courtyard tonight at midnight. Walk quietly and come dressed appropriately.
-E

Midnight? How was she supposed to wait that long?

She took her time getting ready. She had been wearing the same few pieces of rehearsal clothes since she arrived, so finding something new was a treat. There was a pair of black leather pants that felt soft and well worn but looked perfectly pristine. The black shirt crossed at her chest and had ties that wrapped several times around her waist and gave her plenty of freedom to move if she was going to do any more climbing. But the black boots were the best part. They were sturdy, yet the soles were soft enough for her to walk quietly and gave her plenty of flexibility for climbing.

She paced in a loop around her room, and eventually, it was midnight. She crept quietly out of her room, as instructed. She looked like a Priest in the black ensemble, but she did appreciate how she could move in the shadows easier than she had in her bright rehearsal clothes. She found Lady Erenne already waiting in the same reading nook as before.

"Good evening, Ylena," she said quietly. "Have a seat, dear."

Ylena slid into the bench across from her. "Thanks for the clothes. I assume you have a shadowy location in mind for me to visit tonight?"

"Oh, yes. Very shadowed. Tonight, I need you to find a specific room in the temple. You will find at least two of the High Priest's Sentinels stationed at the door. Tell me if you recognize anyone going inside."

"Someone I know? Who do you expect me to find?"

Lady Erenne chuckled quietly. "That is what I hope you find out."

"Okay. That seems easy enough."

"Ylena." Her voice was strong. "Do not underestimate the danger here. This room is guarded by the High Priest's Sentinels. I trust you remember what they look like from the market and what they did to dear Tarley right in front of you?"

Ylena's breathing became ragged. "You were there?"

"You are not my only spy, Ylena. And while Tarley's death was tragic, innocent people like him are executed in this City every day. Keep his image firmly planted in your head so you don't forget where you are. There is no room for mistakes here. Understood?"

"Yes, Lady Erenne. I understand."

"Good. Here is what you will do."

Lady Erenne gave her instructions on how to get down to the room. Ylena had been in two other temples almost exactly the same as this one, and other than the roof the other night, she hadn't explored more than the rehearsal spaces and her room. Roaming around wasn't exactly encouraged, and Ylena hadn't felt the need to try because she had no idea what she would even look for. But a secret room with mysterious guests? That sounded intriguing! Plus, she had on a new outfit, so she was ready for an adventure.

She crept silently down the hallway and tried to stay in the shadows as much as possible. Lady Erenne's directions had brought her to the far end of a series of rarely used storage rooms. She passed the last door and peeked around the corner. At the end of the hall was another door that looked similar to the storage rooms she had just passed, except this one was flanked by two Sentinels. Their matte black armor and unseen faces hidden by masks caused her to shiver. They stood silently, staring straight ahead. She felt too exposed standing in the hallway and just peeking around the corner, so she searched for a better place to keep an eye on the door. The hallways were already dark, but just a few feet ahead, she could see a little indentation in the wall that looked like it had previously been used as a space for cleaning supplies. She moved slower than she had ever moved in her life until she had wedged herself in the indentation and she settled in to watch.

About an hour into her waiting, she wondered if all adventures were this boring. She had seen several people enter the room but only a few leave so far. They usually arrived alone or in pairs. She realized why Lady Erenne said that it would be hard to figure out who they were, because they were all wearing hooded cloaks or hats with masks. She wondered if it was some kind of a party or strange ritual they were attending? The people in the City wore such a variety of clothing that she wasn't sure if these outfits were unusual. What was unusual was how quiet they were. As they approached, she could sometimes hear the people in pairs talking quietly, but when they arrived, they silently waited for the Sentinels to let them in. The guests seemed to avoid looking at the Sentinels, and Ylena couldn't blame them. She couldn't imagine purposefully walking up to one.

Even stranger than the people going in were the people coming out. The oddest thing about the people coming out is that they *did* stop and talk to the Sentinels. Each of them came through the door and handed one of the Sentinels something. She couldn't tell what it was, but they all did it without fail. She was getting bored and realized she hadn't asked Lady Erenne just how long she needed to wait here and watch when she suddenly came fully aware. Someone came out of the room, handed one of the Sentinels a baby, and then went back inside.

The Sentinel took the baby and walked down the hallway, out of her line of sight. He was gone for several minutes, and when he came back, the baby was gone. She wondered who in their right mind would hand a baby to a Sentinel? That was the first baby she had seen since she arrived. She still hadn't figured out where all the children in the City were being kept, but she hadn't expected to see one handed to a Sentinel. She was trying to figure out how she could get around to the other hallway to see where he took the baby when someone pressed in beside her and put a hand over her mouth.

"Please don't scream," whispered Caed. Her eyes went wide, but she nodded, and he slowly lowered his hand. He jerked his head to the hallway behind them, and they both moved quietly back around the corner. He opened the door to the closest storage room and ushered her inside. The room was completely dark except for the sliver of light coming through the crack of the door.

He grabbed her arm and pulled her close. "What are you doing here?" he whispered roughly.

She looked up at him with wide, innocent eyes. "I couldn't sleep, so I thought I'd take a walk."

"A walk?" He looked her up and down, and she felt her breath catch. "You just slipped on some black leather pants to go for a walk down a dark hallway in the temple?"

"And what are *you* doing down here?"

"Uh ... what?" he spluttered. "I'm a Priest. I can walk wherever I want in this temple." He said the last with such arrogance she might have believed him if she hadn't noticed the guilt that flashed across his face. "There are two Sentinels right down the hall. Do you know how dangerous this is?"

"I've seen what the Sentinels can do. But no, I don't actually know how dangerous this is. What is happening in that room?"

He opened his mouth and then shut it again. "Ylena, that answer will take you down a road that we don't have time to discuss right here. Please. Tell me you will go back upstairs?"

She didn't think he'd budge on that answer, so she tried

a different tactic. "I saw one of the Sentinels take a baby. Will the baby be okay?"

He seemed startled into answering. "Yes, the baby is fine. They will grow up here in the temple and become a Priest."

Now it was her turn to be startled. "A Priest baby? That's where babies come from?"

It wasn't until she saw his wide eyes that she realized what she said. "I mean, I know where babies *come from*. I just ..." She prayed the dark room was covering her blush.

He cleared his throat. "Yes, well, that's enough questions. Ylena, please—"

"I know you want me to leave, but I need to know what's happening in this City." Her quiet voice began to crack. "Caed, please, I have so many unanswered questions. Don't leave me to figure this out all alone."

He took her hand with a gentle whisper. "Ylena ..."

She was tired of all the secrets. She thought about all the times she'd asked Grandfather about the City. About her parents. She remembered him sitting beside her at the fire and turning his face away from her when he didn't want to answer. She could smell the smoke and feel the warmth against her cheek as he stared off into the distance, once again leaving her alone with her questions.

Caed sucked in a breath and dropped her hand. "Go back to your room, and don't come here again."

His sudden sharp tone sent a tingle of fear through her, but not enough to smother her anger. She looked into his eyes and asked him the question she had come here to discover. "Are you going through that door tonight?"

He stared at her in the sliver of light and didn't answer.

"Interesting," she said. "Enjoy your night." She bowed her head and slipped out the door.

19

_____

The next morning, Ylena woke early again and went to the courtyard with her coffee. When she crawled in bed the night before, she wondered if she would be exhausted the next morning, but she felt alive with energy. As she drank her coffee, a man who was stocking the bookshelves handed her a small slip of paper that read:

Did you recognize anyone who went through the door?
-E

She gave a relieved sigh at the specific wording of the question. She looked the man straight in the eyes. "No." He nodded and left. She finished her last sip of coffee and went inside.

When Pim came down for breakfast, Ylena asked if they could eat outside, where it was private. She had been plotting what she was going to ask all morning. It was going to be embarrassing and was going to make her feel guilty for not being truthful with Pim, but she needed some information. This was the only way she would find out what she needed to know.

"Pim, I want to ask you something. And it's super embarrassing," said Ylena.

"Oh, fun!" She grinned.

"I've been thinking about that anatomy book." Pim's eyes lit up. "It's just that I grew up with my grandfather, and he didn't talk much about babies and stuff ..." This was actually partially true. When she got her first period, he got a little weird. The next month, when the visitor came to trade supplies, it was a kind woman who sat down with her and talked to her about her cycle, sex, how babies were made, how they were born, how to keep from getting pregnant, how a man could please a woman ... She was quite thorough. Ylena thought it was possible she might even know more than Pim. But she needed some information that should be common knowledge, so she was going to try to cover it up by wrapping it in embarrassment.

Pim was kind, which made the process easier. "Ah! Grandfathers can't be trusted to share all the juicy bits! What did you want to know?"

"I think I understand how babies are made." Pim seemed disappointed that she didn't get to share this info. "But he never told me about how the babies are born? Where do the mothers have the baby? And then what happens?"

Pim's eyes turned sad. "Oh ... because your mom died when you were born."

Ylena was startled at that because it was true. And then she felt dumb because it would have been a slightly less embarrassing conversation starter than the one she chose.

"I understand," Pim said. "I have a younger brother, so I know all about it, but I totally understand why you wouldn't know, especially if your grandfather didn't want to talk about it." Ylena nodded and choked down her guilt at deceiving Pim.

"When a woman goes into labor, sometimes, she goes to a healing center in Perfection Diocese, or sometimes, she has the baby at home and a Perfection Priest will be around just in case. It's very rare that a woman actually dies after having a baby, but it can happen if there is a problem and a Priest can't get there in time." She put her hand on Ylena's. "I'm sorry that happened to your mom."

"Thanks." Since that was basically true, she felt slightly less guilty. "And it's the same for Priests who give birth in the temple?" Ylena hoped that this was a normal question.

She laughed. "Priests can't have babies! Wow! Your grandfather didn't tell you anything!" Ylena blushed at this, because in this instance, it was true.

"Like they aren't allowed to ... um ... you know ..." She kept on blushing, but for a different reason.

Pim laughed again. "Oh, I'm sure they do as much of that as anyone else! It's just that something about their Gifts prevents them from having children of their own. Babies who have been Gifted by the Goddess don't show any signs until they turn one year old, and then that's when they go to be trained in the temple. I know I shouldn't say it ..." She lowered her voice to a whisper. "I'm glad my brother wasn't Gifted. I would have missed him if he had to be raised in the temple. He's even crazier than me, so who knows when my mother will finally let him out of the house? I don't think he can be trusted in public for at least another three or four years. I'd hate for him to uh ... get hurt, you know?"

Ylena blinked at this sudden flow of information that was exactly what she was looking for. It made sense once she thought about how easy it would be for a child to break a vase, or any number of things.

"I'm sure he will be okay. I think your mom did a good

job teaching you everything I never learned. Your brother will be just fine." She gave Pim a comforting smile.

"Thanks," she said. "One question, though ... Are you sure you don't want me to explain how the babies are made? That's the best part!"

Harmony

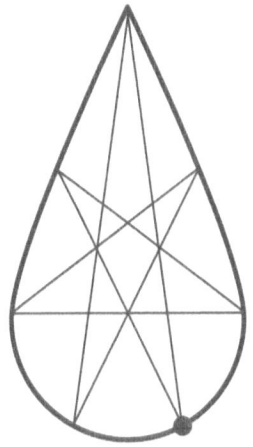

20

When Pim and Ylena heard the announcement that they were moving to Temple Harmony, Pim gave a yell of excitement and ran to get her things as fast as possible.

"I'm so excited to be going to Harmony Diocese!" she told Ylena. "I've really missed it!"

"What do you miss the most?" asked Ylena.

"All the animals, of course! It's just so much more alive there! You'll see." She gave Ylena a knowing smile.

They were soon on their way. They received their usual amount of smiles and waves from the people they passed, but Ylena was more focused on watching for High Priests and Sentinels. Last time, she heard them approaching by the sound of the crowd, or more accurately, the lack of sound from the crowd, but she didn't want one of them to sneak up and catch her off guard.

She was scanning the crowd and suddenly saw a familiar face.

"Grandfather?" she whispered. He put his finger over his lips and signaled with his head to meet him on the other side of the building. She turned to Pim. "I see someone I know. I'll catch up as soon as I can."

Pim smiled. "Don't worry. I'll cover for you! But don't take too long!"

Ylena slipped out of their group and walked to the other side of the building to find Grandfather waiting. She ran and gave him a hug. "I'm so glad to see you! I was worried you would be mad that I followed you, and then I got mixed up in this whole Pageant business—"

He cut her off. "I'm not mad, Ylena. But we don't have much time, so we need to talk quick. I just wanted to check to make sure you are okay and that you will be able to follow through until the end of the Pageant. If this is too hard and you need out—"

"No," she said quickly. "It's fine. I mean, I'm doing well and learning a lot. But there is just so much I don't know. Why didn't you teach me what the City was like? I have so many questions, and I can't ask them without revealing what I don't know."

"I know. I'm sorry." He squeezed his eyes shut. "I've spent the last few weeks wondering if I should have told you more to prepare you." He dropped his voice even lower. "And honestly, this City is so terrible. I didn't want to talk to you about it when you were a child. I thought we'd have more time."

"I know there are awful things here, but there are so many good things, too. If my mother had stayed here instead of trying to give birth to me on the mountain, a Priest could have healed her, and she would still ..." Her earlier conversation with Pim came rushing back, and all the feelings she pushed down then showed up when she saw her grandfather's face.

"Oh, Ylena," he said sadly. "I would have given anything to save her life. Anything." His eyes were fierce. "The Priests would not have helped your mother. That is who she was running from."

Ylena saw Syrene the High Priest and the Sentinels in her mind's eye and shrank back. "What did she do?" she whispered.

"Nothing!" he said sharply. "She did everything right! She devoted her life to serving the so-called Blessed Goddess, and look where it got her! Her fellow Priests would have killed her if we hadn't run to hide on the mountain!"

"Wait ... My mother was a Priest?"

"Umm ... she, uh ..." He wouldn't look her in the eyes.

"I didn't think Priests could have children." She felt pretty smart for having just learned that fact this morning.

He sighed and rubbed his eyes. "Ylena, you should probably catch up—"

"No!" She spoke more forcefully than she had ever spoken to her grandfather. "There is so much you have kept from me. You will tell me at least this one thing before I go."

He saw the hard look on her face and realized she wasn't going to budge. "Yes, your mother was a Priest." He sounded resigned. "And no, Priests don't get pregnant. Ever. Until apparently one did."

"What did she do when she found out?"

"She told your father. He was also a Priest, so that made you doubly unlikely. When your mother told him she was pregnant, something inside him broke. He saw it as a sign that his religion and his whole life was a lie. Your mother came back later to find him dead by his own hand."

Ylena covered her mouth with her hand. She couldn't speak. She knew nothing of her parents for her entire lifetime, and then suddenly, their story was laid out for her in stark detail.

"Your mother knew that if your father reacted that way, the High Priests would react even worse. She knew there was no way they would let her live. She came to me, and I helped her escape the City. We found the cave behind the waterfall. She became even more devout leading up to your birth, constantly singing songs and praying, believing she saw visions of the Goddess ... But none of that saved her. She gave birth to you, and then she was gone."

Ylena felt the tears pouring down her face. Her whole view of her life had shifted in an instant.

"I'm sorry, Ylena. I should have told you. But the thought of those tears are why I kept putting it off. I didn't know how to find the right time to break your heart."

She looked up at him and nodded numbly. "I should catch up ..."

"Ylena, wait." He touched her gently on the arm. "Are you sure you are okay?"

"I just need some time to think about it."

"But I mean, besides what I just said, are you okay? You don't feel sick or ... odd ... right?" He was examining her face in an unusual way. "You haven't noticed any ... strange things happen?"

She thought about seeing a Sentinel murder someone in the street and then seeing one carry a baby. "Grandfather, everything here is strange! I have no idea what is going on!"

For some reason, he looked relieved at that. "Okay, I guess you should catch up. Do you want me to walk with you for a bit?"

"No." She spoke more firmly than she planned. "I can find my way. But thank you."

"I really am sorry, Ylena. For all of it."

She nodded and walked away.

21

Ylena followed the giant crystal spire and cut through some side streets so that she arrived at Temple Harmony just as the rest of the group showed up. She slipped around a corner and stepped right up beside Pim.

"There you are!" whispered Pim. "I hope you learned some juicy gossip out there!"

"I guess you could say that." She sighed. She was saved from saying more because the rest of their group had stopped walking and were huddled up in a circle.

Ylena and Pim moved to the side to get a look. They found a man dressed in a periwinkle suit coat and holding a sparkly cane. At his feet were five pure white, fluffy dogs. Ylena had seen a few dogs around the City, but never like this. These five were lined up in a perfect little row, and as he tapped his cane, each raised their right paw. Lira and a few of the other acolytes held out their hands and shook the pups' paws. The group sighed in unison.

"Oooh!" said Pim. "I've missed this! I told you that Harmony was the best!"

The man said he had picked up these pups from the

Priests and that he was now taking them to his shop, where their new owners would pick them up sometime this week. He tapped his cane again, and the little dogs fell into line and followed him as he walked down the street.

The group chatted happily to each other as they walked up the steps to the temple. As they passed through the arches, they were struck silent again. In the courtyard were trees with small colorful birds flitting from branch to branch. In the grass, a lounging couple was smiling at a kitten playfully running back and forth between them. Under one of the trees, a young man was curled up asleep, and snuggled around him was a family of bunnies.

A Priest appeared to their right. "Goddess's blessing upon you, acolytes."

The group turned and bowed as one. "And also upon you."

"Welcome to Temple Harmony." Ylena looked up and saw that the Priest was a man in a simple black tunic and pants, a silver circlet resting on his golden curls. "If you will follow me, I will show you a part of what the Goddess has gifted us with here in Harmony."

The group followed the Priest eagerly. Pim was right. There was a happiness to the place that was spilling over onto their whole group. They followed the Priest from the temple to a park filled with trees a couple blocks away. Ylena could see hundreds of birds in the trees and heard their gentle coos. The group walked over to one of the tables set up under the trees. A woman in a bright pink tunic stood and bowed to the Priest as they arrived.

The Priest turned to address the group. "We regularly check on the health of all of the animals in the City. The birds can be harder to track down, so once every month, we call them here to check on them all at once. These are all the doves of the City. I just need to check on a few more before they can go home."

He walked to the table, and Ylena saw him do the same hand movements she had seen the other Priests do. Seven blue birds flew down from one of the trees and landed on the table in front of him. He picked them up carefully one at a time, examining their shimmering feathers, their beaks, and their feet. He handed one of the birds to the woman at his side and told her a few quiet words. The woman rubbed the bird's foot with some kind of oil, then took a roll of a small bandage and wrapped the bird's foot. After checking each of the birds, he looked at them. "Okay, you can head back home." Six of the birds flew back up to the branches, but the one with the bandage stayed calmly the woman's hands.

He looked up to the trees. He raised both hands over his head, and hundreds of birds flew out of the trees at one. They circled around each other for a moment, then flew away to every corner of the City. He turned and picked up the bird with the injured foot.

"This little guy will stay in the temple courtyard until he is feeling better, and then he will head home, too. Goddess's blessing upon you."

The group stood staring in awe for a few more moments and then slowly began to walk back. Ylena was once again struck by the contrast of the City: the Priests' Gifts were so wonderful, but they also would have killed her mother. In the midst of all this beauty, how could people do something so evil?

She looked up and realized her thoughts had caused her to fall behind the rest of the group. She moved to catch up but spotted something coming toward her out of the corner of her eye. She held up her hand out of reflex, and a tiny, blue bird landed on her wrist. She was shocked and stared at it in fascination for several moments.

"Oh! Make a wish!" said Pim.

"What?"

"Birds aren't tame enough to land on people, silly! It's a sign of the Goddess's blessing. You should make a wish!" Pim bounced up and down.

Ylena raised an eyebrow. "I just saw a whole group of birds that looked pretty tame to me."

"Yeah, because the Priest was here. He's gone now." Pim waved her arms around the park to demonstrate.

"You're right. That's strange ..." Suddenly, her mind went back to her conversation with her grandfather. *Have you noticed any strange things happen?* She remembered water crashing down around her bath ... The bird cooed at her once and then flew off.

"So, what did you wish for?" asked Pim.

She straightened her shoulders and said, "Answers."

22

***

After fair amount of playing with the animals in the courtyard, Madame Director rounded up the acolytes for their first rehearsal at Temple Harmony. The group quieted when Caed entered the room. He seemed even more of a brooding Priest than usual.

"Good news, acolytes!" said Madame Director. "Now that we have moved on to the next phase of our rehearsals, we will start having musicians join us each day." A few musicians had set up in the corner of the room and were warming up. "It's not quite a full orchestra yet, but I think it will really help fit everything together!"

Madame Director had them start with one of the dance numbers from the second act. The musicians and the acolytes had barely made it through one verse before Caed stopped them.

"No, no, no. That won't do. I think you all need to practice how to do a proper waltz step. Since we have musicians here, you will each pair up, and we will practice with the music." He divided the group up into partners and ended with Pim partnering with Wilder and Ylena standing all alone. "Ylena, you're with me."

Wilder raised his eyebrow at this, and Pim grabbed him by the arm. "Hey, focus on your partner, big guy! Don't worry about them!" He took her by the waist and sent one more glare at Caed over his shoulder.

"Musicians, repeat the entire Third Act waltz until I tell you to stop." He turned to Ylena and raised his arms. "Shall we begin?"

She took his hand, and he put his hand on her waist. He pulled her slightly closer than was traditional and whispered, "What were you doing there last night?"

She tried to avoid his eyes, but that was difficult to do at this distance. "I was ... looking around."

"Have you done that before? Just wandered around the temple?"

"Well, not exactly like that ..."

"And your clothes ... Did you bring those with you? Or did someone give them to you?" She didn't answer, but he continued like she had answered. "Who is it? Who are you working for?"

"I don't need to work for anyone. I have my own questions I want answered." She tossed her hair and avoided his eyes.

He turned her so that his back was to the rest of the dancers. He leaned even closer so that his words were barely more than a breath on her neck. "Ylena, there are some evil people in this City. If you are working for one of them ... If you are working for one of the High Priests ..." His breathing was ragged.

She suddenly stopped moving. "Why would you think that?" Her thoughts were coming in a furious rush.

He still held her by the hand and the waist but didn't try to get her to move. "Ylena, I don't know what you were doing before this Pageant or how you got into any of this, but you are caught in something big. If you are just

137

wandering around on your own, for your own sake, I'm asking you to stop. But if someone else is manipulating you ..."

She felt a sudden flare at anger. Her rational brain taught her it wasn't completely Caed's fault, but he was closest, so he was easiest to blame. She pushed him until he started dancing again, which was tricky since he was the one who was supposed to be leading. "If you think I am being manipulated, tell me what's going on so I can make my own decision. Tell me what's happening in that room, and tell me what's going on with the murdered High Priest." His eyes widened, and he turned her so that she was facing away from the other dancers. "I'm just trying to understand what is happening in this City and what that has to do with me. Give me some answers, please." She looked him in the eyes.

He stared back, and she thought for a moment that he might relent and tell her something. Anything. "I can't. There's too much, and it's not fair that I should drag you down with me."

She stared at him, and her eyes hardened. "Then I guess I'm on my own." She turned her head away from him until he told the musicians to stop.

23

Ylena and Caed were both distracted after their dance, so even though there was finally music, the rest of the rehearsal was fairly uninspiring. Her dinner with Pim and Wilder was hurried, and then she claimed she was tired and went off to bed.

She paced in her room for almost an hour, replaying her conversation with Caed and fuming. Why wouldn't he just give her some answers? He could plainly see she was upset, and yet he still was trying to valiantly claim he was protecting her. How could she be safe if there were traps all around her that she didn't even know were there?

But one thing he said had shook her to the core. Was she working for a High Priest? Was she? Until he'd said that, she'd never considered the fact that Lady Erenne might be a High Priest. She couldn't imagine someone like the High Priest Syrene ever deigning to walk around without a crown on. But Ylena didn't know what all the High Priests looked like. In fact, she had only ever seen one and heard two talking. Who were the others? Could Lady Erenne be one of them?

She was glad to see that there wasn't a note from Lady

Erenne waiting when she got into her room. She wasn't sure what she would say. She couldn't exactly ask, "Lady Erenne, are you a High Priest even more devious than Syrene and Jahan? Are you the one who had the High Priest of Purpose murdered?"

She was angry with Caed about not giving her answers, but she was even angrier that he was right. She was in over her head. And it was entirely possible that she was being manipulated.

She even felt manipulated by her grandfather. He never told her the true story about her mother, even though she had asked him her whole life. He never told her that she was the reason that both of her parents were dead.

Her breath caught in her throat. What was wrong with her? Was she some kind of freak? Her father ... just knowing she existed ... He ...

She dug to the bottom of her wardrobe and pulled out her black clothes. No matter what Caed thought was best, she couldn't just sit around and pretend like none of this was happening. He was right about one thing, though. She was deep in the middle of it. And she intended to find out why.

She looked out her window to see that the sun had fully set, even though the glow of the crystal spire was still shining bright. At this temple, there was a tree right outside of her window, and she followed the path of the branches with her eyes and smiled. The hardest part was trying to figure out how to prop her window open slightly so she could get back in, but once that was done, she was down the tree in no time.

She walked silently through the shadows of the courtyard. She could hear the soft sounds of animals settling into their nests and burrows and was careful not to step on any of their little dens as she passed.

She was counting on two things tonight. One, that this temple had a similar room in a similar location. She didn't know that it was true, but she had a pretty good feeling about it. And two, if she went to the door by the same way she went last time, she would find Caed. She wasn't in the mood to be slowed down by another confrontation, so she knew she had to find a different way in.

Obviously, the people going in and out the doors were taking a different way down to that level. If she could find that, she might be able to get close enough to see inside the door. She continued walking around the courtyard that circled the temple, looking in through the many arches that lead inside. She heard quiet footsteps walking up the steps to the courtyard, so she crouched down into the shadow of a tree.

A hooded figure walked up the steps. Ylena only saw a brief glimpse of a woman's face before the figure wrapped her cloak further around herself. Ylena slid out of the shadow and followed the woman through the arch. The hallway seemed much like any other, but she could see the woman turning the corner ahead to her right. She checked to see that no one was coming behind her and followed the woman around the corner. The hallways were dimly lit at night, so she was able to move from shadow to shadow. She followed the woman down several hallways and suddenly, she could see the door and the Sentinels. She couldn't see inside fully without stepping out of the hallway, but then she'd be in plain sight of everyone in the room. She crouched down in this last shadow before the entrance and tried to decide if there was another way around.

She looked down at her feet and saw a small mouse. She

wasn't scared of mice, but it shocked her enough that she almost squeaked. The mouse appeared to be staring right at her.

"What do you want? I'm busy trying to find another way to see that door."

The mouse immediately perked up on his back legs. Then, he turned and walked into a shadow on the other side of the hall. He stayed somewhere in the shadow for a few moments and then turned and scampered back in front of her again. He cocked his little head, then turned back around and went into the shadow. He peeked his head out of the shadow once more. "Okay, fine. I'll follow you. Maybe this is perfectly normal behavior for mice in the City?"

She looked both directions down the hallway and hurried over to the shadows on the other wall. She looked down and could see the mouse sitting below her. He turned around and walked into the wall. Her eyes widened, and she reached out her hand and realized that what looked like another shadow was an indentation, creating a clever little space to hide pipes that were running up the wall. She looked up and could see that, from this large pipe, several smaller pipes snaked off in different directions. She was fascinated to realize this was how they had running water throughout the temple. She looked back down and saw the mouse was climbing up the pipe.

"Slow down, little guy!" she whispered. "I'm coming!"

Luckily, the pipe was covered in a rough texture, so it gave both her and the mouse enough traction to climb up. She climbed up until she was in the ceiling inside a crawl-space with pipes running in every direction. She could see a faint light ahead, and the silhouette of the mouse was headed that way.

She was much slower than the mouse because she had to pull herself along, above, and around the series of pipes.

Once she made it to the source of light, she found the mouse curled up, asleep. She scooted herself closer and realized that she was looking out of a decorative stone grill. If it was removed from the other side, someone would be able to access these pipes for repairs, much easier than if they crawled through like Ylena did.

She looked down and could see that she was almost directly above the door with the Sentinels. She looked back over at the sleeping mouse. "Thanks, little guy." She blew out a breath. "I think I'll worry about the whole talking to animals thing later." She turned to watch the door.

She observed the Sentinels guarding the room for almost an hour and saw approximately the same number of people going in and out as last time. Her angle still wasn't good enough for her to get a peek into the room, and she was getting frustrated at her lack of progress. Other than a sleeping mouse at her side, she had nothing to prove for this adventure. Just as she was about to give up, one of the people coming around the hallway coughed quietly, and the person at the door stopped and looked in their direction. As he turned his head, his hood slipped a bit, and she saw tight curls framing a dark brown face.

Wilder.

Ylena wanted to believe that she might have been mistaken, but she had been with Wilder every day for months, and she definitely knew that was him. What was he going to do in there? Was this his first time here? Or had he been sneaking down here since the beginning? She didn't know what she planned to do with this information, but she decided she would wait to see how long he was in there before she left.

Ylena woke to the touch of tiny claws tickling her hand. She jerked fully awake and slammed her head into the pipe above her head. She bit her tongue so she wouldn't cry out in pain.

The little mouse sat back on his haunches and looked at her. She looked out at the doorway and realized she had been asleep for quite a while. The guards were still there, but she didn't see anyone passing in or out. She had probably missed Wilder coming out long ago, so she hurried back out along the pipes.

She made it back through the turning hallways, and when she was outside, she was relieved to see that it was still dark. She retraced her steps through the shadows and climbed the tree back into her room. She changed out of her black clothes and brushed the dust that she had collected climbing through the pipes out of her hair.

She lay on her bed and realized that not only did she not discover what was is in that room, she also didn't know what Wilder was doing in there. She fell asleep, and in moments, the sun was up.

24

Ylena was exhausted the next day. Apparently, sleeping curled around plumbing was not very restful. As a result, she was cranky during rehearsal. Since Caed didn't see her sneaking down the same hallway the night before, he must have assumed that she did what she was told and stayed in her room. She had purposefully avoided a confrontation with him the night before, but when she saw the pleased look in his eye during class, she was furious with him all over again.

Wilder tried to be his usual charming self, but she tried to analyze every word he said to see if she could sense anything different about him. He didn't look any different after his night out, which she found totally unfair. She knew that she looked like a mess this morning, with circles under her eyes and hair that still had a few cobwebs in it.

She was tired. Tired of being manipulated. Tired of being afraid. Tired of feeling stupid. She made a quick decision and went to talk to Madame Director during lunch.

"Madame Director, I know it's kind of far from us right now, but I was wondering if there was any way I could go back to the Library?"

"Our schedule is pretty busy, and I don't think we have enough time to send you on an outing like that. However, Knowledge is available to all, as they say." She patted Ylena warmly on the cheek. "What kind of book were you looking for? I bet we can get someone else to go pick it up."

Ylena had planned on roaming around and seeing what she could find, so she had to think quick for a good response. "Um ... I wanted a book about the Priests' Gifts and if they have been studied? You know, like, for research for the Pageant?"

This seemed like exactly the right thing to say. "Oh! You are such a sweet, studious girl! How wonderful! Yes, I will see what we can do."

She was disappointed that she wouldn't get to roam around the Library by herself, so she was even crankier for her rehearsal after lunch. At one point, Lira tried to stick something in her hair, and Ylena turned around and actually growled at her. Lira pulled back in shock and then surprisingly left her alone for the rest of the rehearsal.

During dinner, she even snapped at Pim for teasing her about her attitude. Pim tried to play it off like Ylena had been joking, but Ylena could tell she was hurt. She decided to hide in her room before she snapped at someone enough to get a Sentinel called on her.

She made it to her room and perked up. On her desk was a stack of books. She grabbed them and brought them over to her bed to flip through.

She opened the first one, *Gifted Child Development: Differences in Education of Priests between Temples*. The book was fairly, dry, but it was a thorough scientific study of the Priests' Gifts. She had seen multiple Priests use their Gifts, but that didn't really tell her much about how they worked. The book was clinical, but it was clear.

"*Gifts manifest in children soon after their first birthday.*

Sometimes, the first manifestation of the Gift is subtle enough that it is not noticed, but there are other physical signs. The most notable is that the child's hair starts to turn white. The effect magnifies each time the child uses their Gift. Most children are brought to a temple at the first manifestation of their Gift, so as a result, there are few subjects to test for this phenomenon. However, there have been cases of a child showing the Gift for a full year and then Bonding was refused. The child's hair turns completely white soon before they die."

She flipped through the book again to see if she could figure out what Bonding was. Like many things in the City, it seemed like a word that everyone knew and needed no explanation.

Her next book was a study called *The Mechanism of the Goddess's Gifts: A Comparison of the Gifts between Temples.* At the end of the third chapter, she found what she was looking for.

"In her book, Maeko proposes the theory that tears are not the only way to activate the Gifts of the Goddess, just that they are the most efficient method. There is anecdotal evidence that Priests have been able to use their Gifts by some other strong emotion and not through the medium of tears, but it has not been proved definitively."

Tears? She felt like such an idiot when she read the footnote. Tears were a major part of scripture and even factored in to the Pageant, but she'd once again thought this was a dramatic part of the Pageant or the City in general, not that it was a basic scientific fact that had been proven. She thought back to a couple of the strange things that had happened to her and could remember crying immediately before in every situation. She found it disturbing just how much she had cried recently.

The information was helpful because now she had a framework to understand. The night after she had climbed through the pipes in the ceiling, she had gone outside during lunch and tried to "talk" to a mouse. She tried it for so long that she started to wonder if she had made up the whole thing. But the only difference was that the night she climbed through the pipes, she had cried when she thought about her father. Apparently, she hadn't wiped off the tears. The book wasn't clear about how long the tears lasted or how many tears a Gift required, or any number of scientific things Ylena wanted to know. But the idea that the Gifts are triggered by tears was something simple enough that her grandfather could have explained long ago.

Grandfather. She still couldn't think about him without getting angry. How could he lie to her for so many years? He could have told her about her mother and father at any time, but he chose not to. And what about his question about if anything strange was happening to her? What did he know about her that she didn't?

Lady Erenne had also hinted that she knew things about Ylena before she arrived in the City. Did she know about Ylena's parents? Did she know about the strange things happening to her?

Wilder was sneaking into the guarded room at night. Caed had already admitted that he knew a lot of things he was choosing not to tell her. She was tired of people keeping secrets from her. She was going to figure everything out on her own.

She was trying to decide how she could request her next stack of books without being suspicious when a note slipped underneath her door. She jumped out of bed and ran to the door, but the hallway was empty.

Get dressed and meet me in the courtyard in 10 minutes.
-E

Ylena had to take several deep breaths so she wouldn't scream. Lady Erenne thought she could summon Ylena with just a moment's notice? She wanted to ignore the note and not show up, but a part of her knew how dangerous that could be. Caed's questions had caused her to wonder if Lady Erenne was one of the High Priests, and if it was true, Ylena couldn't afford to make her angry. She put on her black clothes in such a bad mood that she almost ripped the fabric of her shirt. She tied her hair back and climbed out the window.

She hadn't met Lady Erenne is this courtyard yet, so she had no idea where she might be hiding. She silently stalked through the shadows, trying to shove down the anger. She told herself to be calm. She didn't have the luxury of expressing her anger. She walked through one more shadow and found Lady Erenne on the other side.

She was also dressed all in black, but Ylena noted that even though they looked similar, Lady Erenne's clothes were noticeably higher quality than Ylena's. This slight detail caused the anger to flare up even higher.

"Good evening, Ylena," she said calmly.

"Good evening to you, Lady Erenne." She was trying hard to keep the bitterness from her voice, but she wasn't sure if it was working.

"I'm glad to see you've been practicing sticking to the shadows. We have quite a bit of that to do tonight." She turned to go.

Ylena stood in place, just blinking at her. Was that supposed to be a silent command to follow? She thought about asking but didn't trust what her mouth would say if she opened it right now.

Lady Erenne must have sensed that Ylena wasn't following, because she turned around and looked at her. Then, she took a few steps forward and *really* looked at her. "Hmm ...

interesting. Okay, then. Speak up." She crossed her arms and simply waited.

Ylena still didn't trust her mouth, so she thought she would err on the side of extreme politeness. "Pardon me, Lady Erenne. I have had a rough several days of finding out exactly how many people in my life are keeping secrets from me, and while I appreciate whatever this is …" She waved at the space between them. "I honestly cannot handle another secret mission where you learn something valuable and I am left with more questions than when I started."

Lady Erenne raised a single perfectly arched eyebrow.

Ylena wondered if she was about to be executed. She thought it might be more satisfying to be killed for reprimanding a High Priest rather than for simply breaking a vase. Maybe.

Lady Erenne sighed and rubbed her forehead. "I have perhaps forgotten how challenging it is to be young."

Ylena wasn't sure exactly what that meant, but it didn't sound like an immediate execution so she thought that was a good sign.

"Ylena, I am on a mission tonight. I thought it might provide some answers for you as well. Would you consider joining me?"

Ylena nodded slowly.

"Thank you, dear. I would appreciate the company. This will not be pleasant." She turned to go, and this time, Ylena followed.

25

Ylena realized that she didn't know the first thing about being a spy. Following Lady Erenne was like following a master. She was able to hide in the smallest sliver of shadow and could move so silently Ylena couldn't even feel the wind stir. Ylena followed her every move and soaked it all in.

She led Ylena through areas of the City that she never had seen. There were alleys and narrow passageways that she didn't know existed. They moved like two silent ghosts flowing through the City, and Ylena felt alive in a way that she hadn't for days.

She wasn't exactly sure where they were headed other than *inward*. All the temples were located at the edges of the City, the giant crystal spires forming a ring around everything inside. As her group moved from temple to temple, they had mainly stayed on the far edges of the City, but now, she was closer to the center than she had been before.

Lady Erenne signaled Ylena to step into a shadow with her. She whispered, "We won't be able to stay as long as either you or I would like, so please trust me when I signal it is time to go. I won't pull us away just because I want to.

There will be Sentinels on guard, and we have only a short period of time to go unnoticed. Do you understand?" Ylena nodded, and Lady Erenne silently glided out of the shadow.

Ylena knew when they approached their target because the quiet seemed to get ... quieter. There wasn't a sound of a bird or wind through a single branch. It was completely still, and Ylena found it hard to breathe. Lady Erenne signaled her to stop. They were standing in a narrow alley in between two rows of tall buildings. Lady Erenne pointed down the alley, and Ylena could see a pair of Sentinels walk past the opening between the buildings. Then, Lady Erenne pointed up. Ylena looked up and could see that all of the surrounding buildings were completely dark, but five stories above them was a faint glow shining in a window. Lady Erenne began to pull herself up.

Ylena was impressed. There were balconies and pipes and several good hand and footholds running along this side of the building, and Lady Erenne found the most efficient way with no wasted effort. Ylena immediately followed in her exact steps. They started straight up the wall very quickly, but Ylena wasn't sure how she planned to move laterally closer to the window with the light. Lady Erenne pulled herself up into a narrow balcony on the same floor as the light. Quieter than a whisper, she opened the window and slid inside. Ylena soon pulled herself up and stepped inside.

The room was completely black. The window faced away from the closest glowing spire, and not a shred of light filtered in. Ylena closed her eyes and took a quiet breath. She reached out her hand and felt the fabric of Lady Erenne's shirt. She sagged a bit in relief. Lady Erenne took her hand and led her through the room. Ylena was familiar with walking through a dark cave at night, but she usually knew where everything was. She didn't even know what type of room they were in. After several feet, they stopped moving, and suddenly, Ylena could see a tiny sliver of light from the door that Lady Erenne had just opened. It seemed like it lit up the whole room, even though it was the smallest hint of light.

Lady Erenne pulled the door open further, and Ylena could barely see her signal to follow after. They were in a narrow hallway with wooden floors. Lady Erenne hugged the left side of the hall, and Ylena followed. They passed two doors, and Lady Erenne listened at each one before she moved to the next. At the third door, she listened and then slowly opened the door and entered. This room was almost as dark as the first except this time, she could see a thin horizontal light shining to the right. Lady Erenne grabbed her hand, and Ylena could just barely see her eyes. They held hers for a minute, and Ylena nodded. They crept toward the sliver of light and looked through.

Ylena thought they were in some kind of food service room because she could see the crack was at the bottom of a door that raised to pass through dishes to the seating area on the other side. The large room was currently completely empty of furniture except for a large table in the center of the room. Seated around the table was Syrene, the only High Priest Ylena recognized by sight, along with five other people dressed all in black and wearing crowns as tall as hers.

It was a meeting of the High Priests. Except, of course, they were missing the one who was murdered. She tried to glance at Lady Erenne, but she could only see a sliver of her face in the light. Ylena was relieved to discover that even if Lady Erenne was manipulating her, at least she wasn't a High Priest.

Even though Ylena had never seen an ugly person in the City, the High Priests were all unnaturally gorgeous.

When she saw High Priest Syrene in the market, Ylena thought she was beautiful. But with the six of them seated together at the same table, Ylena could see there was something unnatural about them but couldn't put her finger on it.

She recognized the man with the perfectly curled dark hair as Jahan, the man she heard talking to Syrene the night she climbed on the roof. "Temple Purpose has almost selected their new High Priest. We need to talk about what that means for us."

"Why does it have to mean anything for us?" said the golden haired woman with a smooth voice. "The six of us have been working together for the last few months. Maybe we should continue with just six."

The man with smooth, ebony skin spoke up. "We have to bring the new High Priest into our circle so we can maintain the balance."

"Balance, Idra? Curious that you would care about balance." Syrene threw the words out casually as she brushed her long veil off her shoulder.

He turned to face her fully. "Now, Syrene, why would you say such a thing?"

"Only because I know that before dear Ollver died, you were spending quite a lot of time at Temple Purpose. All that attention focused on Priests who weren't your responsibility." She looked down at the table like she was only partially interested. "It just feels out of balance, that's all."

"Is that true, Idra?" asked a man with sharp cheekbones. "Do you have any special connections at Temple Purpose? Perhaps you have an idea on who they will be raising?"

The rest of the High Priests turned to stare at Idra. Ylena wasn't sure if they could read anything from his perfect face, because she couldn't.

Idra's voice was smooth. "Whoever is chosen needs to be

beholden to us. We have to find a way to tie them to the group."

The woman with the golden hair spoke again. "And what do you propose? We are all bound together by a mutually beneficial agreement we established almost two centuries ago. If this new High Priest chooses to betray us, they could unravel everything we have built."

Cheekbones spoke up again. "We will not fall, Merah. We have worked too hard."

"Ollver worked hard, too, Varyn," said Syrene. "That didn't save him in the end, did it?"

They avoided looking at each other for several moments, and Ylena got the sense they had arrived at this point before. Someone at this table possibly murdered the High Priest of Purpose, and they all knew it.

"There is the other matter I wanted to discuss," said the woman with the long braids. "We have each reported suspicious activity over the last few months. I believe there is a group once again planning to sabotage the Pageant in some way."

Ylena snapped her lips shut before she could gasp aloud.

"The two might not be related, Gihla," said Idra.

"You might not recall, but almost two decades ago, there was a similar discrepancy in the patterns leading up to the Pageant that year, and that is when we discovered their plan to sabotage," she said.

"That was a long time ago," said Jahan. "I believe the suspicious activity is a result of the imbalance with Temple Purpose. Once that temple is back fully under our control, the patterns will shift back to normal."

"We have to take this threat seriously!" said Gihla. "If the bonding ceremony at the Pageant fails, the results could be catastrophic. We have to be prepared!" She slapped her hand down hard on the table. Several of the High Priests jumped, and at the same moment, Ylena became aware that there were a dozen Sentinels spaced out through the room. When their High Priests jumped they must have shifted enough for her to see their matte black armor in the dim light.

"We are always prepared," said Varyn coolly. "But we can increase the Sentinel patrols to ensure no one gets out of line."

"I agree," said Syrene. "I suggest we double the frequency of the patrols and send them inside residences and businesses more often. The more they look, invariably, the more they find."

There was a general nod of agreement around the table. They begin to discuss how to better protect their doors, but Lady Erenne signaled that it was time to go. Ylena wanted to stay, but she stuck by what she agreed and silently followed her all the way back to Temple Harmony.

26

Ylena followed Lady Erenne's shadow as they headed back to Temple Harmony. They were still quite a way off when Lady Erenne veered off their path and moved into a small alley behind a line of shops.

"I will head off in my own direction from here. You are more than capable to make it back to the temple safely on your own. I trust you won't get lost?" Her lips formed the barest curve upward.

Ylena looked up at the giant glowing spire in the distance and raised an eyebrow.

"Thank you for accompanying me tonight, Ylena."

"Why did you bring me? Not that I don't appreciate finally learning some answers, but you could have done everything by yourself."

Lady Erenne looked up at the night sky and was quiet for a long moment. "I've been trying to accomplish my goals on my own for quite some time, Ylena. The good thing is that I can usually trust the work will be done properly." Her lips twitched slightly. "But the bad thing is that you end up quite alone." She looked down at Ylena. "I enjoy spending time with you. I see a bit of myself in you. Which is obvious proof of my vanity." She winked.

Ylena smiled. "Thank you for trusting me enough to take me on such a dangerous assignment. You might be the only person in this City who believes that I am strong enough to make it on my own."

"I know that you are strong enough to make it on your own. But I am hoping you are wiser than me and don't try. Good night, Ylena."

"Good night, Lady Erenne." She turned toward the giant spire of Temple Harmony.

"And Ylena? Your requests for books from the Library are one of the many things that are tracked by the type of person you don't want tracking you. Understood?"

She sighed as she nodded and slipped into the shadows.

DISCIPLINE

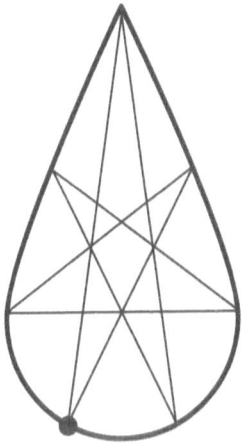

27

The next morning, Ylena returned her books to the temple attendant and told her she was finished researching for a while. She had an extra cup of coffee at breakfast and asked Pim to finish the story she was telling the night before. Pim jumped in with her usual enthusiasm. As she was about to start a new story, Madame Director came to tell them that today they were moving to Temple Discipline.

The thing they noticed when they first left the temple was the silence. The temples were all in the middle of shops and neighborhoods, and there was usually the sounds of talking, laughing, horses pulling carts, but today, the few sounds seemed to echo loudly down the streets. No one asked why it was quieter today than usual. They had been trained to not ask. But Ylena knew.

It took a few minutes before they saw the first Sentinel. He was walking slowly from booth to booth on the street. Ylena didn't make eye contact and held her breath as he crossed to the other side of the street. She had finally just caught her breath again when she looked into a shop window and saw a Sentinel talking to a man in a bakery. Her group continued walking.

She had hoped that the farther away from Temple Harmony they moved, the less Sentinels they would see, but that was not the case. She wasn't sure where the line between Harmony and Discipline was, but somewhere between the two Diocese, they saw two Sentinels dragging a body between them. Their group bowed and waited for them to pass by. Ylena heard a few whispered prayers, and then they continued on their way.

There were more Sentinels in the City than she ever imagined. The High Priests must really be worried if they were willing to mobilize this many Sentinels at once. They mentioned the threat to the City might happen at the Pageant. What did that mean? Was someone in the City planning an attack that night because there would be so many in one place? Or did it have to do with whatever they meant by the "bonding ceremony"?

Usually, moving from one temple to another was exciting, if just for all the sights on the way, but today, every step their group took was slower than usual. When they finally arrived, the temple was a welcome sight, and they were ready to escape the silence of the street. They walked up the steps and through the arches into a courtyard that was both familiar and unique.

Temple Discipline had a courtyard filled with obstacles that could be used to build strength or flexibility. Ylena first noticed a girl hanging upside down inside a circular hoop that was swinging from the branches of a wide tree. A circle of thick vines had grown together to form a large dome, and she could see a man inside jump and grab a vine above his head and pull himself up until he could stretch out on top. There were a few people seated crossed-legged on mats set on soft grass, but most of the people she could see were climbing, lifting, or hanging from something.

Watching the activity in the courtyard was pleasant after the stressful walk through the City. They finally made it into their new yet similar rehearsal space, and Madame Director said that they could take some time to "reflect on" their roles in the courtyard until lunch. Ylena thought that Madame Director needed the break as much as they did.

The acolytes usually got to tour the Diocese when they first arrived, but Ylena overheard a conversation that seemed in code. Madame Director implied that since the City was being so highly patrolled, perhaps a Priest should demonstrate their Gift for the acolytes in their rehearsal space. Ylena was disappointed to not see more of this Diocese, but she was actually relieved to avoid any more Sentinels.

After lunch, Madame Director introduced them to two Discipline Priests. The man and woman were both dressed in loose black linen pants and shirts that crossed their chest and tied at the waist.

"The Goddess's Gift of Discipline appears in a variety of mediums," said the female Priest. "You have perhaps seen your instructor, Priest Caed, demonstrate his Gift of Dance?" The group shook their head. While he had demonstrated a lot of dances for them, he hadn't fully manifested his Gift for them yet. "I hope he will be so kind as to share that with you at some point, because he is quite blessed. Dance is the medium he has studied, and when he chooses, he can use his Gift of Discipline so that he dances with the wind."

The male Priest said, "Today, we will show you one of the other fields of study in Temple Discipline: one of the fighting arts. Luckily, we don't have many practical uses for this since the City is free of violence." Ylena almost burst out with an ironic laugh, considering that she had witnessed Sentinels murdering people in the market, but luckily, she held it in. He continued, "This style of fighting can be learned by anyone, but today, we will demonstrate it using our Gift of Discipline from the Goddess."

The two Priests turned, bowed to each other, and said the tradition benediction, "Goddess's blessing upon you." They remained bowed for about five seconds; then, they both stood and touched their eye. They straightened and began a fight that was like dancing.

Ylena had never seen anyone move so fast in all her life. Both Priests moved with perfectly precise movements, and they each seemed to anticipate the movements of the other. He would kick high with his left leg while she would step backward with her right arm raised to block while punching with her left fist at his ribs while he spun to his right and reached for her neck with his right arm while she spun underneath his arm. They leapt higher than should have been possible, and each jump seemed to fall more slowly than it should.

It went on like this, from move to move, from form to form, without an apparent break. Watching them, she felt like they were living at a different speed than her. Her whole body and mind felt sluggish. She could see the broad movements they were doing and occasionally comprehend the number of subtleties that went over her head. She could understand enough of what they were doing to realize she had no idea what they were doing.

It reminded her of when she had first started learning to dance. Once she had finally started catching on to the broad movements she was trying to learn, she started to realize all the small, subtle movements that she hadn't even noticed the first time. Every time she mastered one thing, it seemed like she discovered a dozen new challenges that she didn't even know existed.

The two Priests were masters of this style of fighting; plus, they were blessed with the Gift from the Goddess. She thought that she could probably watch them fight forever and discover levels upon levels of intricacy that she never realized before. At one point, the female Priest flipped the male Priest onto his back and ended with her forearm against his throat. He laughed. She smiled and held out a hand to him. The both bowed to one another and turned back to the group.

The acolytes bowed as one and responded to the Priests blessing with their own. Ylena was glad to keep her head down for a moment. Their presentation touched her in a way she hadn't expected. Her feelings were on edge from their stressful walk past Sentinels this morning, so she thought that their fight would cause her more anxiety. But instead, their fight had inspired her and stirred in her a desire to move.

The male Priest said, "Our temple is perhaps one of the most interactive, so today, we will be teaching you a few basic katas."

Ylena wasn't the only one excited to learn a part of what they had just demonstrated. The acolytes stood and began repeating a simple strike/block move that the Priests demonstrated. In a lot of ways, the katas were like learning dance moves. And similar to her dance experience, learning the first few steps was exciting but also frustrating. The acolytes' moves looked almost comical compared to the Priests' supernatural grace.

"It takes decades to learn this fighting art, and even then, there are levels of mastery. You can try these moves with a partner, but remember, we aren't looking for injuries here.

Don't make us send for a Perfection Priest for healing. That's always embarrassing." He grinned.

Ylena turned to partner up with Pim, but Wilder had somehow maneuvered into a spot next to her when she wasn't looking. Pim winked and turned to partner up with Wren. Ylena looked at her with narrowed eyes and wondered if she could use this kata to murder her later.

Wilder turned to her with his usual smile. "I guess it's you and me today."

"I guess it is." She still wasn't sure what she thought about Wilder since he had entered the guarded room. She didn't think it was fair to judge him for his secret activities since, at the time, she herself was dressed all in black and being led by a mouse along a series of pipes. That was still very much a secret. However, he entered a room that was guarded by Sentinels commanded by the High Priests. She couldn't find a way to reconcile him with the High Priests.

"Goddess's blessing upon you." He bowed to her.

"And also upon you," she replied.

They both fell into the stance the Priests had showed them. Ylena struck, and Wilder immediately blocked. They both smiled. A breath. Wilder struck, and Ylena blocked. They both nodded and fell into a rhythm of alternating strike and block. Since they weren't good enough to use the moves to actually fight, they still had plenty of breath to talk.

Strike. Block. "You've been a little quiet lately, Ylena. You okay?"

Strike. Block. "Sure," she said. "I've just had a lot on my mind. With the Pageant, you know."

Strike. Block. "Everything else is okay, though? Nothing's happened that's … strange?" he asked.

Strike … She almost missed the block. "Strange?" she said. "What do you mean by strange?"

Strike. Block. "Nothing specific. This City has a lot of strange things in it, and sometimes, that can rub off."

Strike. Block. "Nothing strange happening here," she said with a small smile. "Do you do anything strange at night?"

Strike. He almost missed the block. "Huh? No." He recovered quickly. "Why? Have you been thinking about me at night?" he asked with a smirk.

Strike. Block. She didn't answer.

Strike. Block. "But seriously, Ylena, if there is anything 'strange' that happens, you know my door is always open, no matter how late."

Stri—Dodge, twist, grab, flip.

Wilder was flat on his back, and Ylena was on top of him, her forearm pressed to his throat. She was breathing quickly, but not from the series of moves she had done to flip him over and onto the ground. She leaned in close and whispered, "Tell me what you know. Now."

From the first moment she had met Wilder, he had been confident and always in control, and every single one of his past smiles suddenly felt like statement of power over her. His usual smile was gone, and he was staring at her in surprise.

"I ..." He reached up and touched a lock of her hair that had come loose. "Is this new?" he asked. "This white streak is pretty."

She blinked at him, then sat up and touched the white lock of hair.

The Priest walked over to them on the ground. "I didn't see you flip him, but it looks like you are a quick learner." She turned to the other Priest. "Did you see it?"

Ylena looked around the room and found one person who most definitely did see.

Caed.

28

Ylena stood, bowed to the Priest, and walked to get a glass of water before Wilder had even pulled himself off the floor. She still couldn't catch her breath. What was all that about "strange things happening"? What did he know? Yes, she had noticed strange things, but he hadn't been around for any of them. The rest of the class started to move toward the water, so Ylena stepped into the hallway. Out of sight from the group, she grabbed hold of the lock of hair and stared at it.

"Did you tell him?" whispered Caed. He stepped to her other side so they weren't visible from the room.

"Tell him what?" she asked. She crossed her arms. "I know a whole list of things I haven't told you or anyone else, so you will have to be more specific."

He stepped even closer and raised his hand to the white lock of hair. "Does he know?" He looked into her eyes with worry.

She spoke each word slowly and distinctly. "Does he know what?" Caed had hinted several times that he knew something about her, but since he had never cared to share that information with her, there was no way she was going to tell him anything.

He dropped the lock of hair and placed his hand gently on her arm. "Ylena, I know you are probably confused, and it might be tempting to go to Wilder to try to find some answers, but I don't think he can help you. I don't know what his angle is in all of this, so please, don't trust him with any of your secrets."

"What do you know about my *secrets*?" She pulled her arm out of his hand. His mouth moved, but she didn't let him answer. "You think you should be the only one who deserves answers? Listen to me carefully." She stepped closer until she was directly eye to eye. "I *will* find the answer to every single one of my questions, and I will climb over, or on top of, any person who helps me do that."

She whirled away and left him standing with his mouth open.

Ylena stepped back into place as the group was gathering to learn another kata. She walked up to Wilder and grabbed his arm. She was wickedly pleased to see him flinch. She twisted her lips into a smile and said quietly, "I will not be visiting your room tonight or ever. As you can see, I'm just fine on my own." She could feel Caed's eyes on her from across the room, so she let her hand linger on Wilder's arm. She could practically feel the steam rising off of Caed. She winked at Wilder and walked to her position to begin the next kata.

For the rest of the lesson, she had to keep the mischievous laughter from bubbling up at how easy it was to torment them both at once. She snuck up behind Wilder and put her hands on his shoulders, which caused him to jump and Caed to fume. Once, when Wilder made an offhand comment, Ylena laughed loudly and touched him gently on the arm. It threw him off his guard, and she could see Caed twitching. She was reveling in her newfound power when Pim pulled her aside.

"I am so mad at you right now," she said with her arms crossed. Ylena's eyes opened wide. This was the most aggressive thing she had ever heard Pim say.

"What did I do?"

"This!" She reached up and touched the white lock of Ylena's hair.

Ylena froze in place and couldn't breathe. "Um ... I ..." she said.

"If you were going to see a Perfection Priest, you could have let me know!" Pim said with a stomp of her foot. "I would have liked to get my hair done, too! How dare you come back with such a cute little streak! It's not fair." One side of her lip twitched up.

Ylena released her breath. "You are right. I am a terrible friend." She gave a relieved smile.

"Yes, well, don't let it happen again." She giggled. She looked over at Wilder and then at Caed. "You've sure got the two of them riled up today. I'll forgive you for the hair, because at least you keep it interesting."

29

Ylena was pacing her room, waiting for the sun to go down, with the feeling of fire crackling in her veins. She had dressed in her black clothes but wasn't quite sure where she would go tonight. She just knew she had to get out. Last night, sneaking through the City with Lady Erenne had given her a confidence she didn't have before, and she felt bursting with possibilities. Her day spent battling Caed and Wilder had given her a fierce energy that she needed to utilize.

When the sun finally set, she sprang into action. She propped her window in the usual fashion and climbed out onto the ledge. At Temple Harmony, she'd had to climb onto a tree branch, but at this temple, directly outside her window was one of the many climbing domes that were shaped out of vines. Climbing onto the dome and then down its sides was almost laughably easy.

She made the decision where her first stop would be and walked along the inner wall of the courtyard until she arrived at a large wooden frame with several sets of gymnastic rings. She kicked her foot up onto one of the rings and pulled herself inside of it. She carefully put her feet underneath herself and pulled herself to standing. She grabbed hold of the chain and put both feet on top of the ring. She grabbed hold of the wooden frame and swung herself up to sit on top. She took a few breaths and then stood to balance on the narrow beam. She held her arms out to the side and walked slowly all the way to the end. From there, she could see directly into Wilder's room.

He was sitting at his desk, but she couldn't see what he was working on. His usual smirk was gone, and he seemed lost in thought. Wilder always played like he was confident and flirty and unconcerned with the world, but Ylena wondered what hidden motives he might have. He clearly suspected something about the strange things that were happening to her and seemed to connect that to the white streak in her hair. How could he know anything about that? Pim didn't see anything odd about an adult with a white streak, but to Wilder and Caed, it clearly meant something. Caed was a Priest, so it made sense he might have more knowledge about things like that, but where did Wilder get that kind of information? Did he work for someone in a similar way that she did for Lady Erenne? Could he be working for one of the High Priests and trying to find people like her?

The thought chilled her to the bone. Her grandfather said the High Priests would have murdered her mother and Ylena along with her. She didn't think that would change now that she was an adult. Wilder was trying to get her to reveal dangerous information about herself to him. And she had seen him enter a door guarded by Sentinels. No matter how sweet his smile, she had to keep on her guard.

He finally stood and walked into the bathroom. When he came out, he pulled his shirt over his head and moved back over by the desk. Ylena felt slightly guilty for staring at his bare chest without his knowledge. Then, she added up the number of times she had caught him staring at her appraisingly and felt slightly less guilty. He chose to stand in front of an open window after all, and it wasn't her fault the crystalline lamp was perfectly defining each and every muscle on his chest ... He turned off his light, and she could just barely see him from the glow of the crystal spire shining in. He lay down in bed and rolled over to sleep.

She considered waiting here to see if he eventually went out, but being perched on the end of the wooden frame of the swings wasn't very comfortable, and she had too much restless energy to wait. She lowered herself off the ring and walked through the courtyard shadows again.

30

Ylena walked through the courtyard with the assumption that this temple had the same basic layout as the others. She was crawling with nervous energy, and since there wasn't a mountain to climb, she thought she might instead try to find a space big enough for her latest favorite activity.

She was almost to the dance studio when she heard music. It sounded like the record player Caed played during their dance rehearsals, but it echoed strangely through the empty courtyard. She crept closer and stopped in front of one of the arches that led into the wide room. Sheer, white fabric draped between each of the arches and billowed in the warm night air. The music curled around her as she slipped inside.

The room was dimly lit with only the light shining in from the crystal spire. The light filtered softly through the drapes and formed arches of light on the ground. And through these curving lines of light, barefoot and dressed only in a pair of simple black pants, Caed danced.

He was stunning. Her breath caught in her chest, and she pushed herself close to the wall between arches. She was hidden in the darkness between the arches to her sides and leaned against the wall to watch the beauty unfold.

He spun and twisted with flowing arms and furious legs. If she compared the dancing she had seen before to what he did now, it was like planting a single seed compared to what the Priest had done with the field of strawberries. Ylena could see it. This was his Gift.

He moved perfectly in time to the music. His movements were slow and lyrical and then quicker than she could even see. He leapt. He *flew*. His body didn't seem to follow the same set of rules that the rest of the world lived by. He seemed as solid and firmly grounded as a boulder but moved like he skimmed lightly across a pool of water.

The air seemed to move around him in tempo to the music. She saw him take hold of a breeze and use it to pull himself into a turn. He bent his knees and then leapt straight up. When he could almost touch the ceiling, he grasped another breeze and used it to slowly lower himself back down. He rolled and slid across the floor only to take floating steps back to standing.

She could feel him dancing with the wind that flowed through the drapes at her sides. He pulled and pushed his body, and the wind responded. The wind wove through his dark hair at each turn of his head. The wind slid over the dark shimmer on his skin as he spun through the patches of light. It brushed against his palms, and he pulled it close.

He stood with his hands near his heart, holding within them a contented storm. He opened each finger delicately and lowered his cupped hands to his waist as if in prayer. The wind slipped like pouring water from between his fingers and flowed across the floor.

The breeze approached Ylena hesitantly. It curved around her wrist and then slid away, ruffling her white streak of hair before leaving. With her eyes closed, she could feel the breeze hover near her heart before it caressed her collarbone. She sighed as the gentle breeze curled through her hair and kissed her neck beneath her ear.

She could feel the breeze withdraw, and she opened her eyes to find Caed standing in front of her. He reached up with a gentle hand and wiped a tear from her cheek.

"I didn't know that's what your Gift was like ..." she said.

"When we first met, I thought you were part of the game." He brushed her silky hair away from her face. "I thought someone sent you to cause me to make a mistake. But now I know. I know who you are."

"Who?" The word was a prayer on her lips, softer than a whisper.

He took her hand and used her fingers to wipe away her own tear. He looked at the glistening teardrop on her finger and moved her hand to a small vine that had begun curling into the room. He looked in her eyes as he touched her hand to the vine.

A heartbeat. Ylena took a gasping breath. And then ... life.

The vine branched out over and over, splitting off in new directions. It ran over every arch and down every wall. The vines spread onto the ceiling and looped themselves over the furniture. Small, white roses bloomed amid the bright green leaves. The delicate scent of the flowers filled the room. The vines dripped from the ceiling and covered the entire room until it looked like they were standing underneath a sky of roses.

Ylena looked around the room. Then, she brought her attention back to Caed, who was still holding her hand, still without a shirt. She spoke quietly because she couldn't catch her breath. "I don't know what this means."

"Honestly, I don't know either." He didn't stop looking into her eyes.

She took in a deep breath of roses. "I should go."

He nodded and let go of her hand. "Will you meet me back here tomorrow? I'll tell you ... what I can."

"I would like that." She smiled and slipped out into the shadows.

31

The next day, Ylena heard whispers that a Priest from Order had come to the temple overnight and Gifted them with a room full of roses. Everyone was always careful to call it a blessing, which Ylena assumed was to avoid any more Sentinels roaming around investigating any wrongdoing. Madame Director let their group walk down to the dance studio, and everyone stood looking up in amazement.

"It's so beautiful!" said Pim. "I can't believe a Priest just did this and left. I would totally want to take credit for this!"

Ylena was even more amazed seeing the flowers in the sunlight. The room smelled vibrant and alive. The vines and flowers spread across the walls and ceiling in an unbroken sheet of color. She touched one of the delicate petals and thought about the feel of the wind against her collarbone.

"Ylena?" Pim's voice startled her out of her thoughts. "Come on. We are heading back for rehearsal."

"Of course," she said. She followed Pim through the arches as she put a single rosebud into her pocket.

Rehearsal went better than it had for a long time. They had almost finalized all of the choreography, and with musicians at rehearsal, they could easily rehearse any section as many times as they needed. Wilder was still a bit unsure of how to react around Ylena, but most of her anger at him had faded away, and she just pretended like nothing had happened. He honestly was an amazing singer and dancer, and as a result, it did make her scenes with him easier.

While they were working on one of their last numbers for the day, Caed stepped up to Ylena and Wilder as they stood at center stage.

"Wilder, when Ylena finishes her last verse, you will enter stage left and wait behind her. When she steps back, rest your hand on the small of her back so she knows where you are. Then, she can grab your hand for the spin."

Wilder's smile was back in full force. "Like this?" He put his hand on Ylena's back to demonstrate. Caed walked to their side and waved for them to continue.

Ylena felt his hand on her back and was able to easily grab his hand as she spun to the side. The side where Caed was now standing.

She came to a stop just an inch away from Caed and felt the wind swirl between them. She let go of Wilder's hand and held Caed's eyes.

"Yes. That's exactly how it should be done, Wilder," said Caed as he continued to stare in Ylena's eyes. He walked back to his seat at the front of the room, and they continued with rehearsal.

32

The second the sun set, Ylena climbed out her window. She crept carefully past all the windows, including Wilder's, but didn't climb up to see if he was still inside. When she made it to the dance studio, she could smell the roses, even when she was standing outside. The fabric in the arches was billowing, and she slid inside on a breeze.

Caed was directly on the other side. She stumbled, but he caught her. She looked up at him. "You're wearing a shirt tonight."

He laughed. "Thanks for noticing."

"So, what are you going to tell me? Do you know what the High Priests are up to? Will you tell me what's in the room with the Sentinels?" She pushed toward him with each question.

He fell back and raised his hands. "Wait ... No, Ylena. I still don't feel comfortable talking to you about any of that."

"But you said you know me. That means you can trust me that information."

"I do trust you, Ylena. But I don't trust any of them. If they knew about you ... It's best that you just avoid the High

Priests completely." She definitely did not want to mention that she had recently crept into one of their secret meetings.

He continued, "Plus, there are so many plots and intrigues and games that I'm trying to sort through. It would take days to explain."

She pressed forward again. "I don't have days, but I have nights."

He cleared his throat. "Well, yes, you do. Look, I know you want to know everything, and maybe I'll eventually end up telling you, but can we please at least start with a different topic? I think I know something you will want to learn, and the High Priests are thankfully not involved."

"All right, but it better be good."

He pulled back the drape and led her out.

The temples were surprisingly large on the inside. Other than her rehearsal spaces and the portion of the temple with the mysterious door, she still hadn't seen much. She started moving from shadow to shadow but noticed that Caed was just walking normally. He turned and noticed her in a shadow.

"Ylena, this is my home temple. I know how to sneak around here without even needing to sneak." He gave her a smug look, and she pushed him to keep walking.

She realized that part of his non-sneaking was just knowing which hallways had people in them at this time and which didn't. He led her through empty rooms and storage closets, and then they would walk straight through the center of a large hallway with arching ceilings. Finally, he came to a corner and stopped. He turned to Ylena and held his fingers to his lips to signal her to be silent.

She had no idea what they were sneaking up on. Maybe there were more Sentinels guarding other parts of the temple? They crept down the hallway until Caed stopped them in front of a window. She couldn't see what it looked into, but Caed peeked through the window quickly and then looked back up at her with his fingers at his lips again. Then, he stepped in front of the window and signaled her to follow.

She looked inside and found babies. Rows and rows of babies.

She turned to look at him with wide eyes. He laughed quietly. "Come on," he whispered. "They aren't too terrifying."

He passed the window and walked through the door just beyond. An older woman with rich, brown skin was sitting in a rocking chair and crooning to the baby in her arms. Her hair was like a voluminous halo around head with a silver circlet crossing her brow. She looked up when they entered, and Ylena almost ran right back out.

"Caed! It's good to see you, love! Come here and let me see you!" He smiled and crouched down on the floor by her feet. She brushed his hair back a bit to reveal the Priest circlet. "You need a haircut."

He chuckled. "Yes, Mims."

She put her hand up to his cheek. "You've been eating well?" He nodded. "Good. You've got a nice glow about you. I like to see that. You brought a friend."

It took Ylena a moment to realize that *she* was the friend the woman was talking about. Mims's eyes were still locked on Caed.

"Yes, Mims. This is Ylena. You'll like her."

Mims's eyes flicked up. Ylena was suddenly afraid in a way that was nothing like seeing a Sentinel. She could feel Mims sizing her up, and for some reason, she felt it was imperative to impress her.

A baby from the other room cried, and Caed jumped up. "That's what I was waiting for!" He ran through the door, leaving Ylena alone with Mims.

"Come here, child." Ylena immediately obeyed Mims. Perhaps Sentinels would also obey. She crouched down on the floor like Caed had. Mims looked in her eyes, and then she raised her hand and touched the white lock of Ylena's hair.

Ylena froze. Mims rubbed the hair between her fingers then smoothed it out, pulling it gently along Ylena's cheek.

"When Caed was little, he would bring me little treasures he found outside. A white stone, a feather, a perfect tiny acorn ... I'm not sure what kind of treasure he has brought home this time."

Ylena wasn't sure if that was a compliment or not, so she decided to remain silent.

"Caed is a good boy, so I hope you aren't planning on breaking his heart."

Ylena's eyes widened, and her pulse sped up. His heart?

"Hmmm ... so you haven't really considered that as a possibility. Well, that's both a good sign and a bad one." Mims frowned slightly. Ylena still wanted to win her approval, but she still had no idea what she could say.

"Did he tell you where he was bringing you tonight?" Ylena shook her head. Mims laughed quietly. "I take back what I said about him being a good boy."

"I heard that," Caed said. He held a small blond boy in his arms. The boy's eyes were red from crying, but he was currently fascinated with a small stone statue of a cat he held in his chubby hands. As Ylena watched, she saw it turn into a bird with wings outstretched. He smiled and kissed it. Then, he laughed, and the bird was suddenly a dog.

"Caed!" said Mims sternly. "Wash those tears off of young Piper's face, or he will be playing with his toys all night! You know better." She gave him a frown.

"Yes, Mims." He turned to the little boy and whispered loud enough for Ylena to hear, "You've got time to change it one more time, buddy. Make it a good one!" He picked up a soft cloth from the table by Mims and washed the tears off the small boy's face. He then sat down in the rocking chair opposite from Mims and pulled the young boy against his chest. He wrapped the little boy's fingers around the statue, which was now a bunny, and held the small hand close to his heart, which caused the little boy to settle down. The boy started sucking on his thumb, and his eyes started getting heavy as Caed rocked.

A baby from the other room cried. "I think they sense you are around, Caed, and are all waking up to play." She frowned, but he grinned. She stood up and motioned for Ylena to take her rocking chair. Ylena obediently sat down, and Mims handed her the child she held in her arms. "This is Phoebe. I'll go see who Caed woke up this time."

Ylena didn't have any time to object before Mims left the room. Caed chucked quietly. "Don't worry. Phoebe's tears are all dry, so it's unlikely she will cause a rainstorm over your head."

He must have seen the panic on her face, because he chuckled again. "I'm just teasing, Ylena. She won't hurt you."

Ylena whispered, "I've never held a baby before ... I've never *seen* a baby before tonight."

He gave her a small, sad frown. "I didn't know. You're doing fine. Just hold her close enough that she feels secure and safe. She looks like she should fall asleep soon."

Ylena looked down at the little girl and adjusted her close to her chest. She reached one hand up to touch the girl's hair. She had several streaks of white mixed into her dark hair. Ylena smoothed the girl's hair back and gently stroked the side of her face. The girl stared up at her with big blue eyes and blinked slowly. Ylena quietly began to sing.

It was the same song she sang at her audition. She now

knew that the song was part of the Pageant and probably went a long way to getting her the part. In the Pageant, it's a sad song, but she remembered her mother singing it to her like this, like a lullaby. She poured love and peace into the soft words and saw the little girl's blinks get longer and longer. She could feel the notes vibrating in her chest, close to where she held the girl, and soon, Phoebe's eyes had fully closed. She finished the last line of the song and then began to softly hum.

She looked up to see Caed staring at her. His eyes were locked on her face, and he didn't look away when he asked, "What do you say, Mims?"

Mims stood in the door with another small girl who was mostly asleep. "Yes, I see, son. I see."

33

T he first night they visited Mims and the babies, Ylena had so many questions, but as they said good night to Mims and walked away, she held them all in. She could tell from Caed's expression that something important, maybe sacred, had happened. She didn't know if she would use the word "sacred" with him, since his thoughts on religion were a little odd for a Priest. But every word out of Mims's mouth had a weight to it, and Ylena had spent their walk away from the nursery considering her words.

When they arrived in the nursery the following night, Mims was folding sheets and towels in the room across the hall. "You can sit in the rocking chairs and talk, but if you end up waking up the whole room of babies at once, that disaster will be up to you to solve, understood?"

"Understood, Mims. I promise we will only wake the babies up two at a time." He grinned.

She tsked and shook her head, but Ylena saw a hidden smile on her lips.

Ylena and Caed went into the small room off the nursery and looked through the window in the door.

"There are so many of them," Ylena whispered. "These are all of the babies in the City who have the Gift?"

"Each temple has its own nursery, with more or less the same numbers. When parents discover their child has a Gift, they drop them off at the temple in the Diocese where they live."

"Their family has to give them up?"

His whisper had a sharp edge. "Once a baby exhibits a Gift, they immediately belong to the Goddess. These babies are already considered Priests."

Ylena looked at the babies and couldn't imagine the expectations already on their tiny shoulders.

"After the Pageant each year, the baby Priests will be sent to their proper temples based on their Gift. They will be placed in a family there. A temple mother or father will raise multiple Priest children over the years."

"I don't know if this is too personal to ask, but is Mims your mother?" She wasn't sure if personal questions were off limits, or just questions about High Priests.

"It's not too personal. Yes, I consider Mims my mother, and you could probably tell by the way she gives me a hard time that she considers me her son."

"I can tell she loves you," she said simply.

He turned to her and smiled. "Yeah, I could always tell that, too." He looked back at the babies. "I was her 'baby'— the last one she adopted into her family. After me, she retired to this job in the nursery. She told me she likes the regularity of having babies all the same age instead of keeping track of a family of child Priests who range from babies to adults. "

"So, how many brothers and sisters do you have?"

"I grew up with thirteen older brothers and sisters."

"Thirteen?" Her eyes widened.

"More than that if you add in the children Mims raised before she got to her last fourteen," he said with a wink.

"I never had a brother or sister. I can't imagine what that would be like."

"Loud," he said. "Smelly. Filled with almost equal parts fighting and laughter." He got a sad look on his face. "Three of them were murdered by High Priests."

"What?" She turned to him quickly. "What happened?"

"It was my oldest sister and two of my brothers. Who really knows what happened? It could just be statistics. With fourteen kids, chances are good you will lose a few to the High Priests." She hadn't heard his voice this bitter.

"I didn't think they would kill Priests. I mean, you all seem pretty valuable."

He huffed. "I'd like to think that all the people in the City are valuable, but I guess the High Priests' theology is different than mine." He turned to look at her. "Wait a minute ... Talking about the High Priests was supposed to be off limits."

She raised her hands innocently. "I didn't bring them up!"

He sighed. "You're right. Next topic. I'm surprised you haven't asked me about the white hair."

She looked at each of the babies in their crib. Some of them had a single streak of white like hers, and a few other heads were almost completely white. "If it is something about the Gifts that make their hair turn white, then why haven't I seen any Priests with white hair?"

"The white hair only appears before the child's first bonding ceremony, which is where you come in."

"Excuse me?" she asked.

"The Pageant. That's what all these babies are waiting for. During the Pageant, they will be bonded to the City, and after that, their hair returns to normal."

187

"And if that doesn't happen? If they don't bond with the City?" she asked.

"When children first manifest their Gift, they have one year to be bonded to the City. If they don't, their use of the Gift will drain the life from them, and they will die."

They were finally at one of the things they hadn't spoken about. "Then how did ...?" She held up her lock of white hair.

"Yes," he said. "How have you lived with the Gift your entire life and not had it drain your life away?"

"I don't know. I never had any of these Gifts until I got into the City."

He turned slowly and looked at her. He cocked his head and laughed. "Of course. You didn't grow up in the City."

She finally realized that this was something he didn't know about her. She felt sudden panic at having accidentally revealed that information. How could she stupidly blurt that out?

"Ylena." He touched her cheek and turned her face to look him in the eyes. "I will say this to you again. You are in no danger from me. Learning you grew up outside the walls is fascinating and helps clear up a lot of my questions, but it is not the most dangerous thing I know about you. You are a woman who is Gifted yet who has not been bonded to the City. For this alone, I hope the High Priests never catch even a rumor of you."

He lowered his hand and leaned against the door frame. "The first time I saw your Gift was when you danced true, even though you didn't recognize what had happened. The night I found you in the hallway near the Sentinels, you used the Gift of Knowledge on me, though I wasn't sure if you knew what you had done. I honestly didn't know for sure you had the Gift of Order until you caused the whole room to explode in flowers. I'm guessing you've probably noticed you have several of the other gifts as well?"

She nodded slowly.

"And do you know that, because you have more than one Gift, the High Priests would want you dead for that, too?" She hadn't realized that. He began ticking reasons off on his fingers. "So, you come from outside the City. You are a woman who has more than one Gift. You've not been bonded to the City, and yet you are still freely using your Gifts. Do you understand just how many times over the High Priests will want to kill you?"

She stared at him with wide eyes and then blurted out, "My parents were both Priests."

He laughed so loud he woke up multiple babies, and it took the two of them several hours to get them all back to sleep.

34

Ylena was walking through the courtyard after lunch when she stumbled upon Lady Erenne drinking tea.

"Good afternoon, Ylena," she said.

"Do you know the days I will choose to walk through the courtyard, or do you sit out here every day and I just don't look?"

Lady Erenne gave an enigmatic smile. "I'm old enough to know the patterns of things, dear. Come have a seat."

Lady Erenne was seated cross-legged on the ground at a low table. Ylena scooted around next to her while she took another sip of tea.

"There is a meeting tonight, similar to the last one we visited. This one will be less well-attended but should still be interesting."

Ylena sat up straight with excitement but immediately hunched down when she realized she had already made plans with Caed. "Um ... okay ... Yes, I am available." She would have to think of some reason to cancel with him.

Lady Erenne raised an eyebrow. "Good. I will meet you

here after sunset. Enjoy your day, Ylena." She went back to sipping tea.

~

During their afternoon rehearsal, Ylena waited until Caed was alone by the water fountain. She walked up casually and spoke quietly without looking at him. "I can't meet with you tonight."

He looked at her quickly and then back at his water. "Oh ... Is everything okay?"

"Yeah, I'm a bit tired from rocking all those babies last night. I just need one good night's sleep is all." At his disappointed expression, she added, "I'm sure I'll feel better by tomorrow night!" His expression turned slightly suspicious, so she drank her water quickly and hurried back to rehearsal.

Later that night, she found Lady Erenne in the same part of the courtyard, once again dressed in her outfit of all black. She really liked Lady Erenne's boots, but she wasn't sure if she would be able to run in heels if necessary.

"Shall we go?" said Lady Erenne. Ylena turned toward the steps, but Lady Erenne stopped her. "We aren't headed out tonight. Tonight, we head up."

She led Ylena through the shadows to a door hidden on the inner courtyard wall. The door led into a series of narrow hallways she hadn't been down with Caed. She wondered if he knew these hallways were here, and if so, why he hadn't told her?

The hallway led to a narrow circular staircase, and they began their looping trek up. They passed several floors before Lady Erenne stopped at a door the same color as the stone walls. She placed her ear to the door and then opened it slowly. They stepped into a room glowing with light.

The room was built directly against the crystal, and the light filled the whole room, casting shadows on the far side of everything it touched. Their door was hidden behind a large fountain, so they were able to step into a deep shadow. Lady Erenne shut the door behind them gently, and the stone door blended into the wall so well that Ylena couldn't see its edges.

Ylena peeked out into the large room and was surprised to see it filled with so many fountains. It reminded her of the courtyard in Temple Purity. She soon guessed the reason. Two of the High Priests were seated at a small table, and Ylena could barely hear their conversation over the sound of the fountains.

"Syrene, you know I am not just being paranoid. There is something going on with the numbers. Surely you've noticed they have been falling the last number of years." Her tall crown glittered in the glow from the crystal and made her golden hair shine all the more.

"You are not being paranoid, Merah. I believe there is something going on as well. The question is, who is causing it?"

Merah leaned back and looked at her appraisingly. "I'm sure you have your suspicions."

"I do." Syrene picked up the goblet in front of her and swirled the dark red liquid thoughtfully. "My question is, who has something to gain by lower numbers each year?"

"No one benefits. We all depend on the balance."

Syrene took a sip and set the goblet down. "Maybe one of us believes that their Gift is more valuable. Maybe they seek to use their power to gain an upper hand."

"But why now?" said Merah. "We've held this balance between us for over two hundred years. Who would choose to disrupt it after all this time?"

Syrene stared off thoughtfully. "Two centuries is a long

192

time. Maybe someone got tired of Order." Merah looked shocked. Syrene continued, "I'm not saying I agree with them, Merah. I'm just theorizing."

Merah picked up her goblet to drink, and Ylena felt a cool breeze tickle the back of her neck. She looked up and noticed there was a balcony with an open door on the other side of the table. Caed was on the balcony, listening to the same conversation. Lady Erenne followed Ylena's gaze and saw Caed, even though he didn't see them. Lady Erenne sighed silently and rubbed her forehead.

Ylena saw Syrene shiver, and she said, "Pardon me a moment." She began to walk to the balcony to shut the door. Caed realized she was coming his direction, and he looked around for a way to hide or escape. She saw the panic in his eyes when he realized he wouldn't be able to move fast enough.

Ylena's heart beat wildly with fear. She imagined the High Priest breathing the poisonous dust onto Caed and watching him claw at his neck and stare at her as he died. Tears sprang to her eyes, and she plunged her hand into the fountain in front of her and *reached*.

The calm fountain closest to Syrene suddenly leapt straight up toward the ceiling. The water coalesced into the shape of a Sentinel as tall as the room. He was made from clear water, but the glow from the crystal cast menacing shadows across his shimmering face.

The High Priests stood, completely shocked, staring at the water Sentinel. Ylena looked to the balcony and saw that Caed had somehow slipped away. She sighed in relief until she noticed Lady Erenne's unreadable eyes looking at her. Ylena realized she had just revealed one of her Gifts to a woman she still didn't even truly know. Lady Erenne opened the hidden door and signaled to Ylena to get inside.

Ylena removed her hand from the fountain, causing the

water Sentinel to crash down, and the High Priests cried out. The last thing she saw as the stone door closed was the High Priests standing in shock, their wet hair falling sloppily around their tilted crowns.

～

They made it back down the stairs and through the narrow hallway into the courtyard. Lady Erenne hadn't yet said a word. Ylena decided that since she didn't know what to say, she definitely wasn't going to be the first to speak.

Lady Erenne pushed closed the hidden door, took a deep breath, and turned to look at Ylena. "I'm trying to decide if you are extraordinarily foolish or remarkably clever."

Ylena gave her a little smile. "Maybe both?"

"You openly used your Gift in front of two High Priests. You risked revealing both of us." She looked at her with hard eyes. "For a boy."

"But they would have found him!"

Lady Erenne's voice was unyielding. "If he's playing this game, he knows about the danger. If he figures out the risk you took to save him, do you think he will be pleased?" Ylena shook her head. "I should think not. He's a smart boy, and I'm sure he would have found a way out." Ylena opened her mouth to ask how she knew Caed, but Lady Erenne continued.

"That being said, your demonstration was brilliant and may cause quite an interesting ripple effect." At Ylena's confused look, she continued. "Merah and Syrene are the High Priests of Order and Discipline respectively, and you heard them theorizing on who might have betrayed their cabal. You then used a rather dramatic Gift from Temple Purity." Ylena's eyes widened in comprehension. "Beyond that, the fact that you made it a Sentinel was astounding. I bet that, after we left, they had a hard time deciding if they wanted to call any of their own Sentinels in to investigate. You just lit a spark in the middle of dry brush, and I'm interested to see what catches fire first." In the dim crystal light, Ylena could see a wicked glint in her eye.

35

The next day at rehearsal, Caed cornered Ylena in the hallway. "So, did you get enough sleep last night?" he asked a bit too casually.

"Umm ... yeah, thanks for asking. I'm feeling much better." He looked at her suspiciously but didn't reply. "What about you?" she asked. "Did you just hang out in the nursery like we had planned?" She blinked up at him innocently. He narrowed his eyes slightly but didn't answer.

She went back to rehearsal but was distracted by thoughts of their conversation. Had Caed been planning on taking her to the meeting between High Priests? Or did he just take advantage of the opportunity once Ylena canceled on him? Or if he heard the High Priests were meeting, would he have canceled anyway?

She was so distracted that some of her moves were sloppy enough that Wilder noticed. He pulled her close during their dance and whispered, "Ylena, are you okay? You seem distracted."

"I'm fine. I'll pull it together." She smirked. "I don't want to trip you so you end up flat on your back."

He chuckled. "Thanks, I appreciate that." He was

thoughtful for a moment. "Ylena, I care about you. I think you are really talented, and I ... don't want to see you get hurt." His eyes flicked over to Caed, who stood at the front of the room with his arms crossed over his chest, staring at them.

"Thanks, Wilder. I do appreciate that."

They sang their next portion and then moved into another dance combo when the room suddenly went silent.

Two Sentinels entered their rehearsal room.

They each froze in their dance position and didn't breathe. The Sentinels walked over to where the acolytes stood on stage and stared at them. Ylena could see that Madame Director and Deven both seemed torn between wanting to step forward to help and being frozen in fear like everyone else. Caed's body had gone completely still, and she could picture him forming rescue plans in his mind.

She stood motionless with Wilder's hand still on her waist and his other hand squeezing hers. She was starting to breathe shallowly and thought she might pass out under the Sentinel's faceless gaze. But then she felt Wilder's breathing start to slow, and she tried to match her breaths to the sight of his chest rising and falling. She looked up and saw his face was completely calm. He was staring at the Sentinels, his smile was hidden, and he had no apparent panic. Just a calm, intense regard.

She took strength in his composure. She turned her head slowly to look at the Sentinels. She couldn't see a single feature of their faces, but she felt their eyes on her. One of them raised a hand and signaled them to continue. The acolytes were still frozen in place, but Madame Director was aware enough to quickly cue the musicians.

Once the music started, the acolytes followed their training and performed. The first few notes were hesitant, but they were soon pouring everything they had into the performance. They sang with passion and put every drop of energy they had into the dances. They were in the middle of a song when the Sentinels turned and walked out without a word. The acolytes finished the entire song just to be safe, but when the last note sounded, they all just stood unmoving in their final pose. No one shifted or said a word.

Madame Director finally broke the silence. "Thank you, acolytes. Time for a water break." She walked off.

Ylena and Wilder were holding their last pose, side by side and hand in hand. He squeezed her hand and turned to face her.

"You definitely pulled it together there at the end." His playful words were a comforting bit of normalcy. She chuckled, but it came out a bit too close to a sob.

He pulled her closer and spoke quietly. "Ylena, I believe in you." He reached up with a soft hand and touched her white streak. "When you need me, I'll have your back." He held her eyes for a moment, then walked away.

She took a deep breath and turned to look for Caed, but he was already gone.

36

Madame Director announced they were moving to Temple Perfection, so instead of eating breakfast, Ylena went to the room with the flowers. The room itself looked the same in every temple, except now, this one room was special. The flowers hadn't stopped blooming, and Ylena could see new shoots still forming. She walked to the arch where she had stood to watch Caed dance and touched the soft petals of one of the blooms. She breathed in the scent of the flowers and turned to go.

Caed walked through the arch where she stood. "I thought you might come here one last time before you move on."

"I still can't believe it," she said as she touched a vine. "It started out as such a small vine."

"This is more than a single Order Priest can accomplish on their own. Your skills are exceptional."

"I'm not even sure how I did it. I don't know if I could recreate it."

"You seem to be able to do what is necessary when it's

time. That water Sentinel showed up when it was needed." He raised an eyebrow.

She bit her lip. "Hmm? What's that?" she asked innocently.

He chuckled. "I'm becoming familiar with your Gifts, Ylena. I knew it was you. I'm still curious how you got into the room, though. Besides the balcony I was standing on, there is only one entrance."

"I'm curious about something as well. If I hadn't gone on my own, would you have taken me with you?" She fixed him with a hard stare.

"No."

"At least you are consistent." She crossed her arms.

"Ylena, I've told you, I don't want to get you involved in this. It's too dangerous."

"Listen to me." She leaned in close enough to speak quietly. "You were the one who told me the High Priests would murder me multiple times over if they knew who I was. And I'm the lead role in a Pageant with some sort of mystical function the High Priests are worried about being sabotaged. I'm already involved!"

He started to retort but then stopped and looked puzzled. "What do you mean about the Pageant being sabotaged?"

She searched through the overheard conversations and realized the Pageant being sabotaged was discussed at the other meeting she had spied on with Lady Erenne. "It's just a thing I heard. My point is—"

"Ylena, stop. I know you are involved. And I know you are brilliant and competent and the most Gifted person I have ever met. I don't want to involve you in my plans, because I made them before I met you. I don't know how to reconcile them to … you. I don't know what you mean in all this."

At her confused look, he continued. "I am a Priest of the Goddess. And I don't believe in her. I don't believe in any of this. This system is broken beyond repair. The High Priests have corrupted everything in this City."

The intensity in his voice made her shiver. "I know the High Priests are terrible, but what about you, or your brothers and sisters, or the other Priests that are growing food and healing people?"

"None of our Gifts can outweigh the evil that is being done. If it were up to me, I would tear down every temple in this City, brick by brick." She was shocked by the look in his eyes.

"But the Gifts themselves aren't evil. Can you look at this at call it evil?" She gestured at the flowers draping the room.

"That's my point, Ylena. I don't know what this means." He picked one of the roses and studied it. "And I don't know how to fit you into the world I thought I knew."

"I don't know this world at all," she said. "But I believe there is something *beyond* that I want to understand. I saw you dance with the wind, and it gave me a glimpse of something sacred. Something divine."

"I'm not divine," he said sadly. "I'm just a guy with some clever tricks."

"Maybe you are right. Maybe these flowers are just a clever trick of my own. But I have to keep looking for answers, Caed. I am tied to this City in ways I don't understand, and I won't stop searching for the truth. I'd love to look for those answers with you, but if not, I will continue on my own." She plucked a rose for herself and left.

PERFECTION

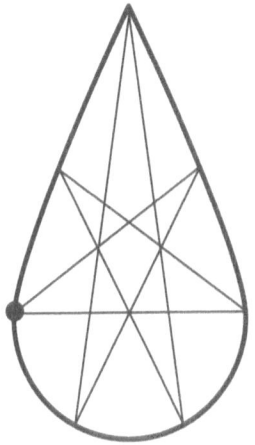

37

Their walk to Temple Perfection was as quiet and stressful as their last trip. They saw Sentinels on the road and in several of the shops, and Ylena felt fortunate that they didn't see the Sentinels drag anyone off this time. A male Priest, whose silver circlet shone brightly above his short black hair and tanned skin, met them outside the temple. After the usual blessings, he led them further down the road until they arrived at a large building. There was a steady flow of people in and out of the wide wooden doors.

"Our healing centers have three purposes: to heal those with physical ailments, to care for those with illnesses of the mind, and to perfect the flesh. If any of you have been feeling under the weather, you might want to stop by one of the healers, but I imagine the rest of you will enjoy seeing the work of the Perfecters."

The Priest led them inside to an antechamber with three separate doors and through the center set of doors, where the majority of people were headed. They entered a room with a high ceiling and sparkling chandeliers. People were sitting in chairs around the room, reading or talking to the person next to them.

"If you'd like to get your flesh perfected, you can sit in these over here, and a Priest will see you soon." He pointed to the right side of the room, where she could see several people waiting by another set of doors. A man and a woman walked out through the doors, and they were smiling and laughing. They had the same look of everyone in the City: Perfect. Smooth skin, long lashes, white teeth. Every person who exited the doors had the same look. In fact, almost everyone who was waiting already looked beautiful, so she had no idea what else they might be waiting for.

"If you'd like to get your hair perfected, you can wait over in this area." He gestured toward another door, and Ylena saw people walk out with their hair perfectly coiffed in a bright variety of colors.

Pim hurried over to her. "I think instead of a white streak, I'm going to go red. What do you think? Do you want to get your hair done, too?"

Ylena wasn't sure what would happen to her white streak if she tried that, so she declined. "No thanks. I think I'll stick with what I have for now."

The acolytes divided themselves up into two groups and sat down to wait, but since Ylena didn't plan on getting perfected, she walked back out into the antechamber. She didn't feel ill, but she wanted to see what the Priests did to heal people.

She walked through the set of the doors on her right, and Wilder followed her.

"You don't want to get perfected?" she asked.

"I already am," he said with a wink.

She rolled her eyes but smiled. They walked into a corridor that split into several different hallways. There was a desk in front of them, but no one was there, so they turned down the first hallway.

Each door had a small window where Ylena and Wilder could peek inside. At the first door, they saw a beautiful woman lying propped up in a bed, staring ahead at nothing. Bright sunlight streamed through her window and fell across her arms lying peacefully at her sides. She seemed calm, but her eyes were blank. The next window revealed a man with dark, curling hair sitting at a table, seriously studying the interlocking pieces of a puzzle. He didn't glance up as they passed.

As they continued toward the next door, they heard a voice behind them. "Goddess's blessing upon you."

They automatically bowed. "And also upon you."

The Priest in front of them was a woman with warm brown eyes and soft brown hair that curled around her shoulders. She was dressed in a simple black shift. "Welcome to the healing center. You are the acolytes who are visiting today, correct?"

"Yes, Priest," Ylena replied. "What happens in here? Are these people waiting to be healed?"

The Priest shook her head sadly. "No, they have been healed as much as they can be. Caring for them is all that remains."

At Ylena's confused expression, she led them forward to the third door. Inside was a beautiful woman who was talking even though no one else was in the room. She stood and waved her arms to make her point about something. Her face changed, and then she wrapped her fingers through her hair at her scalp and pulled angrily. She stormed across to the other side of the room and stared out of the window.

"Everyone in this wing is physically healthy and healed of any illness or injury. But there are some things we can't heal." The Priest stared sadly at the woman who had now walked back to the table and was having a new conversation. "We can heal flesh and bone, but we can't heal the mind."

Ylena looked around at the number of hallways and rooms. "So, they all live here? Alone like this?"

The woman gave another sad smile. "Some of them are well enough that they can gather together for activities, but unfortunately, way too many are alone just like this." She looked at Ylena and Wilder, considering them. "Would you like to talk to one of the residents? He loves talking to people, but he doesn't get many visitors."

Wilder gave her a look that said, "Let's go back," but Ylena followed the Priest to the next room. Something about the silence of the hallway both called to her and terrified her. The Priest led them inside.

A man with pale skin and short, dark hair looked up from his table, where he sat writing in a small notebook.

"Good morning, Walter. How are you feeling today?" The Priest touched him gently on his hand, and he looked up at her and smiled fondly.

"Hello, sweet Alys. You look lovely today, as usual." He turned to face Ylena and Wilder. "And who are these gorgeous young things you've brought to me?"

"Walter!" She tapped his hand. "Don't pretend you are wicked. They don't know how much you shamelessly flirt with people who are way too young for you!" She winked at him.

"Considering I am hundreds of years old, the only people left are the ones who are too young for me!" He laughed.

Ylena looked questioningly at Alys. Hundreds of years old? Alys smiled and said, "Walter has been here longer than anyone else by far. No one knows exactly how old he is, not even him."

He had gone back to writing in his notebook, and he spoke without looking up. "A couple hundred, more or less. It doesn't matter much."

Alys looked down at Walter. "These two young people are acolytes in this year's Pageant. I bet you've seen the Pageant many times."

He looked up from his notebook and considered the two acolytes. "The Pageant? I was in the Pageant when I was young." He looked off into the distance and got a dreamy look on his face. "They were a lot rowdier than they are today. There were no High Priests, so we could get away with a lot more. For my role, I kissed a butterfly, and it turned into a beautiful woman. She was wearing nothing but her long hair and ..."

"Walter!" said Priest Alys. She looked embarrassed and coughed nervously. "Walter sometimes remembers things that are hard to believe."

"Hard for you to believe, Alys, because you have been trained to be so proper, but three hundred years ago, everything was just so much more interesting." He looked Ylena and Wilder in the eye. "I once met a woman who was so beautiful the stars shown like the sun in her eyes. She was asleep when I met her, and she only heard my name in her dreams. She cried for me, but I couldn't wake her up. I think she was also the butterfly that came to see me the other day ..." His eyes were staring off into the distance.

Priest Alys touched his hand again. "Oh, Walter. Your stories are always inappropriate or just heartbreaking." She looked him in the eyes. "Did she ever wake up?"

He focused his eyes on her and said in a worried tone, "Did who wake up?"

"Oh ..." Her smile turned sad. "Don't worry about it,

Walter. I need to take the acolytes back to their group. Are you okay?"

He smiled at her again. "Of course!" He looked down and began writing in his book again. Ylena looked at one of the pages and saw that he was writing random numbers and squiggles. He would suddenly scratch a line out and start a new line. She leaned over to see how many books he had filled when he reached up and scratched the length of her arm with his pen. She shrieked and moved back. It was bleeding a bit, but Alys and Wilder both had terror in their eyes and ran toward her.

"I'm fine!" She held her arm up. "It's just a little scratch. Don't worry about it."

Priest Alys began crying. "I should have never brought you in here! Walter isn't normally violent, so I thought it would be good, but now I've doomed both of us to the Sentinels."

"No!" said Ylena. "We aren't calling any Sentinels. I'm fine. I'll just wrap it in a bandage. I will go, and we won't talk about this."

Alys looked up at her. "You are a blessed child." She wiped her tears. "I think I can manage better than just a bandage, though." She touched her hand to Ylena's arm and closed her eyes. Ylena felt a tingling run up her arm and back down. The scratch was gone, and just a few drops of blood remained.

Ylena smiled and looked at Alys. "That was beautiful. Thank you."

Wilder pulled on her arm. "We should go. Now."

She was surprised at his voice. He hadn't spoken at all since they entered the room, and now, his voice was sharp enough to cut.

Before she could move to follow him, Alys reached up and touched her white streak of hair. "This is interesting. I felt it when I healed your arm. It feels like the babies who arrive at the temple after they first manifest their powers. I don't understand how—"

Wilder stepped between the two of them and blew a fine powder into Priest Alys's face. Her eyes went wide. She grabbed her throat and fell to her knees. She looked at Ylena with confusion and grabbed her hands as she slipped down to the floor. Ylena fell down beside her, trying to understand what was happening, but before her mind could catch up, Priest Alys was gone.

"What ...what did you?" she said to Wilder. "She healed me." She took a sharp breath in. She wiped one of her tears and pressed it to Priest Alys forehead. She closed her eyes and tried to imagine the flowers blooming, the water forming a Sentinel ... but there was nothing. She couldn't feel anything.

"Ylena." Wilder's voice was tender. "She's gone. You can't heal someone who is dead."

She let out a short sob. "Why did you do this?"

"We don't have time to discuss this right now. We have to go." He turned and looked at Walter, who was calmly writing in his notebook. He reached into his pocket. Ylena stood and grabbed him by the arm.

"No! I won't let you!" she growled.

"I don't have enough anyway." He sighed. "We will have to hope that no one believes any of the stories he tells."

He lifted Priest Alys in his arms and headed toward the door.

"What are you doing?" she asked. "Where are you taking her?"

"I'm going to leave her body in the hallway. It will be more believable that a Sentinel killed there. Hopefully, no one will think to ask Walter if it was actually a Sentinel." He glanced out the door and then carried Priest Alys back to the entrance.

Ylena followed after him numbly. He laid Priest Alys on the ground gently and arranged her limbs to look like she had fallen. Her body resembled Tarley's in the market square.

She bent down and touched Alys on the forehead. "Goddess's blessing upon you."

Wilder stood and gently lifted her by the arm. "We have to go. Now."

She nodded and followed him.

38

Pim ran up to Ylena to show off her new hair, but Ylena walked with unseeing eyes as their group headed back to Temple Perfection.

"What's wrong, Ylena?" asked Pim. "Don't you love the red?" She shook her hair, and it floated in the wind.

"Give her some time, Pim. We saw someone who was badly injured and came to receive healing. It was pretty gruesome."

"Ah ... I understand. Not everyone can handle the sight of blood." She nodded knowingly. "I'm going to go show off my hair to Rowan. I'll see what he thinks about redheads." She winked at them, then sprinted ahead.

Wilder stepped closer to Ylena and said quietly, "I'm sorry. I wish that it hadn't been necessary. I was trying to keep you away from the Priests completely, but I thought that wing would be safe. I had no idea you would get hurt. And the rest."

She stopped walking. "You carry that stuff in your pocket? Just in case?"

He gave a dry laugh. "I carry more than just that."

She studied his face. Then, she silently began walking

again.

They arrived at Temple Perfection, but Ylena was numb to the beauty of the courtyard. She barely noticed reservoirs of still water surrounded by lavender. A woman relaxed with eyes closed in a pool with flowing jets of water. They walked into their rehearsal space to find lunch waiting, but Ylena went to her room without speaking to anyone.

Ylena was laying on her bed, staring at the ceiling, when someone knocked on her door.

"Ylena." Wilder's calm voice came through the door.

She didn't answer.

"Please," he said. "We have rehearsal. Seeing a little blood only explains away so much. I can't cover for you missing a rehearsal."

She still didn't answer.

"Skipping rehearsal is something that will get the Sentinels called. Please," he begged.

She opened the door, and he took a step back. She closed the door behind her and walked ahead of him.

He hurried after her. "Ylena, please—"

"No." She didn't turn around.

During rehearsal, Madame Director was obviously frustrated. "Ylena, dear, I'm not sure why you are struggling with this today, but I need to see a bit of expression in your face, please! We could have guest judges here any time!" Everyone knew by the panicked sound in her voice that she meant the Sentinels.

"Yes, Madame Director," she said. "I will try harder."

She sighed. "I know you will, dear. You are a good girl. How about we move to Act Three, Scene Four instead? It is a more melancholy scene, so it might better fit the mood."

Madame Director was right. The sad song suited Ylena's mood. She hadn't realized that the lullaby her mother had sung to her was from this scene of the Pageant. It wasn't truly a lullaby. It was a song about love and death. After her song was finished, she bent down over Wilder, who played the role of the dying Companion. The rest of the cast sang their song, and Ylena could look as sad as she wanted.

"Ylena." Wilder turned his head so he could talk to her without being seen by Madame Director. "I have two goals in my life right now. Initially, my only goal was to protect the success of the Pageant at all costs. But once you arrived, I was given a second task. Protect you. By any means necessary."

"Who gave you these assignments?" The stone floor was cold as she knelt by his side, but that wasn't the source of the chill she felt.

"That's not my place to tell," he said. "But I will do whatever it takes to make sure you are safe and that the Pageant goes as planned."

"But what you did ..." Her quiet whisper caught on a sob. "I can't look at you without seeing her face."

He reached up to the collar of her shirt and pulled her closer. It was in the script, so Ylena didn't pull back, though she wanted to. His dark eyes begged her to listen. "Do you think I'm the kind of person who enjoys what I just did? I have to live with this sin for the rest of my life. The memory of her last breath will probably drag my soul down into the Abyss, but I would do it again in a heartbeat to keep you safe."

It was her cue in the song to stroke his cheek, but her quiet voice was bitter. "Because that's your assignment?"

"No, Ylena." His eyes held hers tightly. "That's not why at all."

39

Ylena felt dangerous all afternoon. She had cried over Alys's body, unable to heal her, and now, the dry tears froze on her hands and face. She wasn't sure if it was possible to wash them off. Washing off the tears felt like washing away Alys's death too easily. She wanted the tears to freeze. She wanted them to hurt.

After sunset, she crawled out the window and crept to the dance room. The rooms were the same at every temple, but this one seemed empty without the flowers. She was careful to not touch any stray vines. Another surprise Gift of blooming roses wouldn't be so easy to explain away.

She walked to the center of the floor and stared at herself in the mirror. She felt a moment of disorientation, tracing her steps from the mountain to this exact place. How could she have lived her entire life not knowing anything about the City, about her parents, about herself? Her childhood stretched behind her in a blur. It felt like someone else's life.

She closed her eyes and sang.

Her voice was quiet but pure, and it pierced through the stone room. Her melody struck the mirror with a clear tone and bounced backward to be softened by the flowing drapes. She harmonized with her echo, a melancholy counterpoint that bounced through the room. She shaped a wordless descant that resonated along the ceiling like a despairing cry.

In the midst of the reverberating room, Ylena danced.

She grasped a breeze and let it pull her sharply to one side, then hung balanced between the breeze in one hand and the counterpoint in the other. Spinning out of the move, she pressed the breeze through the counterpoint until it split into a wild trill. The fluttering notes slowed and dripped through the air before settling into a steady drone. She pulled the low drone around her body like a cloak and slunk across the floor, picking up the notes that had fallen along the way. She shook off the cloak of sound and kicked the broken pieces of notes up to the ceiling. The new melody rained down as she opened her arms wide to soak it in.

This new song was fierce and free, and she twirled as it poured over her. The melody cascaded through her hair and down her neck. She felt the song drip between her shoulder blades and trickle down her spine. The notes struck the floor and pooled in resonating puddles, and she lunged and swept her hand through the puddle in a wide arc. The melody flew back into the air, only to be caught on a hovering breeze. Leaping to the next puddle, she brushed her foot through the bubbling notes. They flew from her pointed toes to twist into the melody still hovering in the breeze. The songs spun together, and she danced inside their duet, letting them pull her from step to step.

She plucked a single note from the air and wrapped it around her wrist. The note followed her as she jumped across a lingering pool of sound to pull another note off the breeze. She wrapped this note through her hair as she slid across the floor and lifted a third note from the puddle. She spun and slid and bounced throughout the room, scooping up note by note, until she was covered in living sound. The notes wrapped around her and vibrated through her in tempo to her own pulse.

She unwound the first note from her wrist and wrapped it inside a breeze as gentle as a breath. Then, she collected the notes from her hair and her ankles and her fingertips and wove them into the breeze. The notes trembled in her hands and tickled across her skin. The woven song came to rest directly over her beating heart. She lifted the delicate melody and held it carefully in the palm of her hand, carrying it slowly toward the arches, not wanting to snuff out the flame of the song, while dragging a cloak of fallen notes around her.

Caed was watching her from the same place she stood when she watched him dance. He was breathing like he had run a long distance, and barely contained tears filled his eyes. She lifted the melody in her palm and placed it gently on his brow beneath his circlet like a benediction. He closed his eyes and drew in a shuddering breath. She saw the song slide over his lashes and down his cheeks to linger in his dark wavy hair. The notes tumbled down his neck and chest and floated in a breeze in front of his heart.

He opened his eyes and studied her face, then reached a trembling hand to touch her cheek. Her frozen tears burned away, and all she could feel was the warmth of his hand. The song hovered on the breeze between them, the rhythm keeping time with their beating hearts.

When he spoke, his voice was quiet but intense. "I don't believe in anything, Ylena. But I believe in you." He slid his hand into her hair and pulled her toward him. His lips brushed hers as softly as a drifting snowflake. He whispered her name as a prayer, and she took his breath and formed it into a kiss. She composed a symphony to the taste of his lips. She wrote an aria to his fingertips on her skin.

The song hovering between them expanded until it wrapped itself around them. The rhythm resonated through her body and shook loose all the notes that had gathered along her skin. Music filled the room until it pressed the two of them against the archway. Her back was pressed against the wall while his body restrained the barrage of the echoing melodies. The music swelled through her until there was only the rhythm of their hearts pulsing through her head. The cadence built until her skin trembled with the sound.

Until the temple itself quaked with the sound.

Suddenly, Caed stepped back and spread his arms wide. He summoned the wind through the arches, causing the drapes to flutter wildly. The storm blew away the last few fluttering notes, but the stone beneath their feet still quivered to the rhythm of their song.

"You should go." He was out of breath. "You can't let them find you here."

The cold air was harsh on her tingling skin, but her thoughts were buried under a storm full of melodies.

He took a step toward her and tipped her chin so she would meet his eyes. "Ylena," he said, "it isn't safe for you to stay."

Her brain finally registered his words. She took a gasping breath in, still feeling a faint rhythm coming up through the stone floor.

"Yes," she said. "I should go." She raised the drapes to leave.

"Ylena," Caed called.

"Yes?" She turned to find him resting his hand on the pulsing stone arch.

"When I told you I wanted to tear down the temples

brick by brick, this isn't exactly what I meant." Her eyes widened, and she felt a thrill of fear. His full lips held the barest hint of a smile. "But I would try it with you again in a heartbeat." She was pretty sure he saw her blush before she made it outside.

40

"Ladies and gentleman," said Madame Director. "Today. Is. Costume. Day."

Her announcement produced a cheer from the cast. They knew what their costumes would look like, but they had to wait to finally try them on until the seamstresses had finished. Madame Director and Deven were bustling around, getting each acolyte their proper costume so the seamstresses could make any final alterations.

Ylena walked over to the rack that held her costumes in a neat row, and Wilder began flipping casually through the costumes on the other side. He met her eyes over the top of the rack. "Have you said anything about what happened yesterday?"

"What? Of course not!" she said. She focused on her costumes to avoid his eyes. "It's a topic I don't really want to talk about."

"Ylena, I did what I did to keep you safe. I don't know all your secrets, and I don't need to know." He looked across the room to where Caed stood talking to one of the musicians. "But there are some people who absolutely should not know."

"I'm not sure what you mean." She pretended to study the sleeves of one of her costumes.

"In case you haven't noticed, Priests enjoy their place as the ones in charge of this City. They want all the knowledge and power for themselves so they can control it." His eyes flicked to her white streak of hair that had gotten wider since last night. "If they find someone ... unique, they will want to control her. Or destroy her."

She met his eyes. "I will keep that in mind."

He nodded and handed her one of the costumes. "Try this one on next. I'll try on my matching one, and we can see how great we look together." He smiled and hurried off.

Ylena took the costume into one of the fabric-draped dressing rooms in their rehearsal space. She had just pulled off her blouse when she heard Caed outside.

"Ylena," he whispered. She grabbed her blouse and held it to her chest. "Don't come out. I just want to talk to you alone."

"Sure," she replied quietly. "What's going on?" She tried to speak in a casual tone but was finding it difficult to talk to Caed while she had her shirt off.

"I heard whispers about something odd that happened yesterday at the healing center around the time your group was visiting. Did you see anything suspicious?"

She sucked in a quiet breath, but tried to cover the sound by pulling her billowing costume down over her head. "Suspicious? What happened?"

He paused. She realized this was probably too close to one of those topics he didn't want to discuss with her, but he finally answered. "A Priest was killed."

"That's terrible." She didn't have to fake the sadness.

"Yes. It looked like it was the work of Sentinels. However, they usually carry away the body, and this time, they didn't. Some of the Sentinels from Temple Perfection came to look, and the other Priests say that they seemed confused."

She began buttoning up her dress. "That's strange."

"Very," he said. "Since you were there, I was wondering if you saw any Sentinels, or maybe you saw someone else acting suspicious?"

"Nope. Everything seemed pretty normal to me." She fastened the wide belt. "I hope they figure out who killed her."

"I never said the Priest was a woman." His voice was flat.

She froze and replayed their conversation. "Oh, I guess that's just what I pictured."

She could see his outline move closer to the fabric drape and he whispered sharply, "Ylena, if you know something about this, you have to tell me. I have a right to know."

She flung the curtain aside, and he leapt back. "Oh, really?" She crossed her arms. "You have a right to know? You demand to know any information I might have, but you can keep all your secrets to yourself?"

He dropped his gaze to the floor. She knew that she had caught him, and she smiled at her small victory.

"You're right," he said. "You should be able to keep your secrets." She bowed her head to him regally and turned to go, but he caught her arm and whispered in her ear. "Here's some information you might want to know." His warm breath tickled against her neck. "No one has mentioned any strange sounds in the temple last night. I think that's a bit odd, considering that I can still feel the floor pulsing beneath my feet."

She walked off quickly so she wouldn't mar her triumph with a wild blush.

41

Ylena returned to her room after dinner to find a note on her bed.

If you are available, will you please meet me in the courtyard after dark?
-E

She chuckled at the polite request. She had snapped last time Lady Erenne expected Ylena to follow along without question, but she had a suspicion Lady Erenne had written this letter with a smirk. Once the sun had set, she climbed out of her window and found Lady Erenne waiting.

"Good evening, Ylena," she said, polite as ever.

"Good evening, Lady Erenne."

"Are you up for a bit of a stroll? There is something nearby that I believe you will want to see."

"Sure." Ylena gestured toward the steps. "Lead the way."

Lady Erenne took them on a curving path, avoiding streets where they found other people. She slowed down as they approached a path that cut through a low stone wall draped with vines. As they stepped inside, Ylena realized what it was.

"A graveyard?" she breathed. She could see rows of stone markers for every one of the dead.

"Yes," said Lady Erenne. "Specifically, a graveyard for the Priests from Temple Perfection."

Ylena stopped walking. The pleading eyes of Priest Alys were all she could see. "Why did you bring me here?"

Lady Erenne's eyes were kind in the glowing light of the spires. "Ylena, you need to see this. Will you come?" Ylena nodded and followed.

Lady Erenne took her down several looping paths until she stopped in front of a grave next to a giant willow tree. Ylena studied the ground but was confused.

"Who ...?" The dirt and grass didn't appear to be new, so it couldn't be where Alys was buried.

"It's your father's grave. He was a Priest of Perfection."

Ylena felt her knees give way. "My father ... How did you ...?" She touched the gravestone and could barely make out the name in the glowing light.

Goddess Bless the Soul
of Priest Ylain of Perfection

"My mother named me after him?" She traced the letters in the stone. "Grandfather never told me his name."

"Your mother's remains are not in the City."

"No," said Ylena. "She is buried under a stand of trees near our cave on the mountain."

Lady Erenne remained silent and sat down beside her.

"He died because of me," said Ylena. She could barely get the words past the lump in her throat. "She told him she was pregnant with me, and the thought of me was enough to cause him to take his own life." She choked down a quiet sob.

"No, Ylena." Lady Erenne placed a gentle hand on top of Ylena's. "You are strong, but you are not strong enough to cause a man to make a decision like that. He could see no way out. You hadn't even taken your first breath. You are not to blame."

"My existence was enough to cause him to question his faith and for my mother to flee for her life. I could be killed for the simple reason that I was born. Why would anyone be afraid of me?"

"People are afraid of what they don't understand. That's one reason the Virtues are so comforting. The more Knowledge we have, the more Order we can create, the safer we feel." Lady Erenne tucked Ylena's white streak behind her ear with a gentle touch. "But if we know everything, there's never room for surprise or wonder or imagination. Despite how you might feel, I've found you to be a delightful surprise."

Ylena's lips curled up gently. "Thanks," she said. "Can I have a moment alone before we leave?"

"Of course, dear. I'll wait on the path."

Ylena took a white rosebud out of her pocket. She pulled off a petal and touched it to the edge of her eye. "Goddess bless you, Father."

She put the petal into the dirt, and it burst into a vine that wrapped around his grave marker. Delicate, white blooms stood out in the crystal glow.

She met Lady Erenne on the path, and on the way out, they stopped by a grave covered with newly grown grass. Ylena prayed a blessing over Priest Alys, and they walked silently back to Temple Perfection together.

42

Ylena pulled her costume off and felt a pin stick her arm. She hissed and removed the costume more carefully. She pulled the pin out with a glare. Her costumes seemed to always have pins strategically hidden in them even though no one else had the same problem. After seeing a smug look on Lira's face after their last fitting, Ylena had a pretty good idea why. She put pressure on the small dot of blood that had appeared. She was not going to let Lira get the best of her today.

She put her regular clothes back on and hung up the costume. She was talking to Pim when the entire room went silent. Everyone dropped to their knees at once. Ylena followed them by reflex and then glanced to see what was happening.

High Priest Idra entered the room, followed by two Sentinels. His ebony skin shone beneath his glittering crown, and his black cape flowed behind him as he walked into the room like he owned it. Considering the fact that this was his temple, maybe he actually did.

"Goddess's blessing upon you," he said in a deep resonant voice.

"And also upon you." The group's reply managed to be both too breathy and overly sincere, but he appeared to be familiar with such responses.

"Madame Director!" he called out.

She stood with eyes bowed. "Yes, High Priest?"

"I would like to see how the Pageant's rehearsals are progressing."

"Yes, of course, High Priest. The acolytes just took off their costumes. Would you like them to put them back on?" she asked.

"That will not be necessary. I'd like to see the scene from the end of Act Two where the Goddess and the Companion pour the tears into the basin." He sat down in Madame Director's chair, and the Sentinels stood directly behind them.

"Yes, High Priest. Right away." She told to the musicians where to begin as the acolytes moved into place.

Wilder grabbed Ylena by the arm and pulled her off stage. He picked up the flower crowns they wore in multiple scenes and put his crown on his head.

"He said we don't need our costumes," she said nervously.

Wilder put the other crown on her head and began arranging her hair underneath it. "Ylena, please, please be careful. He is a High Priest, but specifically the one from here in Temple Perfection. I can't pull the same trick on him and two Sentinels at the same time, okay?" He tucked all the loose strands of her hair underneath the crown so that the large white streak was no longer visible.

The music began to play, and she followed him onto the stage. She pulled the crown tighter onto her head and began to sing.

The scene was pivotal to the story of the Goddess. It involved quite a lot of tears, both her own and what they referred to as the Vessel of Tears they used throughout the scene. Her heart pounded fiercely as she remembered picking up this very same bowl from Tarley in the market that day. She carried it through the scene like her life depended on it, because it obviously did.

When it came time for her to cry, she made sure that her own eyes were bone dry. Her tears caused too many volatile results, even if she didn't intend it. She was able to secretly steal a drop of water from the bowl and place it on her cheek.

She stood with Wilder at center stage with the bowl cupped between both of their hands. They demonstrated their move that would pour the water into a round basin that was built into the stage. For rehearsal, they had a large bucket at the front of the taped off stage area, and they poured the water from the bowl into the bucket. They finished their duet with one last strong chorus, and then that was the end of Act Two.

They stood on stage in silent terror as they waited for the High Priest to speak.

He stood. "That was very nice. I saw a few rough patches during the second verse that I assume you will be working on?" He smiled, but it didn't reach his eyes.

"Yes, High Priest. That is exactly what we will be working on. You are very correct." Madame Director said with a bow and cupped hands.

"Good," he said. "What have the other High Priests had to say?"

She looked up with wide eyes. "High Priest, you are the only one to come to a rehearsal."

"Hmmm ... That surprises me. Perhaps they don't have as much of an appreciation of the arts as I do. I take this Pageant very seriously. I assume everyone knows that?" He turned to look at the group.

They all bowed their heads, cupped their hands and replied as one, "Yes, High Priest."

"Perfect. I'm glad we are all in agreement." He turned to Madame Director with a smile. "I will leave you to it. Goddess's blessing upon you." He walked out, followed by his Sentinels as the group responded the reply.

Madame Director took a deep breath and adjusted her shawl. "Musicians, begin at the same place. We will be running this scene for the next two hours."

Even though she had already ended practice before the High Priest arrived, no one said a word of complaint.

Purpose

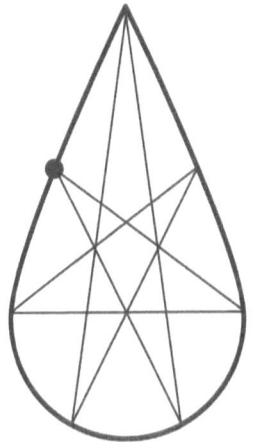

43

———

After the High Priest's visit, they began adding an extra rehearsal after dinner each night. Some nights, they would run the same scene dozens of times in a row. No one complained or second-guessed Madame Director, but they were all exhausted and had a haunted look in their eyes. One night after dinner, she made an announcement.

"Ladies and gentlemen, we will not have rehearsal tonight." There was an audible sigh around the table. "Tomorrow, we will be moving to Temple Purpose for the last step on our journey. Get some sleep, because we still have a long way to go."

After a good night's sleep, Ylena was glad to be walking to Temple Purpose, even if the roads were still crowded with Sentinels. Since they'd had so many late rehearsals, she hadn't left her room at night since her trip to the graveyard with Lady Erenne. It felt good to be looking at something other than their rehearsal space.

They had collected a massive amount of supplies over the course of their rehearsals. They packed up a cart full of their costumes and props that would arrive at Temple

Purpose later in the day. She was sure that it would be much more efficient if they would have just stayed in the same location for the entire rehearsal, but when they traveled through the city from temple to temple, Ylena could see the movement was part of the plan. People smiled and waved at them as they walked, and she felt glad that she could be a part of something that brought at least this small piece of joy.

They arrived at Temple Purpose and met a Priest in the courtyard. Under a large tree, there was a seating area carved from white stone. The chairs were sculpted to look like a bird's wing in flight. She stepped closer and could see individual feathers and fluffy down. She ran her fingers across it and was amazed at the detail. She looked up at the tree and realized the leaves were perfectly still. The massive tree was made of the same white stone but had been painted cleverly to look like a real tree. She looked at the leaves with wonder as they were locked in a perfect frame.

The group began to move back down the steps, and Ylena had to hurry to catch up to Pim. "Where are we going?"

"To see where we will be performing. Keep up!" She smiled and grabbed Ylena by the hand to pull her along.

After they had walked a while, Ylena realized they were headed straight to the center of the City. She was pretty sure she would have known that had she grown up here, so she kept any questions about what they would find when they got there to herself. She didn't really know what to expect, but it wasn't until they arrived that she finally understood how important the Pageant was.

They passed through a final neighborhood of small houses and were faced with a wall of towering, white, stone cliffs. They walked up a winding staircase built into the stone, and at the top, it opened up to a massive stone staircase that stretched down between the cliffs. They walked down the stairs, and she realized the steps were cut into benches. These were all seats. This was how many people would attend the Pageant. She stopped walking and tried to get an accurate count of how many people would be able to fit in the row of seats. Her brain could not comprehend it.

As she stood frozen in fear, Pim took her by the arm and began to walk her down the steps. "I'm guessing you haven't been here before?" Ylena snapped shut her open mouth and didn't reply. "I've actually only been here a few times myself, but it still gives me chills every time."

As they continued walking down the stairs, Ylena realized the same amber glow of the crystal spires was shining from below. A small crystal rose from the ground at the base of the stage, and its top was shaped into a large, glowing basin. The stone that framed the wooden stage flowed around the crystal so that the edge of the basin was nestled directly into the stage floor.

Madame Director invited them to sit together on the stage. Ylena sat down on the polished wood planks and looked out on all the seats; row upon row spread out before her. She closed her eyes and tried to imagine what it would be like for all the seats to be filled. Some of those seats would be filled with High Priests. Her breathing began to speed up. And did Sentinels watch? Where did they sit?

She felt Pim's soft hand take hers, and when she met her eye, Pim gave her an encouraging smile. "Ylena, you will do great. I've only seen a few Pageants, but I'm not exaggerating when I say that you are my favorite Goddess so far."

"Thanks, Pim." She took a deep breath and returned Pim's smile.

Madame Director gave them instructions and sent them off to take a few minutes to explore. Ylena and Pim walked to the center of the stage and looked out at all the seats. The front row of seats was not benches, but rather seven stone thrones for the High Priests. They wandered to the side of the stage and passed inside one of the cliffs that ran the length of the amphitheater. Cut into the cliffs were small rooms with tables and racks built into the walls.

Pim walked into one and pulled the curtain closed behind her. She peeked back through the curtain and said, "Dressing rooms. I'm claiming this one!"

They walked past a few more rooms and turned to find Caed unloading some props onto a table.

"Oh, hello ladies." He appeared to be polishing a book that didn't need to be polished.

"Hi," said Ylena. It felt warmer backstage than she expected.

Pim giggled. "I see something over there that I really want to look at. I'll be over there. Looking at something else." She wiggled her eyebrows so only Ylena could see before she walked off.

"We haven't had much time for anything other than rehearsals lately. I've missed talking to you," he said. "I've missed ... other things as well." She felt his eyes trace their way across her lips, and it was a struggle to not bite her lower lip in response.

He took a step toward her, and she could feel the music inside her surge to life. As he leaned down toward her, she shivered and closed her eyes.

"Hey, Ylena." Wilder stood casually leaned up against the wall behind them. "Madame Director was looking for you." He turned to look at Caed with a smile that didn't reach his eyes. "Goddess's blessing upon you, Priest."

"And also upon you, Wilder." Caed ground out the words between his teeth. "Ylena can find Madame Director on her own. You can run along."

Wilder took a step into the room. "You know, maybe

Priests who care about Purity and the Virtues and all that shouldn't be hanging out in private dressing rooms with acolytes. Just a thought I had."

Caed stepped away from Ylena and toward Wilder. "Maybe you should leave the theology to those who know what they are doing."

"Oh, I know exactly what I'm doing," said Wilder as he stepped toward Caed.

In a short period of time, Ylena had traveled from desire, to confusion, and now, she was fully planted in seething anger. "Are we seriously back to this again?"

Her words seemed to pop the bubble that had formed around them both, and they turned to look at her.

"I'm going to find Pim and then Madame Director, and the two of you can take all the time you want to sort this out. It is clearly more about you than about me." She turned on her heel and left.

44

Ylena made it through the next few days of intense rehearsal carried on a cloud of furious anger. Caed and Wilder had resumed their strange battle, and she was exhausted from falling into the middle of it when she didn't expect it. One day, Wilder's hand lingered on Ylena's back for just a few moments too long in one of their scenes, and Caed made them rehearse the scene a dozen times until he proved he could do it right. Wilder then looked at Caed and said, "Thank you for letting me practice that so many times. I know exactly how to touch her now." Ylena thought Caed might jump up and strangle Wilder on the spot.

Caed must have seethed about it all night, because the next day, he came prepared. When Wilder's hand went a bit off script, Caed stopped the song. "Lira!"

Lira leapt forward. "Yes, Priest Caed?"

"Lira, I assume you know the Goddess's role as well as your own?" Caed asked.

"Oh, yes, Priest," she replied breathily.

"Great. I'd like Ylena to see how this piece will look from

the audience so she understands her role better. Wilder, please continue with Lira as Goddess." He drug a chair next to him and patted it to summon Ylena to his side.

The music started, and Ylena took the few steps to the chair beside Caed. She was taking slow breaths and biting her tongue so hard she thought she might taste blood.

She sat down and saw Lira gleefully savoring every moment of the experience. Ylena was glad to see her happy for once. Wilder was throwing angry glances at Caed, but he was a good enough performer to only do it when Madame Director couldn't see.

Caed chuckled and leaned back in his chair with crossed ankles. He was looking at the stage when he said, "He doesn't know what to do with himself if he can't be pawing all over you."

She turned slowly to face him. "He's not the only one to have had his hands all over me."

His body froze, but he glanced toward her, like an animal that had sensed a trap. "No, he's not."

"If I wanted him to stop, you know I could make him, don't you?" She knew he would replay in his mind the time she threw Wilder on his back.

"Yes, I know that." He spoke slowly, still sniffing for the trap.

"Then I expect you to find another hobby besides monitoring who has their hands on me." She turned to face the stage.

"Ylena—" he started, but he cut off at her glare. They watched the rest of the scene in silence. Then, he sent Ylena back up to resume her place.

∾

The Pageant was three days away when Madame Director announced they would begin evening rehearsals on the actual stage. After morning rehearsal and lunch, their entire group traveled to the center of the City and found themselves on the stage again. They began practicing at Act One and ran it straight through until they stopped for a meal seated on the edge of stage. They watched the sunset together and then began a new set of rehearsals with the lighting team.

Their lighting team was comprised of several Priests from Temple Purpose, along with their assistants. Madame Director called for the acolytes to stand in their positions for their first scene, and Ylena watched the lighting team work. The Priests prayed and touched their tears and then bent down to touch the stone of the white cliffs around the edges of the stage. The stone flowed up like a fountain of water and built a web of white stone that stretched across the front of the stage high in the air. The Priests then tapped into the source of the bright crystalline and formed the stone to connect it to the arch towering above the stage. The glowing liquid flowed along the stone and was pulled through the thin tunnels they formed.

The light from the crystalline shone directly on the stage, and Ylena felt warmed from its glow. The light was so bright it made it difficult to see every seat in the huge amphitheater, and she was soon in love with the crystalline's glare. Wilder's face glowed with a gentle light that made his smile shine, and as she glided across the stage, she felt that the light followed her every step.

She began to think of these Priests from Purpose as the Light Priests. They devised ways to cause the stone to flow in the right place to make sure the light followed its path. They could create wider tunnels to create a brighter light, and when the scene was over, they could wrap the stone around the crystalline to snuff the light completely.

Ylena could have danced in the warm glow of the light all night, but Madame Director called an end to rehearsal and told them they would start again tomorrow. Ylena went to bed imagining the light shining in her dreams.

45

T he nights of rehearsals passed much too quickly for Ylena, and they suddenly arrived at the day of the dress rehearsal. Madame Director let them sleep a little later than usual, and after a late breakfast, they made the walk to the amphitheater.

Ylena walked across the stage and into her dressing room in a state of bliss. The music from the Pageant ran in a constant flow through her mind, and every step felt like choreography. She sat down at the small desk with a mirror and started to brush her hair. Soon, some of the assistants from Temple Perfection would come to style her hair, but for now, she just pulled it up and out of her face. Her white streak had widened into a thick band that framed her face unless she tucked it behind her ear. She brushed it back with the rest, and it stood out in stark contrast to her dark hair.

"I think the white streak suits you," said Lady Erenne.

Ylena turned around quickly to find Lady Erenne leaning against the stone wall next to the rack of costumes. "What are you doing here?"

"I always enjoy watching the dress rehearsal. It's not as

crowded as the Pageant, and it is often a better performance than the Pageant itself."

"You've never told me what it is you want from me," said Ylena. Lady Erenne raised a cleanly sculpted brow but didn't say anything. "You brought me here. You put me in a dress, gave my name to Madame Director, and made sure I was on stage in time to audition for this Pageant. But you've never told me why."

"Can't you feel it, Ylena? Something in the air? The way the pieces are lining up in just the right way?" At Ylena's confused look, she continued, "Something is going to happen during this Pageant. Something that will change the balance. You should be here at the beginning of it all."

"You know what is going to happen?" she asked.

"Not everything. But enough." She closed her eyes and leaned her head back against the stone.

She didn't seem like she would say more, so Ylena prompted, "So, what should I do?"

"Whatever comes next, my dear!" Lady Erenne opened her eyes and smiled. "Whatever comes next."

Ylena stepped onto the stage and smiled. Every part of her felt alive. She could feel each hair on her head singing with power. She could feel magic in her fingertips and her heart beating in time to the rhythm of the orchestra. She had not cried a tear all day, but she felt brimming with energy.

Madame Director talked them through the order of the night and sent them off into the wings to wait for their cue. Ylena stood in her costume of the Goddess with her hair in the elaborate twists the stylists from Perfection had created, and she felt like a goddess herself. She was a tempest contained, ready to burst to life on her cue.

The music began, and she became life itself. Every note followed her wish, and each step she took was a prayer. She was the Goddess, Wilder was her Companion, and her love for him and the City flowed from her every breath. Her song was an invocation rising upon the wind. The earth pulsed with her heartbeat, and she looked out into the night sky and brushed the stars with the palm of her hand.

Her only moment of hesitation was with the Vessel of Tears. She could feel her own tears brimming behind her eyes. All she would have to do is think about a room full of roses, blink once, and the tears would spill over. But her mind was aware enough to realize there was danger there, so she held the tears back and used a fake tear from the bowl once again.

The scene ended as she poured the Tears from the Vessel. The water poured into the crystal basin that glowed with the same light as the crystal spires. The Tears splashed down and caught the light from the crystal before dripping down the sides and into the channels that led below the stone.

The lights faded, and Madame Director clapped. "That was lovely, dears. Get ready for the last act. We will begin in ten minutes."

46

Ylena went back to her dressing room and changed into her costume for Act Three. Her hair stayed in place due to the magic of hairpins and a sticky spray from the stylists from Perfection. She was fastening her final button when she heard someone call her name.

She opened the curtain and found Caed. He was dressed in his usual all black and was silhouetted by the soft light that the Light Priests had run in narrow strips along the hallway. She beckoned him into her room, where she had light from glowing lamps surrounding her mirror.

"Ylena, I'm sorry for my jealous attitude when I see you with Wilder. I thought I was above such behavior, but apparently, I am not."

Her lips curved up slowly, and she savored his words. "A Priest. Apologizing to me. How fascinating."

His eyes flashed but then settled into a glow. "I live to fascinate you, Ylena."

She stepped closer to him. "You may continue." She watched his eyes slide across her lips as she wet them with her tongue.

He crossed the distance between them and grasped her

face in his hands, pulling her gently to his lips, and she closed her eyes and melted into him.

Then, she melted into the floor.

Her bare feet sank into the stone and created footprint outlines which branched out into a pattern of feathers that spread over her floor and up her walls. She felt the layout of the entire amphitheater spread out before her. The stone was waiting for her touch, waiting to be shaped by her hand, and she stepped back with a gasp.

He looked down at the feathers spreading throughout the room and looked up at her with a smug smile. He wiped the tear that had fallen from her lashes when she had closed her eyes for their kiss.

"Ylena," he whispered. "It is dangerous to kiss you."

She opened her mouth to make a saucy comment, but Pim ran to her door and said in a rush, "Madame Director is calling for us onstage … right now." Her eyes were wide with fright. Ylena nodded, put her shoes on quickly, and followed Caed onto the stage.

Ylena turned to see if Wilder was following and almost crashed into Caed's back. He had stopped at the edge of the stage, and before she could see why, he grabbed her by the hand and pulled her to her knees in a bow. Six High Priests stood at the front of the stage, talking to Madame Director.

"We are about to start Act Three, High Priests, but we can of course begin wherever you would prefer." Her head was bowed, and her eyes were focused on the ground.

"Don't make any changes on our account," said High Priest Syrene with a peaceful voice. "We will just sit here in the front row, and you can pretend we aren't here."

Madame Director's throat bobbed. "Yes, High Priest. Please make yourself comfortable. We will start immediately." She turned to face the acolytes. "We will begin Act Three as planned. Give it everything you've got!" Her voice was cheerful, but her eyes revealed the stark terror the whole cast felt.

The acolytes hurried into their positions, and once the High Priests made it to their seats in the front row, the Light Priests dimmed the lights throughout the amphitheater. Caed grasped Ylena's hand and gave it an encouraging squeeze before moving to his customary position in the wings.

Act Three began in full darkness. A single low note from the strings resonated through the amphitheater. The deep note was the floor, and Ylena walked across it. She stopped in the center of the dark stage and sang her own note in return. The note floated down from the stars and was met by a second note from the strings rising from the floor. A pure beam of light shone down from the crystalline far above and landed at her feet. She raised her arms, and the light grasped hold of her hands and trickled down her wrists and forearms. The light gave her note strength to burst into a melody that danced across the stage. The song poured from her lungs and filled the air of the amphitheater, filled the whole sky.

The lights came up on the full stage, and her voice was suddenly lifted by the voices of the rest of the acolytes. Harmony upon harmony rang out through the night. The music crept into every crevice of the amphitheater and chased out every bit of lingering silence until only the song remained. She felt Wilder's hand at her back, and she spun out to his side before he pulled her back to his waist.

As she took a breath, she felt his soft whisper at her ear. "Ylena, be great. But not too great."

Her breath caught, and she almost missed her next note, but she scooped it up like a restless child and held it close. Her next turn brought her to face Wilder, and she saw his wide smile below his serious eyes. She took her melody and clasped it firmly in her hands, but at arms length.

The song wanted to soar, but she kept it at her eye level. She couldn't trust it to move beyond the grasp of her hands. The notes wanted to skip over the stone benches and fly into the City beyond, but she pulled them back to wander in circles close by. By the end of the act, she was exhausted from balancing her song close, but not too close.

The lights faded to black, and Act Three was finished. The acolytes scrambled into position, and when the lights came back up, they had lined up along the front of the stage. They grasped hands, took a single graceful bow, and straightened. Normally, this was where the applause would fill the night, but instead, there was silence. The acolytes were still gripping each others hands, and Ylena thought her hand might break from Pim's grip.

The High Priests stood as one and said, "Goddess's blessing upon you."

The acolytes' reply came automatically, but their eyes were scanning the High Priests to see their reaction.

High Priest Idra turned to Madame Director, who stood at the foot of the stage. "Goddess's blessing upon you, Madame Director. We look forward to tomorrow night. Make sure the acolytes get their rest tonight. We want them to be perfect tomorrow."

Madame Director bowed to them as they walked out. Once they were gone, she turned to the acolytes. "Tidy up your things quickly. We are heading back to the temple to get some sleep."

THE PAGEANT

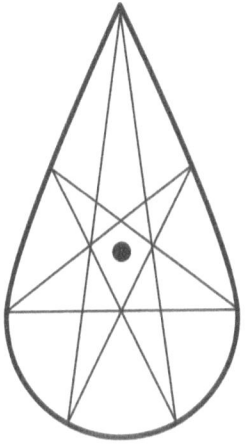

47

The sun had set, and the Pageant would soon begin. Rows of Priests and people from the City had begun to file into the stone benches. Madame Director said they could take a few moments for prayer and contemplation, but Ylena spent the time lying on her floor, staring up at the feathers imprinted on the stone ceiling. She was terrified of the consequences if she or any of the acolytes failed to be perfect tonight, but that wasn't the only reason her heart was pounding in her chest. She imagined the music filling the amphitheater and the warm lights on her skin, and her body buzzed with anticipation.

Caed stood outside her open curtain. "Can I come in?" She nodded from her place on the floor, so he sat in her chair. "How are you feeling about tonight?"

"Like I'm balanced on the edge of terror and joy, and I'm afraid to fall either way."

He nodded and gave her a small smile. "That's understandable."

She traced the feather patterns with her eyes. "I don't recognize myself from just a few months ago. My home on the mountain was my whole world, and now ... I can't imagine going back knowing what I know now."

"I'm glad to hear that. I honestly can't imagine the City now without you in it."

She turned her head to look at him. His eyes pierced her to the core. She turned back to her study of the feathers. "But what am I supposed to do after the Pageant? I've been living in one temple after another this whole time. I don't have a place to live here. If I could find Grandfather again ... Maybe he knows a way that I could live here instead of going back to the mountain after the Pageant."

Caed didn't respond, so she turned to look at him again. He was lost in thought, staring blindly at the wall. She studied the way his dark hair curled around his neck and the hints of silver circlet that glinted around his forehead.

While still facing the wall, he said, "Ylena, I know where your grandfather is."

She sat up straight on the stone floor. "What? Where is he?"

He took a deep breath and turned to face her. "I'm not sure why he hasn't come to find you. I think you should focus on the Pageant before you dive into whatever he is planning."

She felt a fire surge through her veins, but her voice came out cold. "I appreciate your opinion on what you think I *should* do, but if you really want to be helpful, you can explain what you mean by *whatever he is planning*. What aren't you telling me?"

Caed rubbed his forehead. "It's not that simple—"

"Oh yeah, that's right. There's a whole lot you aren't telling me." She knew she was headed down the same well-worn path they had never resolved, but she still had fire in her blood.

"I don't want to get you involved in—"

"Involved? Besides all the ways I am already tied up in this, you hint that my grandfather has some secret plans, and you don't think that *involves* me?"

"Yes, you are involved—"

"Then what is it? Why won't you include me?" They were both standing now, and she took a step closer to him. "Maybe you have no interest in involving me in anything? Maybe you just want to kiss me and see what tricks I will do for you? That way, you will know how to control me."

She saw hurt flash across his face and felt a brief moment of guilt. "Control you?" His eyes changed from pain to anger. "It's obvious you can't be controlled, not even by yourself." He gestured at the feathers in the stone.

Her eyes flared. "I'm wanted onstage."

"I'm sure you are," he said with clenched teeth.

She swept out of the dressing room and found the rest of the acolytes were already gathering backstage. They were whispering excitedly while checking each other's costumes.

"Oh, Ylena!" said Pim. "I'm so excited I can hardly breathe!" Pim adjusted Ylena's stiff feathered collar and fluffed her white chiffon skirt so it fell evenly. "I remember the first time my mother brought me to see a Pageant. It was the most beautiful thing I had seen in my life. I can't believe I get to be a part of it." Pim's smile was radiant, and despite Ylena's lingering feelings of anger toward Caed, she couldn't help but smile in return.

"There is probably a girl out there that will dream about being you someday." Ylena adjusted Pim's already straight collar and smoothed back her hair that was already perfectly smooth.

Pim's dreamy eyes shone with tears. She held Ylena's hand. "Goddess's blessing upon you."

"And also upon you, Pim." She squeezed Pim's hand and walked to her position next to Wilder.

Wilder was standing in the wings, fidgeting with his costume. "Are you nervous?" she asked.

"Honestly?" he asked. "Yes. Yes, I am."

She smiled and adjusted the fold of his vest. "I've never seen you anything other than confident. Well ... confident and then sometimes overconfident." She grinned as she brushed down one of his sleeves.

He chuckled. "True. Being nervous is a new experience for me."

"I think you will be great." She adjusted his collar, and her fingers brushed against his neck. He caught her eyes and tried to hold them, but she patted him casually on the arm and said, "All set!" She turned to face the stage.

"Ylena." His voice was gentle. She hesitated but turned to face him again. "When I auditioned, I knew I was in for a lot of rehearsals and singing and dancing, but I didn't know I would enjoy it as much as I have. I can't believe this is the last time I will sing these songs with you and the last time we will dance like this." He looked at the floor and fidgeted with his vest again. He took a deep breath and looked her in the eyes. "In case I don't get the chance to say it again at the end, there is no one else I would rather have as my Goddess tonight."

She blushed and looked down. "Goddess's blessing upon you, Wilder."

"And also upon you, Ylena."

48

The Light Priests covered all the bright crystalline light with stone, and only the glow of the crystal basin remained. The amphitheater fell into darkness, dropping the crowd into silence. The silence held for the space of seven heartbeats, and then a high note rose from the strings. A note from the horns. Trills by the winds. A chaos of sound with no form.

A clear voice rang out:

> *"First, chaos reigned.*
> *There was no pattern. No form. No purpose."*

The Priests from Purpose slid the stone into position, and the crystalline flowed to cast a soft glow across the stage. Crawling up the backdrop and along the edges of the stage was a chaotic mess of vines and flowers and trees piled on top and in front of one another. Priests from Order stood backstage with their hands holding individual vines and roots. Water flowed everywhere, across the vines, pouring from above, and in shooting fountains scattered across the stage. Priests from Purity knelt with their hands in pools of water in the wings.

The voice called out again:

"But out of the chaos ... came a miracle."

A fountain of water at the center of the stage was glowing brighter than the rest. The light from the crystalline seemed to make the water glow from within. The fountain pulsed with a rhythm that began to slowly raise out of the chaos of sound.

"The Goddess was born,
and SHE shaped the chaos into order."

The fountain exploded in a fury of light and water, and Ylena stepped from the center. Her white dress was completely dry and flowed softly in the breeze. The orchestra began to play a soaring melody timed to the words.

"SHE set the stars in their place
and told the rivers where to flow."

Ylena held out both arms, and the Priests caused the water to stop flowing and froze it in place. She raised her hands over her head, fingertips graceful and catching the light. The water appeared to follow her command and floated high above the stage to coalesce into a single glowing pool above her head. She brought her hands together and moved like she was pulling taffy from the sky. The water began to flow into the perfect circles along the edges of the stage like the Priests had practiced.

"SHE showed the sun and moon their paths
and taught the plants how to grow."

She lowered her head and slowly pulled her arms down and cupped her hands at her waist. Then, she knelt and slapped her hands down onto the stage. The Priests crafted new vines that wove themselves around the chaotic plants and bound them up into living pillars and archways spaced evenly around the stage. The trees branches filled in until they were perfectly uniform with the smell of flowers and fruit filling the amphitheater.

"The Goddess shaped the world to HER Will,
and all of creation found its place."

She stood and lifted her arms to the side, and the rest of the acolytes began to dance onto the stage. Their moves began as chaotic, sharp movements, but as they drew closer to Ylena, their movements smoothed and began to happen in time. When they were all standing in straight lines, they began to dance in unison. Ylena danced the same movements as the rest of the group, and they were a picture of cohesion and unity. The music soared, the acolytes raised their arms as one, the lights faded, and the audience cheered.

Ylena lost herself in the performance. She had no thoughts of Caed or secrets or her grandfather. And even though they were seated in the front row, she had very little thought of the High Priests. She wanted to stop and savor the excitement, but there wasn't time. There was only one note and then the next. One dance and then the next. One costume and then the next.

She had a few moments longer to change into her costume for the last scene in Act Two due to the large musical number with gymnasts from Temple Discipline twirling on vines hanging high above the stage. Her cue wasn't until the Priests from Harmony released the doves to fly in patterns above the crowd.

She noticed Wilder fidgeting with his costume again, so she walked over to check on him. He jumped slightly when she touched his arm.

"You're still nervous?" she asked.

"I guess I'm not as much of a natural at this as you are," he said with a smile.

"I don't know about that!" She laughed quietly. "But I am really enjoying myself." She peeked on stage to see if the doves were flying yet.

"I noticed they chose the new High Priest."

She turned around quickly. "What? How do you know?"

"The seventh throne is filled. It's hard to see with the lights so bright, but I noticed when I was downstage."

Ylena shivered. Six High Priests were bad enough. She didn't think the City needed another.

He smoothed back a perfectly smooth piece of her hair. "I'm sorry, Ylena."

She blinked at him in confusion, but the doves began to fly, and she followed him onto the stage.

She soon forgot his strange apology and jumped into the scene. Her steps felt light, and she moved through the dance with an ease she never expected she could have on her first disastrous day of dance lessons. She almost laughed at the thought, except that this was the part where she supposed to cry.

She danced offstage, and Madame Director carefully

handed her the bowl that represented their Vessel of Tears. Their eyes met, and Ylena could see the pride reflected there. She couldn't stop herself. A single tear began to trickle down her cheek. She felt stricken with panic, but Madame Director misinterpreted her wide-eyed look. "You've got this, dear. Go make me proud." Ylena nodded carefully, trying to will the tear to stay in place.

She carried the bowl out onto to the stage. She walked carefully through the musical procession and drew comfort from Wilder's presence at her side. They stood together at front center stage and sang their duet. As she sang, she scanned the audience and glanced at the seventh chair in the front row of High Priests.

It was Lady Erenne.

Ylena managed to keep singing, but she couldn't stop staring. Lady Erenne looked back at her with dark, knowing eyes. She looked just as regal as she always did, but now, she had a tall crown to back it up.

She felt the bowl in her hand move and brought her attention back to Wilder. This was the part where they both tipped the liquid in the bowl into the glowing crystal basin at the edge of the stage. As they tilted the bowl, Ylena noticed that Wilder had a small bottle in his hand, and he poured the liquid into the basin at the same time. Her eyes widened, but she didn't stop singing. She tried to focus on her voice while staring at both the crystal basin and Lady Erenne and also keeping track of the tear drying on her cheek. They finished the last note, the lights lowered, and the crowd once again cheered.

Wilder hurried off stage in the darkness. Ylena ran to catch up.

Madame Director called out to the acolytes, "There's only a slight musical interlude before Act Three begins, so change quickly!"

Ylena handed the bowl to Madame Director and followed Wilder backstage. She saw him grab a bag out of his dressing room and continue down the hall.

"Wilder!" she called. "Where are you going?"

He stopped but didn't turn. She saw his shoulders sag. She stepped in front of him to look him in the face. She saw such sadness there she staggered.

"What's wrong? What did you do?" she asked.

"Ylena, I'm sorry. I don't have time to explain. Please, come with me. Right now. Walk out of here with me. It's the best way I have to protect you."

"Protect me from what? What did you do?" Her voice was rising in a panic.

"I did the best thing I could do to guarantee our survival. I don't exactly know all the effects of what I just did. So, we need to leave. Now." He grabbed hold of her arm and tried to lead her down the hall.

She shook him off firmly. "I'm not leaving. I can't leave the rest of the acolytes. What will happen to them if we aren't on that stage for Act Three?"

Ylena could hear Madame Director calling for her from the stage.

He sighed. "I'm sorry, Ylena. I really am." He turned and hurried down the hall and out the door.

49

Ylena was still staring at the closed door when Madame Director found her. "Ylena! You have to get on stage! Now!" Madame Director pushed Ylena in front of her, and Ylena numbly moved along. She vaguely noticed someone was pulling her out of her costume and putting her in another one. Pim was buttoning her up when Madame Director called out, "Why can't I find Wilder?"

"He's gone," said Ylena with a flat voice. "He walked out the door and isn't coming back."

Madame Director's eyes went wide, and she looked like she might faint, but she pulled herself together in her usual fashion. She shook Ylena by the shoulders. "Pull yourself together!" Ylena's eyes finally snapped into focus on Madame Director's face. "Listen to me. You have one job. Be the Goddess. Get out there and sing so Goddess-damn beautifully that the High Priests forget all about Wilder's role. Do you hear me?"

Ylena took a deep breath. "Yes, Madame Director."

"Good." She straightened her shawl and nodded once. "Make me proud."

Ylena walked out onto the dark, silent stage. The darkness had lasted longer than seven heartbeats, and Ylena hoped that alone wasn't enough to send the High Priests into a fury. The musicians were still waiting to find out if they should begin, so they hadn't started the low, droning note that was supposed to cue the scene. She closed her eyes and heard her note echo in her mind. She took a deep breath and sang. The single note stood alone in the night air. She was exactly on pitch, but her note had a hint of sadness inside that she couldn't clear away. She held the note, clasped firmly in her hand, until the drone from the strings rose up to meet her.

Warm light from the crystalline lights landed perfectly at her feet. She pressed her open palms gently into the light and let the glow strengthen her. She sang, and her melody fluttered around the amphitheater and settled on the listeners' shoulders like a cloak of butterflies. Just when she thought that her voice was the only one in the whole amphitheater, the voices of the other acolytes rose up around her. Their combined voices chased away the hint of sadness from her song and gave her melody the wings it needed to fly through the amphitheater and beyond.

She felt a strong hand at her back that spun her out to the side. She laughed in relief, believing Wilder had returned, but when she twirled back in, she was met by Caed's serious eyes instead.

Caed was in Wilder's costume, and he had his flower crown pulled down to hide most of his face. He looked nothing like Wilder, but she prayed that the City's ability to live in denial would work in their favor. The Sentinels didn't immediately rush the stage, so she continued to dance without missing a beat.

She wanted to thank him for stepping into Wilder's place, to tell him she was worried that he was putting his life at risk by joining them, to apologize for what she said earlier, but they were on stage and under the bright lights in front of thousands of people, so she could only try to say it with her eyes. His eyes locked with hers, and she knew he understood.

He grasped her by the waist and pulled her into a waltz across the stage. Except for a few moments in dance rehearsal, she had never danced with Caed. She had watched him dance, and he had watched her, but they had never truly danced together before. His footsteps were confident and sure, and Ylena felt that, when he was leading her through the steps, she could relax and savor each individual movement.

She saw tears on his lashes and felt the salty remains of the tear still burning her cheek. Fear flashed through her. The audience only had the barest of illusions that Caed was Wilder. Floating up on a breeze would surely break the fantasy. They needed to stick to the choreography, and their feet needed to stay firmly on the ground. He looked into her wide eyes and nodded. Then, he winked, purposefully letting a tear slide off his lashes and down his cheek.

Their feet moved in the planned steps, but Caed twisted his fingers and flicked a wisp of air to stroke her cheek. She almost lost the next step, but she slid into it just in time. When they faced one another for the next combination, she looked into his eyes and signaled *Challenge accepted.* She brushed her cheek in a way that looked like choreography and took a breath in.

The air around her spread out like a web under her control. She could pull a breeze close to help her spin faster or let the breeze carry her higher on a leap, but she chose instead to use it for other purposes. She floated a breath of cool air up along Caed's neck and let it settle to rest behind his ear. She was delighted when she saw his slight shiver that he hid with a smooth jump. She sprang into her next steps with determination and focus.

She was surprised when he didn't attack during their next combination, so she was caught off guard when he struck during her solo. She stood at center stage for her aria when she felt a whisper of air touch her at the hollow of her throat. She almost sighed but held on to her melody. Her notes climbed higher and higher into the air, but as they soared, the whisper sank lower and lower. It clung to her collarbone, and she tried to hold still as she sang, but with every breath she took, the lower the whisper fell. Her body began to tremble, and she thought she might pass out, but she hit her last high note with her final gasp of power. As she finished the note, the whisper danced up her neck and brushed across her lips before it blew away into the night.

Then, Caed was by her side. He grasped her hand and pulled her close. She leaned back in his arms, and he traced the line of her neck with his eyes. He took a step, and her body responded and followed him across the floor. They moved with the wind flowing around them, blowing through their hair, caressing their face. Ylena didn't need to breath, because the air was part of her and lived comfortably in her lungs. Their feet stayed on the ground, but they could spin and then stop with such precision. Ylena wanted to laugh with the joy of it.

She wanted to dance with Caed on this stage forever and never have this night end. She brought her attention back to the music long enough to realize that the Pageant was drawing to a close. She didn't know what that meant for her future in this City, for future dances like this with Caed. She was happy in the midst of the dream and didn't want it to be over.

They had danced to separate sides of the stage, and Caed summoned her to himself with a breeze that wrapped around her and spun her to center stage. He caught hold of her and gathered her in his arms, holding her close and gently lowering her back into a graceful dip. Her back arched, and she closed her eyes on a sigh. As she closed her eyes, a tear dripped off her lashes and splashed down into the glowing crystal basin.

A heartbeat.

The glowing spires at the center of every temple in the City flickered and went out.

50

The light from the liquid crystalline and every crystal spire was gone. Everyone was staring out to the edges of the City, trying to understand what happened. It had never been this dark in the whole history of the City, and the people began whispering nervously.

A cold wind blew through the crowd. Colder than anyone except Ylena had ever felt. The wind from the mountains blew in over the walls and cut through the crowd like a knife. The whispering grew louder and louder, and Ylena stared into the dark sky with fear. A snowflake landed on her cheek and mixed with the tears she was afraid to touch. In the crowd, she saw people with expressions of shock as they reached their hands up to touch the gently falling snow.

Someone in the crowd screamed. Followed by another. Then rows of people began to run up the stairs to leave. The crowd was pushing each other down in their rush, which lead to more panicked screams. She squinted in the dark to see the faces of the High Priests and found fear and anger. Unbridled anger. Her head snapped toward Lady Erenne, who mouthed a single word. "Run."

She spun toward Caed and saw snowflakes sparkling on his eyelashes. He grabbed her hand and pulled her backstage.

Ylena stumbled blindly after him. He led her in the dark through the wings and up the narrow spiral staircase leading up to the catwalk. Their footsteps were loud as they ran upward, but the sound was drowned out by the screams. She could hear the High Priests yelling orders and the Sentinels stomping on the wooden floor of the stage.

At the top of the staircase, Caed began to climb even higher onto the railing, but Ylena pulled him to a stop. "Caed!" she whispered. "We need to find Pim! We have to help the others escape!"

Caed's face was barely visible in the light of the moon, but she could read his expression: resigned sadness. She gasped and tried to pull away, but he grabbed her and held her close. "Ylena, if they didn't already have an escape planned, they aren't going to make it out."

She pushed his hands away and started back down the stairs when she recognized the screams. She had never heard Pim or the other acolytes scream in fear, but she knew it was them. Ylena tried to scream, but Caed took the sound from her lungs and cast it away on a breeze. He held her in his arms as she shook in soundless terror.

She was high above the stage and hidden behind curtains and vines, but she heard them scream. She heard them fall.

Loud footsteps rang across the stage, and the Sentinels began searching backstage and in the dressing rooms. Caed took her arm and pulled Ylena's frozen body beside him as he began climbing higher. Her hands moved by instinct to climb further up into the rafters high above the stage. He pulled her next to him behind the ropes and pulleys used to control the curtains. They were balanced precariously on a narrow rail, but he held them in place with a steady wind.

Ylena sagged against the ropes and let the wind hold her. Caed took her hand but didn't speak.

Most of the audience had abandoned the amphitheater, so the sound of the Sentinels backstage was clear. They knocked over props and ripped down curtains. Without the light of the crystalline, the backstage area was in complete darkness, and they were wrecking everything in their search.

Their search for her.

"Ylena and Wilder are the two that are missing." Ylena recognized High Priest Syrene's voice. "Sentinels, get out there and find them."

"I don't believe the Sentinels are only yours to command, Syrene," said High Priest Idra.

The golden haired High Priest, Merah, spoke up. "Are you saying we should just let them go?"

"Of course not," said Idra. "I just don't appreciate Syrene commanding all of our Sentinels. Do you?"

"Fine," said Syrene. It sounded like she spoke with her teeth clenched shut. "Do whatever you want. I'm leaving. I will direct my own Sentinels to find the last two and finish the job while you stand around squabbling."

She could hear the Sentinels stomp off the stage, then whispering and the fluttering of robes, and then everything fell silent.

Her body trembled as she stood balanced atop the railing. Caed leaned closer and whispered almost silently. "We have to go now. Can you climb if I let go of the wind holding you?"

She nodded, and he released them both. She began climbing back down to the catwalk. He tried to lead her, but she shook him off and crept down the staircase. She picked her way through the mess the Sentinels caused backstage until she stood in the wings and looked out.

Madame Director and the rest of the acolytes were lined up along the front of the stage. They were sprawled out like they had taken their bows and fallen where they stood. The amphitheater was silent. A faint trace of snow covered all the seats, and she could see footprints leading out. A cold breeze struck her bare arms, and snowflakes swirled through the air.

She walked slowly to where they lay. Pim's hand was outstretched, and Ylena hesitantly reached forward and touched her wrist. It was completely still and growing colder by the moment. She sucked in a harsh breath and swiped at the tears at her eyes. She touched them to Pim's forehead, praying harder than she ever had in her life. But her prayers were met with silence. She smoothed back Pim's hair that was still perfectly smooth, and wept. "I'm sorry. I'm sorry. I'm so sorry, Pim."

She looked over to where Madame Director was hunched over, her arms wrapped protectively around Lira. She tried to quiet her sob with her hands, but she couldn't stop her pointless tears from falling.

"I'm so sorry, Ylena." Caed was kneeling by her side. "Please, we have to leave now while they are fighting amongst themselves."

Ylena stood up slowly. She walked over to the crystal basin that had stopped glowing. "Did I cause this? Did I break it all?"

"I don't know, Ylena. I don't know why this happened."

"I saw Wilder pour something in when we dumped in the water from the bowl. Did he cause this?"

Caed had a thoughtful look on his face. "He poured something in ... Interesting." He turned his attention back to her. "The bowl didn't hold water, Ylena. It held tears from all the young Gifted babies in the City, the ones Mims cares for and all the rest from every temple. Since their tears were poured in, their hair will return to normal, and they can freely use their Gifts now that they are bonded to the City."

"Do you think he poured in something that will hurt those children?" she asked.

"I'm not sure. But the spires went dark only after your tear fell in."

She lowered herself to the ground in front of the basin. She whispered, "I have apologized a lot lately, and now it looks like I need to apologize to a whole City. I'm sorry." She reached out her hand and touched the cold crystal. "You are a beautiful City. I'm sorry I broke you."

The light of the basin flickered on, followed by every spire in the City.

51

Ylena stood quickly and backed away from the crystal basin. Its normally warm, amber glow was now a soft purple, along with every spire in the City.

Caed was looking from spire to spire. "Okay .... Yeah .... We definitely need to go now."

Ylena closed her open mouth and nodded. Instead of going back to the catwalk, he led her backstage. The crystalline lights were back on, and she could see him stop in a room filled with racks of costumes. He grabbed a cloak and handed it to her, then led her to yet another door and ushered her inside.

"I have an idea. Save a few tears, because we are going to need them." She blinked in confusion but followed him up a hidden staircase that led them up toward the top row of stone seating. When they arrived at the top, he pointed to the small door set into the wall. "This leads out to the top of the seats," he whispered. "I don't know if they have Sentinels stationed at this exit, but I don't want to find out." He touched his hand to the stone on the other wall. "On the other side of this is a sheer cliff face that probably no one other than you would ever try to climb. Open this door and escape down the cliffs and into the City."

"Open the door?" she asked. His hand was on a smooth stone wall.

He mimed wiping a tear.

"Oh," she said simply. She stood beside him and rubbed a finger beneath her eyes. She laid her hand on the stone next to his and took a breath. The stone became a liquid held in place by her hand. She moved her fingers and coaxed the stone to flow out from beneath her touch. Caed pulled his hand back as the white stone poured along the outside of the cliff. The snowflakes had stopped falling, but the wind was still cold as it blew past them.

Caed looked out past the cliff and pointed. "If you climb down, you can cut through that row of trees and houses and make it straight to Temple Purpose."

"You're coming, too," she said firmly.

He smiled sadly. "No, I can't. I'm not sure if they are looking for me, but if I don't show up in my temple tonight, someone will notice. You have to hide, and I will come find you as soon as I can."

"But I need to escape beyond the walls and get back to the mountain. They will find me if I stay here." Her voice was rising in panic. "The Sentinels know my name, and everyone in the City knows my face! I am not going to make it out of here! I'm going to die like Pim and the others." Her breath caught on a harsh sob.

He pulled her face so close to his that their warm breath mixed together in the cool air. His fingers tangled in her hair, and he held her eyes locked in his. "Ylena, you will live. Do you understand? I need you to live. Promise me."

She breathed in the scent of him and brought her breathing back under control. The heat of his body pressed close to hers sent sparks through her that snapped her thoughts into sharp focus.

"I will live," she whispered.

He nodded once. "After you get to Temple Purpose, head to the door guarded by Sentinels. Wear the cloak and sneak inside. Then, find your grandfather. I will join you as soon as I can."

"Grandfather is in Temple Purpose? What do—?"

There was a sound from inside the amphitheater.

"Close this door behind you," whispered Caed. "I will find you." He grabbed her behind the neck and pulled her in for a kiss. He tasted like snowflakes and salty tears. She wanted to fall into the kiss, but he stepped back.

She gave him one last look as she pulled herself out onto a rough ledge of the cliff. She looked back inside at Caed, who was staring at her with longing. She touched a part of the stone that she had melted, and it flowed up and over her hand. The hole closed like it had never been there, and Caed was gone.

She began the slow climb down the cliff, moving faster than she ever had before. If she got to a spot that didn't have a good handhold, she just formed the stone into a shape exactly where she wanted it. She had tears upon tears with enough power to flatten the entire cliff to the ground, but she thought that might be noticeable.

She made it to the bottom and pulled on the black cloak from the costume rack, feeling safer once she was hidden in its folds. She hurried from the cliff into the surrounding trees and blended in to the night.

She had walked to Temple Purpose in the dark the last few nights, but she had been with the rest of the acolytes and hadn't needed to hide. She thought of Pim's laughter echoing through the night air and had to lean against a building until the sobs that were threatening to burst free finally settled back into the bottom of her gut.

Few Sentinels roamed the streets. They didn't seem to be searching in an organized way. She wondered if the Sentinels had ever been asked to hunt someone before. She had only seen them strike people down in broad daylight. She made it past them easily and was soon in the temple.

She kept her cloak pulled down over her face as she swept through the silent hallways. It was quieter than last night since the whole cast of acolytes that slept in this temple would never be coming back. She floated from hallway to hallway until she was close to the door with the Sentinels. She wasn't sure what she would do if the Sentinels asked to see her face. They hadn't been looking at faces the last time she was here, but now that they were looking for her and Wilder, maybe they would check everyone going inside.

She peeked around the corner quickly and didn't see any Sentinels standing by the door, but as she turned the corner, she found two Sentinels crumpled on the ground. No one else was coming in or out the door, so she stepped inside.

CURTAIN CALL

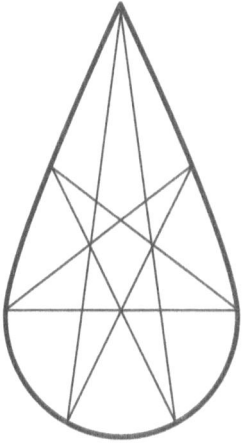

52

The hallway was dark after the door closed behind her, but she pressed forward until she came to a set of stone steps going down with crystalline lamps lighting the way. She walked down the circular staircase for so long that her legs were aching and she felt dizzy. The light from the lamps got swallowed up in a purple light as she finally reached the bottom. She walked through the doorway, and everything she thought she knew fell away beneath her feet. She stood on the edge of a city underground.

The same crystal spire that ran through the center of the temple above ground continued below the white stone and was driven still deeper into the ground below the underground city. The now purple glow of the spire lit up the huge cavern that glowed with the light of crystalline lamps. She could see people walking down streets between buildings of both stone and wood and was struck by how ... normal it seemed. The cave walls looked surprisingly like the City above, almost as if the white stone that built the City had been pulled directly out of this part of the ground. As she walked further down, she heard laughter and yelling unlike in the City above. Late at night, the City was quiet with only a few workers passing on the streets, but down here, there were people everywhere. Laughing, screaming, singing, fighting.

She joined the people walking on the street and headed toward the crystal spire. She saw people kissing in the shadows. A man talking to himself as he walked. A child sitting on the side of the road and eating something he picked up out of the gutter. A woman passed out in the middle of the sidewalk. A man pushing another man up against a wall. A woman grabbing a man by the hand and laughing as she pulled him along.

She looked up to the stone arching far above her and tried to picture the perfect people asleep in their beds at this very moment. Did they know this existed? Did they know what they were walking above every day?

The High Priests knew. These were their doors and their Sentinels. They knew there was a City underground, and they allowed it. And from their overheard conversation, she believed this was their goal. This was the power balance they had talked about maintaining.

She passed several dark storefronts with shadowy figures inside. People came out with eyes that were fogged over and smiles that didn't move. She stopped in the middle of the street and didn't know where to go. She thought she would find Grandfather in a secret room hidden in the temple, but she had no idea that she would suddenly have a whole city to search.

"Hey, little girl." A wrinkled old man without any teeth grabbed her by the arm. "Would you like to come play?" She shook off his hand and took a quick step back in disgust. "Don't be like that, pretty girl. I know some fun people." She turned and ran.

She ran down a number of different streets until the

beating of her heart began to slow. As the fear receded, she felt the sadness start to take over, but she shoved it down until she could find somewhere she could safely cry. She thought for a moment she might be lost, but she realized the crystal spire was just as reliable of a landmark here as upstairs. She began a slow walk back toward the light, keeping to the shadows. She had a lot of shadows to choose from. She was grateful for the dark cloak Caed had given her. She pulled the hood up to hide from more people who had a similar look as the toothless old man.

Caed had told her to find Grandfather, so it must be possible. She walked down the street, looking from face to face, trying to decide who to ask. If she asked the question, would everyone know she obviously wasn't from here? Did that matter down here? Her breath started coming in quick bursts, and she thought she might pass out. She sat down on the side of a sidewalk in the glow of the crystal spire and tried to catch her breath.

"Ylena? Is that you?"

She looked up and found Grandfather standing next to her.

"I'm so glad you made it, Ylena. Welcome to the Underneath."

To Be Continued in *Dance with the Night -
City of Virtue and Vice: Book 2*

The Underneath

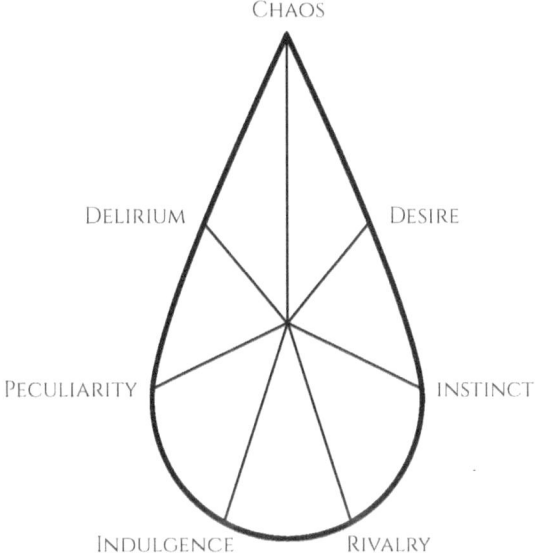

CHAOS

DELIRIUM

DESIRE

PECULIARITY

INSTINCT

INDULGENCE

RIVALRY

When best friends fall in love,
the results are magical.

Do you want a FREE friends-to-lovers
stand-alone novella with a happily ever after?

Sign up for my newsletter to get a sweet story from the
Shining City and to receive updates on new releases.

Scan the QR code to sign up
and get your free short story today!

**When best friends fall in love,
the results are magical.**

ACKNOWLEDGMENTS

This isn't my first book.

When I was in fourth grade, my friends and I co-wrote a book based off of a true story. The hook: A girl drops her orange slice on the cafeteria floor. A confident, young boy approaches the giggling table and asks the girl to "go out." She agrees, but only if he eats the orange slice. With a sparkle in his eye, he takes a bite. We titled it, "The Orange Crush." (We didn't know about trademarks back then.)

When I was in eighth grade, I wrote a fantasy novel based off of a similarly thrilling junior high adventure. I don't remember the actual events, but the book was about two girls discovering magic and elves and boys. I changed the actual names before I shared the story, but after so many years, I can't remember who is who. However, there is a donkey that I assume was based off of an ex-boyfriend. There is noticeable glee when Young Author Me calls the donkey a jackass.

After that, I took a thirty-year break from writing books. I wrote scripts, short stories, and songs. I wrote sermons, ad copy, and stunning email messages. But if it weren't for some truly fabulous people in my life, this book wouldn't have happened.

Thanks to Aaron for asking the fateful question that caused me to consider writing a book.

Thanks to my fan club president and actual Light Priest, Jamal. Your encouragement, imagination, and fanaticism have gotten me through some rough patches. I'm glad you live in this world with me! (I'm still waiting to read that fanfic!)

Thanks to my early beta readers. Joy, Nathan, Alicia, and Angie. Thanks for your feedback and encouragement!

And to Kent ... You gently held this story as I told it—cherishing it like your own but never claiming it. Thank you for believing in my mind and my creativity, and for loving me even when it's hard. You are the essence of every love story I will ever write.

And to you, dear reader: Thank you for escaping into this fantasy world with me. I hope you laugh and cry and swoon as much as I did writing it.

Subscribe to my newsletter for giveaways, new releases, and more at www.susannahwelch.com/newsletter

ABOUT THE AUTHOR

Susannah Welch lives in sunny South Florida with her brilliant husband and a magically hypoallergenic cat. She enjoys singing and dancing and showing off. She likes her stories with a little bit of drama, and a whole lot of sparkle.

facebook.com/susannah.welch.author

instagram.com/susannahwelchauthor

www.ingramcontent.com/pod-product-compliance
Lightning Source LLC
Chambersburg PA
CBHW031645100726
47898CB00006B/1982